LAKELAND HEATWAVE:

Body Temperature and Rising

K D GRACE

Published by Xcite Books Ltd – 2012

ISBN 9781908086877

Printed and bound by CPI Group (UK) Ltd, Croydon, CR0 4YY

Cover design by
The Design House

Lakeland Heatwave: Body Temperature and Rising
is dedicated to the Natural World, the
true source of magic and mystery
beyond imagining.

Thank you, with all my heart!

THE LAKELAND HEATWAVE SERIES

9781908086877

9781908262789

9781908262202

Reviews

"I am a huge fan of K.D. Grace's explicit, well-crafted writing (I've selected and published her work in multi-author "Best" collections), and this novel did not disappoint me. It's the first of a hardcore paranormal trilogy, and many readers think it is her best work to date." **Violet Blue**

*****

"Body Temperature and Rising is my favourite of K D Grace's books so far… So if you're looking for a well-written, pacy and smokin' hot paranormal romp, I'd point you towards this book. One warning, though. As soon as you've read it, you'll want to read the next book immediately. I know I do!" **5 out of 5,   Erotica For All**

*****

"This is powerful, sexy writing from the extremely competent K D Grace. The story contains a compelling narrative. And all of it is set in the most beautiful scenery in the natural world. You really will love this book." **Erotica Readers & Writers Association**

*****

"For the love of all things steamy, this is one HOT read. Steamy, sexy and some other words that start with S and mean hot things, Body Temperature and Rising is definitely a wild ride. If you don't like the sexy, stay out of the sex coven." **Reading the Paranormal**

*****

"Crossing my fingers that there is more to come in this series and soon! Body Temperature and Rising is steamy hot with an involved plot. Definitely give this paranormal erotica a try!" **BookingIt**

Acknowledgements

Very special thanks to Brian and Vron Spencer. Your boundless love and enthusiasm for the Lake District is contagious. Thanks for all you've taught me, and thanks for your help in exploring and experiencing, and I hope, bringing to life on the page, the magic of the English Lakes. You two are the best!

Thank you, Renee and Jo and all of the lovely Ladiez at Sh! Not only are you a fount of information, fun and encouragement, but you're an endless source of inspiration to me. Hugs and kisses and my deepest gratitude.

Thanks to the amazing Miranda Forbes, who does the work of four people, and to the incredible Hazel Cushion, and all the fabulous people at Xcite Books for making *Lakeland Heatwave* a reality.

Thank you, Lucy Felthouse, for cracking the PR whip, when necessary, and for staving off more than one panic attack for this neurotic writer. I couldn't have done it without you, EP!

Thank you, Kay Jaybee, for just being there for me and being your fabulous self. The journey has been so much better because of you.

Thank you, Raymond, for believing in me and being proud of me and easing the journey. There's no one I'd rather have by my side. Volim te mnogo!

Chapter One

OUT OF NOWHERE THE clouds descended, blocking the midday sun and the view of the Borrowdale Valley below. The path ahead of Marie vanished in a roil of thick mist. She shivered, then squinted at her compass. Damn it! The weather forecast had promised sunshine for the day, unseasonably warm, it had said, just like it had been all week. She reassured herself that there was no real way she could get lost on Maiden Moor and High Spy, so close to civilization. Then why did the mist feel so unsettling?

She shifted the pack on her back and tried to remember if this was the route she had taken with her parents. But that was fifteen years ago, and there had been no fog.

The world around her fell silent, as she stepped cautiously forward. She heard no bird song, no breeze, and stranger still; on what was a frequently walked path, she heard no other people. It was as though she were the only person left in the world. As she followed the flank of the fell around, the silence deepened still further until even the sound of her own breath seemed muted in the mist. Goose flesh rose along the back of her neck, and she shivered. A few more steps and the sound of a woman's voice, half whispered in the mist, stopped her in her tracks.

'Anderson? Are you there?'

The knot in her stomach tightened at the possibility of this Anderson being lost to his companion in the fog.

'Anderson?' The voice came again. It didn't sound particularly frightened. 'Anderson, I need you.'

Marie was about to round an outcropping of rock that obscured the path when, directly in front of her, the mist

1

cleared, and she caught sight of the woman calling for this Anderson guy. Her dark hair was pulled back in a heavy pony tail, and her legs extended for ever from underneath kaki walking shorts.

Marie was about to make her presence known when out of the fog, almost as though he had materialised from nowhere, stepped a dark-haired man with a closely trimmed beard. He was broad shouldered, a little taller than the woman, and dressed in a black suit of vintage cut.

Damn tourists, Marie thought. What the hell was he thinking coming on to the fells dressed like that? Her irritation was interrupted by an intense tingling of heat below her navel that flashed hot, took her breath away and nearly drove her to her knees before it cooled to a warm buzz and skittered down low inside her pelvic girdle. Just then the man scooped the woman into his arms and kissed her with an open-mouthed tongue-fondling that left Marie's insides feeling like warm toffee. Instinctively she stepped back, not wanting to interrupt the reunion.

'I was worried when you weren't here,' the woman spoke between breathless kisses.

'Tara, my love, I came as soon as you called. You must not worry so.'

She released a sigh that was almost a sob. 'I have good reason.'

'Of course you do, my darling. But worry will not ease our situation. So we shall do what we must. And I will do whatever it is you ask of me.'

There was something in the way the man spoke that was strange. The accent was very British, and yet not. And the way he moved against the woman, the way he protectively pulled her to him, the way his mouth made love to hers banished Marie's irritation that they'd chosen her path for their reunion. Irritation was replaced by longing that ached down through her torso to mingle with the strange buzz that had migrated to the soft spot between her legs, and the air felt suddenly warmer. The man's hands joined the reunion. He slid the strap of the woman's tank top down to spill a bare breast heavily into his waiting palm. He paused to knead it and fondle it as though he had never seen anything more exquisite. Then he took as much of it into his mouth as he could. The woman released a shrill gasp as though cold water had been poured onto her. 'I can feel it,' she breathed. 'We were right.' Then she held him to her, letting him nurse at her in hungry nibbles and slurps.

Marie should have left, and yet she stood riveted to the rock beneath her, feeling heavy and pliant, as though something had suddenly filled her and was moulding her and shaping her from the inside with fiery hands. Her breasts tingled at the rub and tickle of the man's beard against Tara's tender flesh, at the tug and pull of pursed lips on swollen nipples. She felt almost as though it were her breasts at which he nursed.

Marie clasped her hand over her mouth to hold back a gasp of appreciation as, from the man's trousers, the woman manoeuvred the longest, thickest erection she had ever seen. Not that she'd seen that many erections When had there been time? She could almost feel the hot stiffened twitch of maleness against the woman's hand.

As the mist floated around them revealing, concealing and revealing again, he slipped his other hand into Tara's shorts. She caught her breath and nibbled her bottom lip as he found what he was looking for. Then she squirmed and twisted against him, practically sitting on his hand, as he stroked her. The look on her face was one of deepest concentration.

For a moment the mist thickened around the couple, and Marie held her breath listening desperately to hungry grunts that she felt deep in her belly and to little throaty moans that tingled down low, down where she shifted almost unconsciously into the dampening press of her panties against her labia.

When the mist cleared again, Anderson was sliding Tara's shorts down, kneeling to kiss and nibble her calf as he lifted one exquisite leg free from both shorts and a pale lace thong that was definitely not what Marie would consider standard walking apparel.

He lifted the freed leg higher until Marie was afforded the perfect view of the woman's distended lips, glistening like the heavily-dewed hawthorn flowers she'd cut this morning for a vase on her kitchen table. Marie was certain her own pout had to be at least as wet. The heat and the buzz between her legs intensified, and the slippery ache overrode the guilt at being an unwelcome voyeur, as she wriggled and strained against the seam of her walking trousers and her much more practical panties.

Anderson lifted Tara's still booted foot onto his shoulder in reckless disregard for his pristine suit. He moved forward cupping Tara's arse cheeks in large kneading handfuls, guiding her into enough of a squat to position her splayed cunt so that his tongue had easy access. Then he buried his face deep into the woman's pussy, as though he planned to split her in two with his tongue and the wedge of his face. The woman trembled and pressed back hard against the rock, surely just to keep from collapsing under the overwhelming pleasure of what Anderson's mouth must feel like eating at her so deeply.

Marie was amazed that, totally surrounded by fog as they were, her view was still perfect, even enhanced. She could almost feel the distended press of the woman's nipples as she tugged and pulled at them with the hand not curled possessively in the man's dark hair. She could almost smell the slippery sheen of the woman's heat coating the man's beard. And the rise and fall of his chest matched her own hungry need for oxygen. A single droplet of precome glistened on the head of his uncut cock. It lewdly jutted and danced between his legs like an escapee from his dapper trousers. It boldly proclaimed freedom with each bounce and shudder against heavy balls pressed tight in their own effort to escape confinement.

It was as if the world in the mist now contained nothing else but the three of them. And the world the three of them inadvertently shared had shifted into slow motion, as though every detail were magnified, intensified and stretched to the breaking point all at the juncture between Marie's thighs.

Even in her fantasies nothing like this had ever happened. Marie moved very carefully, feeling the rock shift under her feet as she eased her cold hand down the front of her trousers and into her panties. She shuddered at her first touch. Her

4

knees felt weak as water as she wriggled her fingers in between her pussy lips, already drenched and swelling. She couldn't hold back a sigh at the velvety feel of herself, at her salty sweet aroma infusing the fresh fell air.

In the crescendo of her lust she wondered if even the crotch of her trousers would bear the mark of her heat when she was finished, but it didn't matter. It didn't matter if her juices flooded and ran down her legs to puddle on the path beneath her, she could not have pulled away if her life depended on it. It was as though she were the invisible third party entangled in a rutting threesome too far gone to disengage.

Anderson tongued his way up over Tara's belly, his face shimmering with her moisture, moving upward to suckle each of her nipples in turn before he pulled her to him and whispered against her ear.

Marie froze, her hand still in her knickers. She held her breath, but she couldn't make out the man's words.

Tara nodded and spoke breathlessly. 'Yes, I know. I feel it. Such a powerful lust. We can't hide it. There's no way.' She gave his cock a caress, and it jumped at her touch.

'I fear it is far too late for that now.' He turned her to the flank of the rise, where she bent, resting her arms against the rock, exposing the half-domes of her arse cheeks to Anderson and to Marie.

Tara lifted one knee onto a boulder. As Anderson helped position her, Marie caught an exquisite glimpse of the dark clench of her anus. As he spread her and she shifted her hips to accommodate him, the engorged lips of her cunt pouted into view again, open and anxious before him, before Marie.

As Marie watched his fingers move over the slick spread of the woman's open folds she wished it were her cunt Anderson was caressing. But at the same time she wished she could touch the soft smooth skin that opened itself so pliantly to his probing. Marie could swear she smelled the tide pool of the woman's arousal, different from her own, yet so delicious that it made her mouth water. Anderson postured over Tara, his cock like a sword pressing downward in his hand. His open fly exposed only his cock and the squeeze of his balls, which somehow made the act seem all the naughtier.

Suddenly the air around her chilled. The world tilted, and Marie felt dizzy and confused as though she had just awakened from a dream to find herself somewhere other than where she should be. Hands cupped and splayed her, hands she couldn't see. An erection that wasn't there pressed anxiously at her cunt. Her heart hammered, everything below her navel surged hot and trembled. The press of flesh and the smell of sex enfolded her on all sides as though she were drowning in a heavy demanding caress, one that pushed at her, prodded at her, nuzzled at her, threatening to overwhelm her.

'Please, Anderson I can't contain it. Help me.'

It was the sound of Tara's voice that pulled Marie back from cold panic, just as Anderson thrust home. Then the world warmed again and swung back into focus. Once more the sounds of pleasure filtered through the thick, otherwise silent air. As Anderson mounted Tara with a desperate grunt, it stopped mattering whether they knew she was there, and Marie felt strangely included in their intimacy. She pressed herself harder and harder into the palm of her hand, pinching her nipples until they ached in empathy with the growing rush building just behind her clit, a storm surge threatening to burst the dam and rip her apart.

Tara's hair had come free from the pony tail and fell in a dark curtain around her face. Marie could almost see the heatwaves radiating up the woman's spine, higher and higher, as though Anderson jack-hammered them into her with each joint-cracking thrust of his cock.

It was obvious Anderson was straining close to the edge when Tara pulled away from him and turned around, grabbing his cock and keeping the rhythm steady. He dropped onto a bolder, then she knelt in front of him and began to slide his swollen erection between her breasts, faster and faster. Her eyelids fluttered and her lips moved rapidly, like she was saying something, chanting something over and over again, something Marie couldn't quite make out. Not that she needed to with the sensory overload already throbbing through her whole body. Anderson braced himself against the rocks,

6

thrusting with abandon between the tight grip of Tara's breasts, every muscle tense and quivering, until at last his whole body shuddered. 'Oh dear Goddess,' he gasped.

Tara pulled back, guiding his cock so that his viscous load splattered across her breasts in high arching spurts. Marie felt fire spread through her chest and down over her belly in empathy with the couple, and she humped herself harder, whimpering, gasping desperate to come.

The look on Anderson's face was ecstatic as he unloaded. Then he joined Tara in whatever it was she was still repeating over and over again. While they chanted, he caressed and massaged and stroked, spreading his semen as though he were spreading lotion over Tara's body, even up her neck and onto her cheeks and forehead. All the while Tara undulated and moaned beneath his touch and continued her chant.

'My seed covers, but the power still resides in you,' Anderson breathed. 'And shall we release it now, my love?'

Tara only nodded and continued her breathless mutterings.

Before Marie could wonder what they were on about, he lifted Tara onto an outcropping of rock that was just the right height. 'Then we shall complete what we have begun. Let me release it for you now, my darling, allow me the pleasure of finishing it.'

My God, the way the man talked, Marie thought. He could convince a woman her cunt was lined with gold. She could probably come just on his words alone.

He buried his face once more in Tara's pussy, and once again, Marie felt as though she had been physically pulled into their intimacy.

With her gaze locked on the writhing couple, Marie tugged and pinched at the heavy nib of her clit until it buzzed with raw heat close to pain but much closer still to pleasure. She shoved and twisted and thrust the rest of her fingers into her grasping cunt until she reached the precipice, lingered there for a moment, then free-fell into a long dizzying orgasm, just as Tara convulsed her own release in breathless guttural grunts.

Marie's legs gave under her, and she sat down hard, letting the aftershocks wash over her. Oxygen rushed back into her starving lungs. Muscles, strained to the point of collapse, relaxed and softened. The strange fire between her hip bones subsided to a warm thrum, and as the mist descended around her again, she managed to crawl to a mossy spot. Suddenly it didn't matter how far she still had to walk or how thick the mist was. She could no longer hold her eyes open.

Just before she dozed, she thought she heard Anderson say, 'There. That's better, is it not?'

Chapter Two

IT WAS THE CHILL that woke Marie from a dream of delirious wet sex with the couple on the path. The wet she was feeling, however, was not the slippery warmth of sex, but the chilling, heavy damp of the fog that curled around her like a smothering blanket. She jerked her hand from where it nestled in her panties, still sticky from her orgasm. Quickly she straightened up and cleaned herself as best she could then she fumbled with the compass to get her bearings. A glance down at her watch reassured her that she had only slept for a few minutes.

There was no sign of the amorous couple. She listened intently, thinking they surely couldn't have gone far, yet she heard nothing but thick cottony silence. Now she was not so anxious to hide herself from them. Now she would have welcomed their companionship.

Her stomach growled. She popped a handful of trail mix into her mouth, took a sip of water, and headed on. The picnic she'd planned for her lunch when the day had been heavy and warm wasn't likely to happen with the mist hanging over her. All she wanted now was to make it safely back home. She took another bearing on the compass just to make sure, secured the plastic map holder around her neck and trudged forward.

The next half hour she walked in the maddening fog. The pace was slow, with frequent stops to check map and compass. A light, but relentless rain slowed progress further. Though the map assured her she should be nearing the monstrous cairn at the top of High Spy, she couldn't fight back the fear that somehow she had missed it, that somehow in spite of nearby civilization, she was lost. In the barren featureless fog, for all she could tell, she might have been transported to another planet while she slept.

She had planned to walk the whole Newlands Horseshoe today, which would have returned her within easy walking distance of her cottage at Lacewing Farm, but she wasn't even half way there, and going back the way she'd come was beginning to make a lot more sense. Whichever direction she chose, she would be navigating completely by compass. The way back looked no different from the way forward. It was only when she reached into her anorak that she realised she was in trouble. The compass was nowhere to be found.

Fighting back panic, she searched her rucksack, all of her pockets, even down the front of her shirt, in case the cord had broken and it had fallen inside. But there was no sign of her compass. For the first time since the day had begun, she felt truly alone in the mist.

It would be all right, she told herself. Keswick was just down in the valley below. These fells were usually crawling with tourists. She really wasn't alone. Her anorak wasn't the most waterproof. She hadn't expected bad weather. But it would do. She had at least a little food and water. She could hold out until the weather cleared a bit then she would just continue on.

But what if the weather didn't clear? No one knew where she was.

The knot that was already a fist in her stomach tightened still further. Her landlord, Tim Meriwether, for the most part, pretended she didn't exist, and she hadn't been here long enough to make any other friends. No one would miss her, not even the couple she had watched.

She knew where she had been from her last compass bearing, so she simply sat down in the middle of what might or might not have been the path and hunched around herself. She'd be all right. She was cold and wet and miserable and the rocks were not exactly gentle on her back side, but she would be all right. She would!

It had to have been a dream, although how she could have dozed under the circumstances, she couldn't imagine. The dark figure approached silently through the fog, little more than a

10

shadow, and yet her pulse quickened, her nipples ached, and her pussy felt heavy and receptive. Still barely visible in the mist, he walked a tight circle around her, looking down at her, inspecting her, caressing her cheek with a large hand. 'It was you.' His voice vibrated up through the pit of her stomach, as though he had taken up residence just below her navel. 'It was you. Exactly as I suspected.'

He moved to stand close behind her, so close that his heat radiated against her back. As she leaned into his warmth, he reached down to caress her breasts. She arched up into his irresistible touch as his hand moved up over her shoulder, her neck, her throat. Almost before she knew what was happening, the pressure of his touch became more insistent, more demanding, almost bruising and the heat was replaced by an icy chill.

Arousal congealed to cold fear. But just as she gathered herself to run, it was a gentle touch on her arm that woke her, and she looked up into the dark eyes of Anderson. For a sharp second the strange heat between her hip bones flashed hot, then settled to a warm thrum. 'Come with me, out of the rain.' He offered her his hand and helped her to her feet. She was amazed to find that he was still in the black suit, no anorak, no water proofs, no proper walking boots.

'I lost my compass,' she said.

'I'm very sorry to hear that,' he replied.

Almost before she knew it they were descending. 'Not to worry,' he spoke close to Marie's ear. 'I am as familiar with these fells as I am with my own face. Once we are safely down to Grange, Tara will be waiting for us.'

He made no attempt to explain who Tara was, nor did he introduce himself. That was her first clue that he might have been aware of her voyeuristic escapade.

'We shall be down very quickly,' he added, turning his face into the storm.

But they weren't.

The weather worsened to a downpour. Bent double in the wind, Marie was soaked to the skin and shivering by the time Anderson pulled her into a cave that she hadn't even seen until they were safe inside. He took her just deep enough to be out of the weather, but not beyond the reach of daylight. There he settled her onto a rocky ledge and sat down next to her.

'We shall wait out the storm here.' He offered her a smile and gestured around the cave, which she could now see was a disused quarry. 'There are many such caves and quarries around the Lake District,' he said. 'Some are fenced off for the protection of curious tourists, and others, such as this one, are unknown to all but a few.'

'And your girlfriend, won't she be worried?'

The tolerant smile he offered made her aware of her mistake. 'Tara knows what I would do in such weather.' Then he added, 'Though she is very dear to me, Tara is not, as you put it, my girlfriend.'

Before she could say anything he chuckled softly. 'I know that you saw us together, and there is no need to apologise. Neither of us was upset that you enjoyed our love making. In fact we rather hoped it would please you. Besides, one must certainly expect such encounters when one chooses the middle of a well-travelled path for a rendezvous. Now remove your shirt for me, please.'

When she balked, he added, 'You're cold and wet. I only wish to make you more comfortable and prevent you catching your death.' He had already shed his jacket and handed it to her. She was astonished to find it completely dry. 'You may wear this.'

When she made no effort to put it on, he sighed and scooted closer to her. 'Please, we must get you dry and warm.' He unzipped her anorak and pushed it off her shoulders, then tugged the hem of her shirt out of her trousers. His hands were unbelievably warm grazing her bare skin. She lifted her arms, and he slid the wet shirt off over her head, then he reached behind her to unhook her bra while his other hand deftly dealt with the buttons of his black shirt. 'Now please, put this on.' He slid the jacket around her shoulders like a blanket, shoved his shirt open and turned so he could pull her against him.

She wasn't sure why, but it seemed such a natural thing to slide her arms around him, beneath his shirt, which was as dry

12

as the jacket. As she settled in close, his chest expanded against her bare breasts, and his breath hitched.

'You are freezing. I think you very much need my body heat.'

'And you seem to have lots of it to offer,' she spoke between chattering teeth, suddenly very aware of the gouge of her tightly puckered nipples against his warm chest.

He laughed softly, and she felt the deep low rumble of it clear through her centre. 'My dear, you are welcome to as much heat as I am able to generate.'

The urge was overpowering. She rose on her haunches and kissed him. Out of the clear blue, she just lifted her mouth to his as though it were hers to take, as though she owned it. And he responded in complete acceptance of her possession, warm lips yielding, encouraging, inviting, making room for the flick of her tongue, welcoming her with the flick of his own.

'You taste of her,' she whispered when she came up for breath.

He cupped her face in a large hand and ran a callused thumb over her bottom lip. 'But her taste pleases you, does it not?'

She nodded. 'I can see why it pleased you so much.' She was suddenly, painfully aware of her brazenness. What the hell was the matter with her behaving this way with a man who was, for all practical purposes, a total stranger?

She was about to apologise when he pulled her hand to his lips and suckled her fingers, the ones that had been in her panties not all that long ago. He held her in a gaze deeper than the quarry that now protected them. 'Your taste also pleases me. Even more so than I imagined.'

The thought made her pussy tense with delight. 'You imagined my taste?'

'Of course I did, but experiencing the aftertaste of someone's pleasure, though nice, is never as enjoyable as tasting for oneself.'

She had no time to do more than squirm at the heat of his comment before he pulled away to remove her boots and wet socks, lingering to chafe her cold feet between his hands, then he opened her trousers with amazing ease. She lifted her arse as

13

he slid them off, along with her panties, then he settled her onto his lap. 'Your bottom will not appreciate alighting upon a cold slab of slate,' he said. He guided her to wrap her legs around his waist and arranged the tail of his shirt to cover them. Then he shifted to better balance himself and offered a soft sigh as his hands slid to her hips.

A quiver of a gasp escaped her throat as she found herself sitting spread and gaping against the erection his trousers clothed, but certainly couldn't hide. The flash-fire burn below her belly flared again then hummed low and warm as though someone had adjusted the flame. At the sudden shock of it, she buried her face in his shoulder and clenched her teeth to keep from crying out with the startling friction.

'I believe my trousers will bear the imprint of your lovely womanhood when the weather clears and we leave this place. Do you mark me as your territory? I am honoured.'

His insinuation made her pussy even slicker, and she was sure he was right. She was making a sticky mess of the front of his trousers. She rubbed herself against him taking in the size of him beneath the soft black fabric, and he grunted hard and shuddered at her efforts. 'Maybe you should take them off, save embarrassing stains and allow me a little more of that body heat you're so generous with.'

He offered her a wicked smile. "My dear, my delicate bare bottom is no more fond of sitting on cold slate than is yours, but perhaps we can find an acceptable compromise.' He ran a hand between them, jostling her slightly in his efforts to open his fly, releasing his cock and heavy balls. The whimper that escaped her lips was involuntary as she pressed upward to renegotiate for space.

He held her gaze. 'Are you certain this is what you desire?'

'Aren't you?' She raked herself against him once more, and he shuddered.

'I am. Very much.'

She was relieved. She had never been more sure of anything in her life. She didn't know why that should be. Perhaps it had something to do with the burning ache at her centre that had awakened again and crawled up over her sex, up the vertebrates of her spine like an eruption of rising sparks. She scrambled to reposition, her bare feet pressing onto the chilled slate until he lifted her bottom. She tugged at the length of him, shifting her hips as his thumb brushed open her pussy lips. 'Oh my dear, you are very ready, indeed,' he breathed. 'Such soft luscious wetness.'

She nipped his neck impatiently and squirmed around the probing of his fingers.

'Then I shan't keep you waiting.' With practised ease he pressed the head of his penis upward until it exerted a firm pressure against her slippery hole. Then he shifted his hips, and with a quick thrust he slid home.

'Oh my God,' she forced her words between her teeth. The fire flared inside her with a feverish heat that made her feel as though she would self-combust, then it steadied itself like the flame adjusted in a lantern. 'You're big,' she sighed.

He moved a hand forward to rake and circle the urgent rising of her clit. 'I have been told that I am not inadequate. I haven't hurt you, have I? It was not my intention, but you appeared so anxious for me to penetrate your tenderness that I was loath to keep you waiting.'

In truth, it had hurt, but the sudden gush of pussy juices at the ridiculously romantic and chivalrous way he spoke went a long way to ease the pain of accommodation. She imagined he could pick up more than a few chicks at the local by talking that way. But then again, she could hardly picture Anderson chatting up women at the pub while the footie blared on the big screen. She wrapped her arms around his neck and shifted against him. 'My tenderness hasn't been penetrated in awhile, that's all. I'll adapt.'

'I shall do my best to make adapting pleasurable for you,' he said, holding her gaze as though just by looking in her eyes he could tell how her body was responding to his heft, to his tweaking and tugging at her clit. Eye contact was hardly necessary for him to tell that he was getting the job done and very nicely at that. Still the feel of his gaze provided its own kind of stimulation, dark molasses eyes studied her, warmed her, took her into him as surely as she had taken his cock.

Once she had grown used to the size of him, she became aware of more than his fullness. She became aware of his warmth spreading inside her, almost as though his cock had a built-in heating element, and he had cranked it for her benefit. Her pussy gripped and relaxed, sucking at his heat.

'Mmmm. My manhood has never been so well sheathed.' His eyelids fluttered. A sigh caught in his throat, and he swallowed it back as a little moan. 'I do hope that adapting is as pleasurable for you as it is for me.' At first, he made no effort to move or to thrust, allowing her to dictate the pace. He slid a splayed hand over her belly and up her ribs to cup her breasts, leaning back to afford himself a good look. His hand was nearly large enough to accommodate the whole of her weighty breasts each in turn.

She gasped as his rough thumb stroked her nipples. 'You came on her breasts.' She sighed.

'Sometimes she wishes it that way. She takes pleasure in it.' He lowered his mouth to suckle and swirl his tongue in a tight press around her areola. His breath was hot against her swell. 'Pleasing her pleases me. And pleasing you, I think shall also please me. Very much indeed.' He rose to take her mouth again, and the first shiftings of his hips pushed the heat up even further inside her.

'I've never watched anyone have sex before,' she said when she came up for air.

'I have many times, but I much prefer to participate. I would ask that you hold tightly to the jacket, my dear.'

He lifted her and rolled until she was beneath him, the jacket protecting her back. He positioned himself on his knees, pushing into her at a steep angle so her butt was in the air and her legs were wrapped around him. 'Now I shall do my best to take away the chill.' He thrust deep, deep enough that it felt as though he would penetrate clear through her. In her peripheral vision the cave suddenly shifted and shimmered as though it were in firelight. She was sure it was just her eyes playing tricks on her. Perhaps there was lightening outside reflecting off the walls.

There was no time to dwell on it. Anderson moving inside

her demanded her full attention. At the steep angle at which he penetrated her, it was as though he poured himself into her, super heating her from the inside. And the more heat he gave her, the more she demanded. She thrust up to meet him, straining and groaning, her thigh muscles tightening and trembling around his ribs until it was a wonder that he could catch his breath. The harder she gripped and thrust the harder he thrust back. She became a mindless bundle of desire, gabbling and mewling and grinding while the whole cave danced like an inferno just outside her field of vision.

'The depth of your need is astonishing.' His voice was a breathless whisper. 'Enough to ignite the whole world and burn it to a cinder, enough to hold my manhood prisoner and never let it go, a condition in which I would rejoice.'

'God, you're a fucking poet,' she gasped. 'It's better than talking dirty.' The words barely escaped her lips before searing heat blasted her with an orgasm that, indeed threatened to burn her to a cinder.

'That's it my love. That's it my darling. Sharpen your fire on me. Take the release you need, and let me be the instrument of your pleasure.' His last words were swallowed back in a harsh grunt. His hips crushed into her, and his cock felt like a battering ram. She could feel it twitch and release his own pleasure inside her, molten hot, searing her insides with the mark of his desire.

'Ah, you are a goddess,' he whispered. 'I am in ecstasy.'

The world tilted slightly as he rolled again and wriggled and shifted until her body rested completely on top of his, his cock still nestled in her cunt.

'Anderson?' She gasped when she could manage to form words again.

'Yes my love.'

'Did you study Shakespeare?'

'No. Why do you ask?'

She snuggled closer to him, her cunt still gripping his cock possessively. 'It's just the way you talk. It's so …'

'I studied the romantics. They were all the rage when I was among the … Let us just say I find them satisfying.' He ran a warm hand down to cup and caress her bottom, and she wriggled into his touch.

'Studied the romantics. Of course you did.' Her last words slurred as though someone had given her a powerful drug and it was taking its delicious toll on her. 'What a great way to pick up chicks.'

He chuckled softly. 'I would like to tell you that picking up chicks, as you put it, was not my intention, but that would be a lie. Now my love, rest and get warm. The storm will pass soon, and then you may go home.'

She wouldn't have believed it under the circumstances, but it was an effort to hear his words as he kissed her ear. She fell into a deep, dreamless sleep wrapped in his arms, resting on top of the slow rise and fall of his bare chest. Still fully impaled.

She woke with a start to find Tara leaning over her pushing her hair away from her face. 'Wake up sleeping beauty. Storm's cleared. Time to get you back home.' She held out Marie's panties teasingly on one finger.

Blushing hard, Marie grabbed them away and shimmied them up over her hips.

Surprisingly, Marie's clothes were all dry and warm. While Tara watched her unabashedly, she scrabbled into them and looked around the cave expectantly.

Tara offered a knowing smile. 'Anderson asked me to convey his deepest apologies, but he couldn't stay. He had a pressing appointment and he was loath to wake you.' She shrugged. 'His words exactly.'

Marie tried to mask her disappointment, but Tara was too astute. 'You completely and totally captivated him. Also his words. And if it's any comfort to you, Anderson is not the fuck and run sort.'

Once Marie was dressed, Tara produced a flask of tea and a very large cheese scone from her rucksack. 'I figured you must be starving after your ordeal.' Her eyes sparkled as they raked over Marie's dishevelled condition.

Marie tore into a scone. In truth, she was ravenous. 'I lost my compass,' she said.

'I know, Anderson told me.' She handed Marie a cup of tea.

'I can't believe I didn't stir. I mean he was …'

'Underneath you, yes, I know, and inside you.'

Marie's blush returned with a vengeance. 'You saw?'

Tara bent to adjust her boot laces. 'Hard not to really. And in all honestly, I'm a bit of a voyeur, something you would know a thing or two about.'

Marie blushed harder, but before she could apologise, Tara continued.

'Anyway, good sex often causes a person to sleep soundly. And you were fucking Anderson, so it was most definitely good sex. Now finish up so we can get back to the car park before dark.'

'Before dark? How long was I asleep?'

'A couple of hours, I'd guess. Now come on, let's go. It's not a hard walk down, but I don't relish stumbling around on the wet, slippery slate after dark.'

Outside the quarry, the low sun shown jewel bright on the freshly washed fell side. Tongue Gill tinkled musically down along the path that descended steeply on loose grey slate. As they walked, the path turned slightly to the left until the top of Castle Crag peeked around the breast of the fell, its forested top looking like elaborate bird plumes in the rain-washed sunshine. The rest of the descent was without incident.

At the car park in Grange, Tara nodded to a pale blue Land Rover. Once they were both belted in, she heaved a satisfied sigh. 'Now, off to Lacewing Farm, isn't it?' She offered an apologetic smile. 'Yes I know where you live. My sisters and I are your neighbours, and we're very nosey. In fact they'll be very excited when I bring back all the day's news about you.' She started the engine. 'The talk around the dinner table will be delightful. You must join us. Not tonight obviously. That would ruin our gossip, wouldn't it? But soon.'

As they headed out of the car park, Marie couldn't resist asking, 'Anderson tells me that you two are just friends.'

'That's right, very old friends, actually.'

'Fuck buddies?' Marie spoke around the shudder of her

pulse in her throat even as she mentally kicked herself for pursuing what was none of her business.

Tara offered an amused smile. 'I suppose you could call us that.'

It didn't take long to get to the farm lane that led to Lacewing Cottage. Tara stopped the Land Rover and turned to her companion. 'I'm assuming you know Tim Meriwether.'

'He's my landlord.'

'Surprised he'd rent to you. He's not exactly friendly to strangers.'

'Guess I made him an offer he couldn't refuse,' Marie said.

'Fuck buddy?' Tara asked.

In spite of herself, Marie laughed. 'Only in my dreams.'

Tara raised a dark eyebrow. 'What's in your dreams is just reality in the form of a riddle.'

Marie chuckled. 'In my case, what's in my dreams is usually in the form of a bad joke.'

Tara glanced down at her watch. 'I've got to get home. My sisters'll be waiting for me.'

'I never had a sister. It must be nice,' Marie said.

'Well, they're not my physical sisters, but I still think of them that way. There are three of us. We call ourselves the Elementals.' Tara held her gaze. 'We're witches.'

Marie's heart did a little tumble in her chest. 'Witches?'

Before she could question further, Tara pulled her into a tight embrace and kissed her with plenty of tongue that tasted of tea and cinnamon. Then she took a card from her rucksack and slipped it into the breast pocket of Marie's anorak, lingering for a caress of the breast beneath. 'This is my card. Call me. I figure after what happened to you today, once you've had a chance to sort through it all, you'll be needing our advice.' She kissed her again and waved as Marie stumbled out of the Land Rover, wishing like hell she could somehow replay what had just happened with slo-mo for the tonguey bits and the groping. Her nipples tingled at the thought.

Voyeurism, sex with the hottest, if strangest man on the fells and now, she had kissed a girl. Well, the girl had kissed her, actually, and done a damn fine job of it. For the first time since her arrival from Portland, Marie didn't feel terrified of the path she had chosen for herself. She had been damn good at the job she'd left, and she knew that her friends and colleagues thought her insane for walking away. In truth, it was the first sane move she had made in a long time. Her investments had set her in good stead. Financially she could survive for as long as she needed to without an income. That gave her time to rest, time to recover. Then when she stopped feeling like raw meat in a butcher's window, she'd think about working again.

Spontaneity had always frightened her, and yet here she was thousands of miles away from everything that was familiar, and in less than twelve hours she'd had more sex than she'd had in the last three years. She could almost believe that she had made the right choice after all, that she would get better, that she might eventually have a life.

Inside the cottage, Marie started some coffee and squinted down at the card in the fading light. It read

Tara Stone
The Elementals
Practitioners of Sex Magic

Not for the first time during the course of the strange day, Marie wondered if she was still dreaming.

While the coffee brewed, she went about the business of unpacking her rucksack, which was soggy inside and out. The sandwich she had packed would almost pass as soup in its not-so air tight bag. She wrung water out of her hat and the extra socks she always carried. She opened the front pouch of her rucksack to pull out the ten pound note she kept on hand just in case she wanted a pint at the end of a good walk or some other treat at the local. Next to the soggy bill, right in plain sight, was her compass.

Chapter Three

MARIE COOKED THAT NIGHT, something she never had time for in her other life, and it really was beginning to feel like another life now. The knot in her stomach from the load of work she never got finished had almost gone along with the constant tightness in her shoulders from the competition that was never less than cut-throat and the fear that somehow she would be found lacking.

It was just stir fried vegetables over rice, but the vegetables were fresh and the rice was a healthy brown mix she'd bought at Booths on her last trip into Keswick. She had promised herself she'd eat healthier. She had promised herself she would get enough exercise, and living so close to the fells she could do that without an expensive membership in a gym she never had time to use.

She ate slowly, savouring the flavours and textures that weren't fast food. While she ate, she studied the OS map that had survived the day's drenching by being safely tucked in its plastic case. She ran a finger down the route Anderson had led her on, along Tongue Gill, a descent that had taken them past the disused quarries at Rigghead. No doubt it was a very interesting route when there was no mist. Not for the first time she wondered how Anderson had led her so competently and found the quarry so easily with no compass, no proper equipment, and dressed like he'd just come from a costume party. Not only that, but how had he known to look for her?

A chill passed up her spine as she glanced down at her compass lying on the table next to the map. How could she have missed it there in her rucksack in plain view? Could she have really let the weather shake her that badly? She recalled the dark figure's chilling caress in her dream and shivered. She was very glad Anderson had woken her when he did.

Still, there had been none of the usual heart palpitations, no hyperventilation, no cold sweats. She smiled to herself. Strange, when there really was something to stress about, when there really was a serious threat to life and limb, there had been no panic attack. She simply sat down in the rain and fell asleep. Perhaps she really was getting better.

She'd been sleeping a lot lately, making up for lost time, no doubt. And as soon as the dishes were done and the kitchen tidied, she was ready to sleep some more. She slipped into her nightshirt, thinking of her love making with Anderson, thinking of how he tasted of Tara when she kissed him. The woman's scent had been all over him, the scent of another woman's pussy. Strangely she couldn't recall his scent, that heavy base note of semen and male heat that made the smell of sex so heady. He had come inside her. She felt him. He'd come hard, and yet she couldn't actually recall his scent, or their blended scent.

Her own scent had been strong, urgent. She would have thought anyone within a city block could have smelled her excited pussy. Even when she got home, she had been loath to hurry off to the shower and wash away her sexy aroma. She was a woman who lived through her sense of smell, and yet she couldn't recall Anderson's scent. If not for Tara's card on the kitchen table she would wonder if she dreamed the whole experience.

Once in bed, she lay on her back, one hand up under her nightshirt cupping her breast while the other pushed and insinuated wriggling fingers between her pussy lips, still yielding and slippery even after a leisurely bath.

It was in that position she woke to the awareness of a man sitting on the bed next to her, a man who, from the looks of his clothing, must have been at the same costume party as Anderson. His fly was open and he was stroking a substantial hard-on. Instead of being frightened, as would have been the normal response to a stranger rubbing one off on her bed, she simply admired his pale hair and the way his large hand moved over heavy equipment. She liked it when she conjured sexy men to visit her in her dream world. Better yet she had conjured one obviously ready to play.

She watched through half closed eyes as he shoved his trousers open further and worried distended balls free from the press of his underpants. With one hand, he caressed the length of his cock, with the other he cupped himself and stroked with his thumb.

It was still there, that strange thrumming warmth between her hips. It was almost uncomfortable, and yet somehow it felt right, especially when she was so turned on. Had it been there when she fell asleep? She couldn't remember.

'I heard them talking about you,' the man said. 'They didn't say how strong you are.' He groaned out loud and shifted to slide his trousers down so that his pale arse settled onto the duvet, allowing easier access to himself. 'Even if they had, I would not have believed them.' His voice was a harsh whisper. 'I long to know what you look like beneath the duvet, beneath the nightdress. Please let me look at you.'

So far this dream was shaping up well. She was happy to play I'll-show-you-mine-if-you-show-me-yours. Strangely, Dream Guy sounded like he'd studied the same romantics Anderson had. Who'd have thought antiquated poet-speak could be so damned hot? She eased herself into a sitting position against the headboard and pushed back the bedding. The nightshirt lay high against her thighs, barely covering her cunt.

She was amazed at how well she could see in the moonlight drifting through her window. She could see the shape of him, the anxious rise and fall of his chest, the parting of his lips. She could feel his gaze on the hem of her nightshirt. She scrunched and raked at it until her hand rested against her pubic mound obscuring his view, and he groaned his frustration. Slowly, carefully she raised her bottom and shifted until the nightshirt was out of the way and her bare buttocks pressed against the smooth cotton of the sheet.

His gaze on her felt almost physical, as though with his eyes alone he could gently nudge her open. 'Please let me see,' he whispered.

She had played the voyeur with Anderson and Tara earlier. Now it felt wonderfully wicked to play the exhibitionist. She shifted her arse again and slowly, teasingly, opened her thighs, still nestling her hand in her curls, stroking and caressing, making herself wait until that magical moment when her fingers first slipped between the swell of her lips.

'I can smell you,' he said. 'The scent of your sex is intoxicating, please, please let me look at you.'

This time, she moved her fingers down over the hard rise of her clitoris and in between the pout of her lips, her breath catching, her hips jerking with that first electrical touch. Then she spread her labia as wide as she could manage with two fingers and opened her legs still further until she was certain Dream Guy could see every detail of her dilating pussy, every fold of her slippery landscape.

He gasped at the sight, and she could see his balls tighten and jerk with the intake of breath. He shifted a fisted hand down the length of his penis, lingering for his thumb to caress and circle the head, its slit opening and closing with each stroke. She could feel the gentle rocking of the mattress and wasn't sure if it was from her dream lover, who was now grinding his arse against the bed with each stroke, or if it was from her own bearing down.

'Touch yourself for me,' the man said. 'My desire is to watch you pleasure your lovely womanhood.'

There was a strange man sitting on the foot of her bed watching her masturbate. The very thought made her juices run thick and hot. With her left hand, she inserted two fingers deep into her wet cunt. With her right hand, she stroked and thumbed her clitoris in tight little rubs until it ached with urgent expansion.

'Breathtaking,' he gasped. 'Absolutely breathtaking. Now play with your bosoms for me.'

What was it about the selective use of euphemisms that was such a turn on? God, why didn't more men study the romantics? She chuckled breathlessly. 'Perhaps you would like to play with my bosoms for me?'

He shook his head almost as if she had asked him to drink poison. 'Oh I may not. I may only watch, and for now that must be enough.'

'Suit yourself.' Who understood what went on in the dream world? It didn't matter though, if he wanted to watch her play with her bosoms, it was definitely something she could get off on.

Keeping her eyes on his, and making sure not to obstruct the view of her pussy, she quickly lifted the shirt over her head and felt his gaze lock on her heavy breasts, nipples and areole at full attention. While one hand still busied itself at her pout, the other tugged and pinched her nipples in turn, cupping her weightiness and kneading the firm, warm flesh.

Dream Guy intensified the stroking of his cock until the whole bed shook with his efforts, and she could see the precome glistening on the head of his penis.

'Fuck me,' she grunted, inserting a third finger into her gaping pussy. 'I know that's not very poetic, but I want to come on your cock.' She reached to pull him to her, but he jerked away and stood quickly, shaking his head.

'What? What's the matter? I have condoms if you're afraid –'

'It is not the use of prophylactics, no. It is just that … I cannot. I want to, but I may not make love to you. Not like this. You have not been prepared.'

'How much more prepared do you want me to be?' She spread the fat slippery swell of herself and lifted her hips to prove her point.

But he only shook his head harder. 'You must believe me. I may only watch your pleasure. For now, it is enough. It must be enough. Please do this for me.' He pumped hard against his hand. She could tell he was getting close, and that made her want it all the more.

She cried out in frustration, then threw open the drawer of the bedside table and pulled out a thick, penis-shaped vibrator. There was no need for lube. She was sopping. She rammed it home and turned it up on full power.

Suddenly the room was filled with the breathless duet of

two people urgently approaching orgasm. Marie arched back against the stack of pillows thrusting the vibrator in and out of her clenching cunt and pinching and stroking her clit while the man shifted on the bed, his trousers dropping to his knees. As he watched her, he stroked and jerked his erection with accelerating speed. Every muscle in his body tensed for the coming explosion until at last he grunted loud, bucked against his hand, and shot a viscous arc of semen across the tangled duvet. Marie's orgasm tore up through her like an earthquake, and she collapsed back onto the pillows, closing her eyes as the waves rolled over her.

When she woke up, honeyed sunlight was streaming through the bedroom window. She rubbed her eyes and sat up. As she did so, the vibrator slipped from between her thighs and she gasped at the slick warm feel of it being expelled. Jesus! Had she had a wank on the vibrator in her sleep? The heat of the dream came back to her and her still-wet pussy quivered. Almost without thinking, she slipped the vibe back inside her and absently worked it as she looked around the room. Her nightshirt was tossed in a heap on the floor. Her pussy tightened and gripped at the vibrator as she remembered Dream Guy coming all over her duvet, but there was no tell-tale stain. Of course not, she chided herself. It was a dream.

She pulled a heavy sigh, lay back on the pillows and settled in for a nice morning diddle while she recalled the driving lust of the dream and how amazingly real it had felt. Back home her dreams had all been about failing, or being fired, or being publicly humiliated in front of the senior staff. She could get used to having luscious wet dreams of sexy men as her unconscious's tool of choice.

After an orgasm that nearly shook the mattress off the bed, she had a quick shower and made tea and toast for breakfast, adding a bowl of juicy strawberries in her efforts to eat healthier. In her wildest dreams, she never could have imagined so much sex could happen to her so quickly. Last night's dream alone was better than anything she had been able to manage in the sex department for several years now. Surely it was a good omen.

She had just settled in to enjoy her breakfast, when she heard a crash coming from the stables. She jumped and nearly spilled her tea. There was another crash. A horse whinnied. And the fire from last night raged up through her belly nearly doubling her over before it calmed. Then she heard a gruff man's voice.

'He's going to be so angry. Hurry, if he finds us this close to his horse, he'll never help us.'

There was a harsh groan and some bumping and banging about and another man's voice came from right beneath the kitchen window. 'But we didn't do it! It wasn't our fault.'

'Well, he'll never believe us, will he? You know how he is.'

Neither of the voices sounded like Tim Meriwether's. Marie rose and moved to the window. Tim's mare shifted skittishly around the end of the paddock. But before she could focus too much attention on the mare, she heard a muffled grunt, and her eyes caught upon the two men directly beneath her window, both dressed like farmers, both with their trousers down over their hips. There was another grunt as the taller of the two shoved his straining cock up the arse of the other, who was bent over holding himself open. He groaned, 'It won't be enough. It's never enough.'

'It'll have to do, won't it? Besides, now she's here. Maybe she can convince him.' The man behind thrust hard then reached around to stroke the formidable cock of the man he was fucking.

'Tara said leave her alone. Tara said she's off limits.'

'Tara's just scared, that's all. She'll change her mind,' the man doing the humping said with a hard thrust.

Marie barely managed to stifle a gasp and hop to the side of the sink, before the burn between her hips flared again. Clutching her stomach, almost absently, she moved as far out of view as she could get and still watch. God, she could have never imagined she would be moving into a voyeur's paradise when she rented Lacewing Cottage. Yesterday Tara and Anderson, this morning two strange men going at it in full view. OK, she wasn't exactly an innocent, but she'd never seen two men fucking al fresco before. And what did they have to do with Tara anyway? She craned her neck for a better view.

The man behind, pulled out his cock, spat on his hand and rubbed saliva the full length of his erection, then he spat into the man's gaping hole and shoved back in. 'You see? It's good, isn't it?'

'It won't be enough,' the man bent over in front said, caressing his balls and pressing back hard against the thrusts. 'It's never enough. Damn it, why won't he help us?'

'Stop whining. It'll be all right. You want to come in my mouth? I'll let you when I'm done. You'd like that, wouldn't you?'

There was another loud crash, and a shout. 'How many times have I told you, stay away from here. I don't want you here. Now get out!'

Marie quickly stepped away from the window, heart pounding in her chest. She recognized Tim Meriwether's voice. She would have never thought Tim to be gay, nor could she figure why two strange men would be going at it in his stable yard. Clearly Tim wasn't happy. What the hell was going on?

'Look what you've done. Get out of here before you cause more trouble.' Then things went quiet, except for the nervous whickering of the mare and Tim speaking soothingly to her.

Cautiously, Marie stepped out on the porch. In the paddock in front of the stable, there was now no sign of anyone but Tim trying to calm the skittish mare. The stable door gave a hard slam on its hinges in a sudden chilled gust of wind that caused them both to jump and the horse to shy sideways. Tim cursed under his breath, then everything went still again.

'Need a hand?' she called out before she had a chance to think that she might be catching him at a bad time.

He looked up with a start and offered her a pained smile. 'You OK around horses?'

'Don't know. Never tried. But I'm not scared of them, if that's what you mean.'

'Close enough. Can you open the stable door for me? As you can see I got my hands full. The mare's pretty spooked.' He nodded to the stable.

29

From her first day on Lacewing Farm, Marie had taken comfort in the earthy smells of horseflesh and hay. Even the pungent bite of animal dung, which sometimes made her eyes water, reminded her that she no longer lived in a world sanitized of everything that didn't involve money and greed. No, horses didn't frighten her at all, not after what she'd lived through in the business world. She slipped in behind the man and the mare and opened the door then stood aside while Tim led the now calming animal into her stall. In no time, he had her quietly munching grain.

'There, that's better, isn't it?' He scratched the mare behind an ear and the horse whickered softly. Then he turned his attention to Marie. 'Thanks for your help. She was really spooked. She's never been this bad before when … She's usually very calm.'

'Not a problem. What were those guys doing in your paddock anyway? I mean really, that's pretty nervy, isn't it? Maybe you should call the police.'

Even in the dim light of the stable she could see the colour had drained from his face. With fingers suddenly unsteady, he fumbled with the lead he'd taken from the mare's halter and dropped it on the floor. He didn't bother to pick it up as he turned to hold her gaze.

'What? What's the matter? I mean I don't mind, or anything. It's none of my business if there are men having sex in your paddock, or even if you're – '

'I'm not! Gay. If that's what you mean. And they're not my friends.'

'Sorry, I didn't mean to offend you.'

'You saw them?'

'Of course I saw them. It was impossible not to. They didn't seem to mind at all having a shag right in front of my kitchen window.'

He shoved a hand through sun-bleached brown hair, badly in need of a trim, and shifted from foot to foot. 'Come here.' He motioned for her to follow him out into the paddock. 'Where did you see them?'

She moved to the edge of the stable wall, where it was

closest to her window. 'They were standing right here. They were scuffling around and arguing, something about it wasn't their fault, but you'd be mad – at least I assume they were talking about you.'

Tim grunted. 'Oh they were talking about me all right.'

She continued. 'Then the one pushed the other one up against this wall, and the next thing I know they're under my kitchen window and ... Hold on. Something's not right.'

He said nothing, only watched her.

'There are no foot prints, no sign of scuffling. Look.' She lifted her feet and set them down a couple of times as though she were doing a strange rain dance. 'The paddock isn't muddy, but it's soft. Look, you can see my foot prints, and I can see yours even from here. But ...'

He came to her side. 'But you can't see anyone else's footprints, right?'

She shook her head and felt a tremor run up her spine.

'Bless you, Marie Warren!' He surprised her by scooping her off her feet into a bear hug. When he sat her back down, she grabbed for the wall to keep from losing her balance.

'What?'

'God, I thought I was losing my mind.' He began to pace back and forth in front of her. 'I mean those crazy women told me that this would happen. They told me they could help me, but they wouldn't let me do anything, and I told them to sod off because they're all completely mad and I thought I was getting that way too. This is such a relief. I mean if you can see them too, then I'm not the only one, and maybe it's not as bad as they say.'

'Tim, what on earth are you talking about?'

He turned to face her, his blue eyes glinting silver in the intense morning sunlight. Then he took a step closer, the smile disappearing from his face. 'You did see them, two men. Two men ... having sex.'

'Of course I saw them. Like I said, how could I not?'

He moved another cautious step closer, approaching her as he had the spooked mare only minutes before. 'Marie, no one else has ever seen them.'

31

The warm morning suddenly felt icy. 'What do you mean no one else has ever seen them?'

'No foot prints, no sign of them, one second they're here then they're gone. Think about it.' He took another step closer. 'They're ghosts.'

'Ghosts?' She found herself pressed back against the wall, suddenly cold, suddenly trembling.

'Come on.' He folded her hand into his and gently guided her back to her house. 'I'll explain everything, or at least as much as I can -- over a cup of tea, maybe?'

Inside her kitchen, no one said anything until the kettle had steamed and they were both seated across from each other staring into their respective cups. The remains of Marie's breakfast sat untouched, forgotten with the morning's events and Tim's revelation.

'How can they be ghosts,' she asked at last. Her voice sounded thin and wispy.

'What do you mean how can they be ghosts. They're dead, that's how.'

'But I've never seen ghosts before. I've never even had any déjà vu or anything like that let alone seen ghosts. Have you always seen ghosts?' She would have preferred to sound a little less hysterical, but she couldn't quite manage it.

'No. I haven't always seen ghosts.' He held her gaze, then he released his breath slowly. 'It all started a little over three months ago. I had taken the mare out for a ride and I had just put her back in the stable when I heard a commotion behind the barn. When I went to check it out, I found two people ... two people shagging under a tree. Later, the woman approached me and gave me this.' He dug in his pocket for his wallet and pulled out a battered card identical to the one Tara had given her last night, but the name on it was Fiori Numan. 'She told me if I'd seen what she was sure I had, then I would be needing the help of the Elementals soon.

'For the next three nights, I had what I thought were incredibly arousing dreams. I'd wake up and there'd be people in my room, people ... masturbating,' he spoke the word through barely parted lips. 'And they'd want to watch me

32

masturbate.' He forced a laugh, 'something I was more than willing to do.' He took a large gulp of tea and looked down at the card lying on the table. 'When I started seeing them while I was awake, I realised something wasn't right. They were always either masturbating or having sex with each other, like the two blokes in the stable yard. They always seemed to be frustrated. They were always asking me for help.'

She leaned closer, heart pounding in her chest at the thought of her own real-as-life dream. 'Did you go to the Elementals?'

He nodded. 'They explained to me that I was seeing ghosts, ghosts who knew I could help them, ghosts who needed my help.'

With trembling fingers, she pushed the card Tara had given her across the kitchen table toward him. She held his gaze. 'Yesterday I had a similar experience.' She didn't tell him about her sexy encounter with Anderson afterward.

'From Tara? That's a surprise.' he said, looking at the card. 'And she wants you to go and see her?'

'Why?'

The muscles along his jaw tightened and relaxed, and he avoided her gaze. 'I don't know. She just never seemed very social, like she never wanted me around.'

'She seemed fine to me,' Marie said. 'You said they told you that the ghosts needed your help. Just what exactly did they want you to do?'

'Because I can see them, supposedly I can be taught some sort of spell that will give them ...' He blushed hard. '... will give them sort of temporary bodies so they can have sex.'

'Have sex?'

'Yeah you know.' He paid an unwarranted amount of attention to arranging and rearranging the two cards on the table. 'A physical body is necessary for sex, and that's the only way they ever get any satisfaction.'

'Then they have sex with each other?' she nodded to her kitchen window to indicate the two ghosts going at it earlier.'

He shook his head, still refusing to look at her, but pointed a callused finger at the two business cards lying next to each other on the table. 'Sex magic, Marie. They're practitioners of sex magic.'

'Jesus,' she whispered. 'You mean those two wanted you to …'

'To have sex with them.' He heaved a shaky sigh. 'Them and any other horny spirit who shows up at my door.'

'Jesus,' she whispered again. 'But you have to learn the spell, don't you?'

'Among other things, yes. Until I do that, until I'm properly trained, I can't give them what they need.' His jaw set tight as he picked up the card, and she noticed his knuckles were white. 'And Tara, who was she with?'

'She was with this guy … but he couldn't have been a ghost because I … Because he …' The room suddenly felt icy, but the heat below her belly flared and burned up through her, crackling along her spine. She could hear her own startled yelp at the feel of it, but it seemed a long way away. She set her teacup down hard, sloshing the contents onto the saucer, suddenly feeling as though all the oxygen had been sucked out of the room. Her pulse went into overdrive and began to flutter in her chest. Anderson had no scent. Anderson's clothes were old-fashioned and they never got wet. Why hadn't she thought that strange? She shoved back the chair, nearly upsetting it in making space to lower her head between her knees as the world began to spin.

'Bloody hell, Marie, what's the matter?' Tim was immediately on his knees by her side. She could barely hear him over the harsh flutter of wings in her ears. Anderson appeared out of the mist as if by magic. Anderson needed no compass to navigate the fog. Anderson spoke like someone from a Jane Austin novel. 'I can't breathe,' she gasped.

Tim sprung to his feet and disappeared out the door of her cottage in a flash. Great, now she'd frightened him away right when she really didn't want to be alone. She could feel the cold sweat break out on her forehead and the back of her neck. She knew it was a panic attack, she knew it! She wasn't going to die, but for fuck sake, it always felt like it! Maybe she was going to die, maybe she was already dead, maybe that's how come Anderson could take her, how come she was so desperate

34

to have him.

She heard the crash of footsteps up the porch and from her position between her knees she saw Tim's jeaned legs before he dropped into a squat and held a paper bag to her nose and mouth.

'Breathe into this. Just breathe, Marie. It'll be OK. Relax now. Just relax. Breathe.'

For ages it seemed that her world was reduced to breathing in and breathing out. At some point, Tim had placed a cool cloth across the back of her neck. When at long last she sat up, he handed her a glass of water. She took it gratefully and offered a weak smile.

His face was pale, lips set in a tight thin line. The muscles along his jaw looked tense enough to bite steel. 'This ghost Tara was with,' his throat rose and fell as though he were attempting to swallow something vile. 'Did he ... Did he hurt her?'

She shook her head.

He dropped to his knees in front of her and grabbed both her hands in a suicide grip. 'Did he hurt you?'

'No! No. He didn't hurt anyone.' She pulled her hands free. 'He, he fucked her. And then ...'

He nodded expectantly.

She took a heavy breath as though she were about to dive into deep water. 'And then he fucked me.'

Chapter Four

'WHAT DO YOU MEAN he fucked you? Didn't you know? I mean how could you not know? And you don't have the spell. He couldn't have been a ghost. How could he have been a ghost?' Tim, who had been so calm until now, suddenly seemed on the edge of hysteria himself. 'Bloody hell! What did he look like? Was he big? Thick-chested like a body-builder? Did he carry a bullwhip?'

'No! He was tall, slender. He wore a black suit and looked quite, well rakish. No bullwhip.' She shoved him away. 'And he was as real as you are.' And as sexy. She felt that thought in places nowhere close to her head. 'At the time, I had no reason to suspect anything unusual.'

'Damn them!' He pounded his hand against the table and the teapot rattled. 'I know they're all barking, but I can't believe they'd do this to you.'

'It's the only explanation.'

He plopped back in the chair next to her and folded his arms across his chest with such force Marie was certain it must have hurt. 'Why? Tell me why you think you had sex with a ghost.' He blushed hard even as he said it. 'I mean was he so hot you just couldn't resist? Did he hypnotise you into shagging him? What?' He caught his breath and straightened his shoulders. 'I'm sorry. That was rude and out of line. I'm sorry.'

He stood and paced once or twice. In a gesture that was surely pure nerves, he topped off the teacups with now tepid tea. 'It's just, well you have to understand, my experience with ghosts wasn't ... well it wasn't nearly as pleasant as yours seems to have been. I mean I obviously didn't know the bloke Fiori was with was a ghost until later. He's a local ghost. I see him around here all the time now. But he wasn't the problem. He wasn't …' His voice drifted off as though he had lost his train of thought. He sat down again, this time calmer, and slugged back his tea. 'Tell me why you think the man you were with was a ghost?'

Marie relaxed into her chair and told Tim about the experience of Anderson, minus the sexy bits. 'And I dreamed. It was so real.'

'And sexy?'

She nodded, feeling the heat crawl up her face.

'But there was no … I mean you didn't actually …'

'We didn't fuck, no.' She stared into her tea avoiding his gaze. 'There was just masturbation.'

'Marie,' he leaned forward and laid his hand on hers. 'Marie, it wasn't a dream.'

She jerked her hand away. 'I know that now, Tim. I know that.' She forced the chair back with a loud screech and grabbed up Tara's card and her cell phone from where it lay on the credenza.

Instantly he was at her side. 'What are you doing?'

'What does it look like I'm doing? I'm calling Tara. She'd got a helluva lot to answer for, and I want to hear it.'

He grabbed the phone away from her. 'Please don't. Please don't do that.' He laid it down where it had been and guided her back to her chair, where she glared at him expectantly.

He ran a hand through his hair and blew out a sharp breath. 'Marie. They're all mad over there. Trust me when I say it's best you don't get mixed up with them.'

'But they can explain what's going on, and they bloody well need to, I think.'

He raised a hand. 'They'll only tell you a load of rubbish, and nothing will change, and they'll make excuses …' His voice drifted off again, then he looked up as though suddenly remembering where he was. 'Please, Marie. Wait. Just give it a little time. Give it till tomorrow, then …' He offered a smile and forced enthusiasm into his voice. 'I reckon tomorrow we'll both just be laughing about it all, and anyway, they're only ghosts. A bit troublesome sometime, perhaps, but harmless.'

His voice wasn't very convincing.

'It's freezing in here,' Sky breathed as she ducked into the cave chafing her arms. 'Really Fiori, couldn't we have just done this in the suite. It would have been so much more comfy.'

Fiori looked up from lighting candles around the perimeter of the chamber. 'The magic will be stronger outside and even stronger underground like this. You know that. Besides if Tara can handle it, you and I surely can.'

Sky joined Fiori in the preparations. 'And you really think we need stronger magic for this? Sounds like a done deal to me from what Anderson said.'

Fiori shot Sky a warning glance and half whispered, 'You know why we need stronger magic.' She threw a quick glance over her shoulder at Tara who sat on bare rock at the far side of the chamber, legs folded beneath her, her breathing that of deep meditation. 'If Anderson is right, then we'll have to protect Marie. We'll have to protect both of them now.' She worried her bottom lip with her teeth as she finished her task, and the two women sat down on the cushions spread over ruined slate.

'But if it's true, then maybe we won't need to protect her at all maybe she's –'

'I know, but she doesn't know that yet, does she, and you know how Tara feels about risking someone else.'

'I hate dream magic,' Sky said. 'Even when it's not me doing the dreaming. It's just all so nebulous, isn't it? And this time, we already know the answer, don't we?'

Fiori shushed her and glanced back over her shoulder to see if Tara had overheard. 'Her mind's made up about it, and surely you can see why.'

Sky released a long, shaky breath. 'Of course I can see why, and I'm as afraid to hope as she is, but we have to. Hope I mean.' She looked around the chamber again. 'Where's Anderson? He was inside Marie Warren. He felt her essence. We can't do this without him.'

The words were barely out of her mouth before the ghost materialised in the chamber and sat down across from the two of them. 'I'm here.' He offered that dark, delicious smile that

Sky was always happy to lap off his face when he gave her a chance. Sadly she wouldn't get the chance tonight. There'd be plenty of sex and she'd no doubt have a blistering orgasm, but it wouldn't be due to Anderson's delicious cock. Once again, Tara would have that privilege. Since he was the only bloke in the coven, he always had his work cut out for him, but then it didn't really matter because the only bloke in the coven just happened to be a ghost and was deliciously tireless and always at the ready for any ritual that required an erect penis.

'There now. I think we're ready.' Tara roused herself from her meditation, plopped down next to Anderson, and offered everyone a distant smile. She rubbed her hands together slowly then fondled the pentacle resting between her breasts. She was already naked and, even in the constant 63 degrees of the cave, her body glowed, and a soft dew of perspiration caressed her upper lip and the valley between her pale breasts. Sky knew that for Tara, the ritual had begun hours ago, and her smile was not the only thing about her that was distant. She had been in the Ether preparing. She was only partially in the waking world, and in her altered state, she was as close to a ghost as she could be and still draw living breath.

Tara carefully released the red ribbon that held back an eruption of wild dark hair, which she shook back over her well-muscled shoulders. Sky felt her heart clench at the sight of her coven sister so vulnerable. She knew how hard it was for her to allow such vulnerability after all that had happened. Then the power that Tara wore like armour, and wore so well, settled back around her, and she looked at the members of her coven with dark eyes, pupils dilated from her spell work and meditation. 'We can begin then.'

Oblivious to the cold or the discomfort, Fiori positioned herself on a flat slab of bare rock that slightly overhung the soft sea of heavily-stuffed pillows and cushions so incongruous with the rest of the surroundings. It was her job to witness and be prepared to bring the dreamers back from the dream world if need be.

When they were ready, Anderson rose and slid out of the dove grey robe he always wore in ritual. Sky slipped free of her pale blue one and both she and Anderson reached for Tara at the same time. As the magic progressed, Tara would become the chalice for Anderson's filling. It would be for her to dream the dream. If it were true, if Marie Warren really was a ghost rider, and anywhere nearly as powerful as Anderson believed her to be, then Sky could barely allow herself to imagine what that might mean. It was Sky's task to help the two into the dream and assist them as needed.

She eased Tara down into the cushions and kissed and caressed her breasts until her nipples felt like stalagmites rising up from the cave, a thought that, under the circumstances, didn't really seem all that strange. Sky knew that the herbs Tara had taken in the mulled wine earlier were already thinning the veil between the physical world and the Dream World, while heightening her senses at the same time. She had never known her coven leader to call upon so much powerful magic for something that should have been a simple dream encounter, and that made her more than a little nervous. Sky could hear Tara's breath like a wind in the cave as she kissed down her belly and opened her legs, which she no longer had the will to do for herself.

In her peripheral vision, Sky could see Anderson kneeling at Tara's feet, one hand resting on his thick erection, the athame in flesh, ready to enter the chalice and bless it. Sky pushed Tara's knees wide apart, and in her mind's eye, she knew that Anderson now viewed Tara as the Gateway, the chalice into which he would pour his experience of Marie Warren and release the magic that would begin the dream.

Without a word, Anderson positioned himself between her legs, lowering his face to kiss her heavy clit and tease open the pout of her labia, reverencing the Gate, before he covered her with his body, taking his weight onto his arms as he shifted and rocked until his cock found her slick path and slipped inside as though it were as anxious to find shelter as Sky had been when she entered the cave.

Sky heard herself groan as though she were a long way away. She felt the drag of memories that weren't hers slide and shimmer at the edge of her consciousness until she grasped onto them. She heard Anderson's breath catch as Tara gripped him. Lovely that, a ghost's breath, so much more precious than anything the living could imagine. Sky pinched Tara's nipples hard knowing the pain would help focus her. Then she felt a flood of sensation that coursed through Tara, and the harder Anderson thrust, the clearer the images of Marie Warren on the fells became. And the harder Tara rode him, the further away from consciousness he took both of them until only Sky remained fully alert to witness the events that had taken place on the fells.

Sky watched as Anderson, consciousness only, reached out to touch the woman huddled down on the path in the rain. And both Sky and Tara felt the jolt of his shock as clearly as if it had been their own. The very touch of this woman made Anderson hard all over. But it wasn't sex, it was flesh. And it was instantaneous, without the Love Spell. Her touch alone had enfleshed him, even without her knowing it, even without him willing it so. That couldn't be right.

But there was no time to dwell on it. The memories rushed forward like fast moving water, and then Sky and Tara were in the cave watching Anderson lift the woman onto his lap lest she catch a chill from the cold stone. And the woman took his mouth, holding him there in the flesh as easily as she breathed her own breath. The passion she generated sizzled and danced along the walls of the cave like fireworks, and she didn't even know it. Sky had never seen Anderson so open to anyone.

With a little tremor of her heart, she realised how vulnerable he was now making himself to his coven. They were the ones closest to him and yet even they had never seen him as he was with Marie Warren. Sky felt the acceleration of Anderson's heartbeat, the excitement of his thoughts as this woman held him so perfectly, so exquisitely. She held him inside her when he entered her, she held him there in the container of flesh and bone that, without her knowledge, she had created for him, so perfect, so tight fitting that the heat of him radiated like life itself. And he spilled his semen in her in great heavy splashes steaming like fire into the chalice that held him tight.

Then he lifted her on top of him, holding her close to the

pounding of his heart, wanting to keep her awake so he could feel the flesh she had given him just a little longer. But knowing her exhaustion and knowing his own rawness at rubbing up against such power, he had let her drift into unconsciousness. And as she did so, he had allowed himself to evaporate like the mist on the fells when the sun came out.

For Tim, sleep didn't come easily, even after an endless scouring of Raven Crag with Keswick Mountain Rescue for the lost tourist who just hadn't bothered to tell anyone she'd changed her mind and gone shopping in Windermere instead. She seemed dazed and confused, not at all sure why she'd made such a silly decision. She had wondered mindlessly into a pub at closing time and announced that she was lost. The whole thing had made Tim nervous. Maybe the woman was on something, maybe she had some mental problems no one wanted to talk about. He didn't know, and in the end they had all nervously laughed it off.

To Tim's disappointment all the lights at Marie's cottage had been out when he got home. He had planned to invite her over for dinner that evening, to help her get her mind off the ghosts, and admittedly, maybe on to something a little more amicable. He hadn't planned on a call-out from Mountain Rescue. Several of the volunteers were away on holiday, and he was close to Raven Crag, so in spite of an uneasy feeling about leaving Marie after such an unnerving revelation – especially after he had convinced her not to call the Elementals – he'd felt he had to go. And now it was late, and her house was dark, and he'd had to eat the lamb stew in the slow cooker alone.

Her car was out front so he could only assume she was sleeping soundly, the morning's ghost incident happily forgotten. He was relieved about that, at least. He was afraid she wouldn't let it go that easily, and he had worked hard to disentangle himself from the nasty mess of three months ago and to learn to cope with the constant comings and goings of ghosts. The ghosts he could live with. He just didn't want anything to do with the Elementals and especially not with whatever it was that seemed to have attached itself to them. They'd tried to convince him the man was just another ghost, but in his gut, he knew better. Could they really think him that naïve?

He tossed in the bed and readjusted the pillow. Marie might be sleeping soundly, but he sure as hell wasn't.

It was hard to ignore the small-breasted ghost sitting on the chair at the foot of the bed tugging and pinching at the plumped nipple that peeked over the top of her deep-cut bodice. With ghosts always being the order of the day, sometimes he succeeded in shutting them out and sometimes he didn't.

The slight tilt of this ghost's head and the way her pale hair fell slightly over one eye made him think of Marie. She was smaller breasted than Marie, and her hair was short, but if he looked at her in the low light through heavy eyelids and used his imagination, he could almost imagine Marie sittingthere watching him hungrily. He could almost imagine Marie about to strip off her clothes, crawl beneath the duvet and snuggle her luscious nakedness up against him. Real body heat, alive and breathing and needing the way he needed, that's what he wanted. Most of the time he just got on with it and didn't think about it, but right now, right this moment, he wanted Marie naked and slick with need, gagging for it as badly as he was.

He was embarrassed to think it might have been his cock that possessed him to lease the cottage to her. With all the craziness going on around him, the last thing he needed was a tenant, but he'd not been able to resist. In spite of his efforts to minimize contact with her for her own protection, he'd been horny for her since he first laid eyes on her – a real flesh and blood woman with sultry eyes that made him think of a fast-moving storm above the high fells. And her voice was just a tiny bit too low for a woman's voice. He could listen to her talk about the weather and get stiff. It was hard to chase away thoughts of her pouty-lipped smile and what he wished she'd do with that mouth of hers. Then there were her full breasts, which more often than not were crowned with nipples that jutted like heat-seeking missiles. And, oh, he wanted to give them some heat to seek, especially tonight after he'd actually spent time with her, talked masturbation and sex with her.

OK, the context hadn't been ideal, but still, thinking about it now when he was chasing sleep and struggling to keep his mind off why she had come to him in the paddock this morning, he'd cherry-pick the sexy bits of their encounter, and it was the heat he chose to remember. His cock stretched and stiffened beneath the duvet, into his searching hand.

'You sleep naked, Tim Meriwether,' the ghost in the chair purred. 'I know that you do. Let me see your cock. Please let me see you.'

'Go away, Lisette,' he sighed. 'I don't want you to see me.'

'Yes you do.' She moved to sit on the edge of the bed. 'You know you do. I'll show you my pussy. It's so wet. You could help me if you would.'

'I can't help you and I don't want to see ...'

He stopped talking because Lisette wasn't listening. She never listened, and in a way that always gave him an excuse for the wank he knew would follow, and he needed an excuse tonight.

Lisette slid her flapper skirt gracefully, almost demurely up over her hips. 'I haven't worn any panties tonight. I left them off just for you, Tim Meriwether, because I want you to look at my cunt.' She shifted on the duvet and lifted one shapely leg onto the bed making it impossible for him not to see the glisten of her swollen pussy lips. 'I want you to see what you're missing; I want you to see how you make me suffer.' Then she plunged her nimble fingers into her split and began to thrust and stroke, eyes fluttering, breath that was not real spilling desperately between the full painted bow of her mouth.

God, Tim thought, if she were real, if she were flesh and blood right now, he'd never be able to resist. He'd crawl between her splayed legs and hump her brains out. But she wasn't real, she wasn't flesh and blood, not like Marie. He tugged at his cock and ground his arse against the mattress.

The ghost gave a throaty chuckle. 'I know what your hand is doing against that lovely hard cock of yours.' She leaned forward, 'And we both know it'll feel better if you throw off the duvet and let me watch.' The ghost excavated the other tight breast from the flimsy front of her dress and gave it a hard squeeze. 'Come on. I'll pretend to be your Marie for you. I don't mind. You can even call me Marie and tell me what you want to do to me.' She leaned close, fingers shoving hard into her gape for emphasis. 'I know you want to fuck her.' She nodded to his hard-on hidden in the folds of the duvet. 'I know that's for her, for her warm round body.' Her thumb went to work on the nub of her clit. 'I could have a warm round body if you'd listen to the witches, if you'd do as they asked, and I would let you fuck me until I was raw, until I couldn't walk. You'd like that, Tim Meriwether. I know you would.'

'Then why don't you go to the witches and let them take care of you,' he said between gritted teeth as he cupped his balls and kneaded them almost to the point of pain.

'I don't crave women flesh, Tim Meriwether, and it's you I want.'

Almost as though his body had a mind of its own, he heaved off the duvet without missing a stroke, and the ghost gasped her appreciation. He shoved himself upright against the headboard, spat on his hand and rubbed his saliva over the hot length of him, too impatient to dig in the bedside table for the lube he kept handy.

Lisette shifted her weight back and lifted her hips until he could see the whole of her cleft clear down to the shadowy clench of her anus. She wasn't what he wanted, and he hated it when he gave in to her tauntings, and yet that was also a part of what made their little trysts so nasty. It was a game of substitution really.

'If I were flesh, you would fuck me now, wouldn't you, Tim Meriwether? I know you would, and I would be slippery enough and pouting enough to accommodate your heavy cock.' As if to demonstrate her point, she thrust another finger into her sucking, slurping pussy until all that remained visible of her hand was her thumb rubbing against her marbled clit. 'You can see it,' she grunted. 'But you can't feel it any more than I can, you selfish prick. I make you come every time, but I only get to watch.'

He was getting close, thinking about Marie, thinking about

her and the ghost on the fells, thinking about her masturbating in her bed. Had she played with her pussy before she fell asleep tonight? Had she fondled and tweaked her lovely breasts. Had she thought about him? He reached for the hand towel he needed more often than he cared to admit these days and convulsed his heavy wad into its folds just as Lisette vanished with a little yelp. He felt like he would come for ever. The hard shudders prying him open from the inside somehow felt dark and raw, like he'd been holding it too long, like even the relief that washed over him and eased him over the edge into sleep was somehow not enough, could somehow not ease the spreading darkness. The thought niggled its way into his consciousness just before he plunged into the dream world. Perhaps this was just a little bit of what the ghosts felt. Had Lisette made him feel that way? But before he could contemplate further, he slept like the dead.

Chapter Five

BRIEFLY, SKY BECAME AWARE of Anderson still nestled inside Tara, though his breathing was now the deep even drag of sleep, which he didn't need but could enjoy at will. Sky lay snuggled close, her head on Tara's shoulder, her hand cupped around a breast. She knew she was asleep. They were all asleep. Only Fiori stood sentinel in the waking world, as silent and unmoving as the stone on which she sat.

Then Sky was under again, back in the cave with Marie, only this time it was through Tara's eyes she viewed the woman, and in spite of the carefree enthusiasm Tara presented, Sky could feel the doubt, the tension, the clench of fear deep in the coven leader's belly all overlaid by way more sorrow than one person should ever have to bear. But waking up from her lovemaking with Anderson, Marie Warren was blissfully ignorant of all of that.

Then there was the good-bye kiss in front of Lacewing Cottage, and the dream flared with heat and passion, all on little butterfly wings. It wasn't entirely sexual. There was a heavy dose of excitement and nerves, the kind associated with that very first kiss. The energy of the memory crackled and buzzed with exhilaration that could only be felt in the presence of magic, and for a moment, Sky wasn't sure if it was her own excitement or the excitement of Anderson and Tara in the dream world that she felt. But it was there. It was clear, much more clear than most dream magic tended to be. She floated along on the feeling until it dissipated and flattened and cooled.

Then it chilled, like the first hard breath of winter in Cumbria. Her eyes fluttered open to the grey half-light that might have been dawn, but the sunlight couldn't reach them inside the cave. Fiori's candles had bathed the chamber in shades of orange and rose, not this dull flat grey. She stirred to find Tara and Anderson gone. The smell of sex thinned around her, and she was cold, so cold that her teeth chattered. Fiori still sat sentinel on the rise of stone casting a dark, hulking shadow across the dream bed.

Shivering, Sky grabbed for a blanket. She was about to ask Fiori why she had let the others leave before the magic had run its course, but her words died in her throat as the shadow rose around Fiori until she was completely eclipsed in the enormity of it. Sky's stomach knotted and threatened to rebel as the owner of the shadow, now standing directly behind the unaware Fiori, rested a huge palm along one side of her pale face. He hunched just enough that with the other he could grope Fiori's bare breasts none too gently. Fiori's eyelids fluttered and she stretched upward and backward like a cat into his embrace.

At last he spoke. 'I paid a visit to Lacewing Farm this morning. Afraid your friends, the sodomite farmers took the blame for upsetting Mr Meriwether's exquisite mare.' The man tisk-tisked. 'Such filthy wretches. Your Marie is lovely, by the way. That's right, I had a good look at her after I sent her landlord and his Mountain Rescue friends off on a wild goose-chase for a missing walker.' He shook his head sadly, all the while his hand roamed over Fiori's body like a rodent searching for food. 'Yes, Marie Warren is very lovely, indeed, but weak. Disappointingly weak, really. I had so hoped for more of a challenge.' And with a sigh that was almost sensual, he raised both hands to the sides of Fiori's face, tightened his grasp and twisted until there was a sickening snap.

'Sky, Sky!'

It was hard to hear her name being called over the screaming. It was only as she fought her way up into the waking world between Fiori and Tara that she realised she was the one doing the screaming. 'It was Deacon,' she gasped, when she could speak. 'He was right there behind you, Fiori. I saw him. He spoke to me. He wanted me to know that he could hurt us, that he could hurt them – Tim and Marie. Marie,' she

48

gasped. 'Is she all right?'

Suddenly Anderson materialised on the cushions, still naked. 'Both Marie and Tim are sleeping peacefully,' he said without preamble, 'though Tim only very recently according to Lisette. There was indeed a strange Mountain Rescue call out, and Tiggs and Finny assure me that they were not responsible for the incident with the mare. It would appear that Deacon has graced Lacewing Farm with a visit in spite of all our efforts to curtail him.'

Tara laid a warm hand on Sky's arm. 'We all saw it, Sweetie. He intended that we should.' They all looked at Fiori, who had said nothing since Sky came up from the dream. She sat, still naked, nibbling on her lower lip. 'Don't worry, I'm all right.' she said, raising a hand to her neck. 'I've already been there, remember?' She forced a smile, but her face was ashen, her lips pale and set tight.

Tara released a long, slow breath and ran a hand through her dishevelled dark hair. 'Well, this changes everything then, doesn't it? I mean we can't bring her into this.'

'It changes nothing,' Fiori shook her head slowly. 'We have no choice but to bring her into it. It's what we expected all along, and you have to stop pretending otherwise, Tara. Marie is already in it, and so is Tim Meriwether. It's only made worse by the fact that neither of them knows. If we want this to stop, then we have to take a stand now, and like it or not, there's no way of excluding the two of them from the solution.'

'Especially not when our dear Marie may very well be a part of the problem,' Anderson said. He squared his shoulders and gave a curt nod. 'I will go to her.' He raised a hand before Tara could speak. 'And I will be sure to stay hidden. Sadly, I fear she will not be happy to see me under the circumstances, so it is just as well. It seems that the incident with Tiggs and Finny, along with a consultation with Tim Meriwether has led our Marie to the logical conclusion about the state of my physical existence. Poor timing, I fear, but there is nothing for it, is there?'

'Be careful, Anderson,' Tara said. 'If she can enflesh you just by touch alone without even knowing what she's doing, we

49

don't know what other powers she may have. But –'

'I know,' he said. 'It is of the utmost importance that we keep her safe.'

The hulk of a man was standing behind a woman with hair the colour of the flames that danced around them. He took her face between his hands almost tenderly. He was saying something about Lacewing Farm, something about Tim, and he mentioned her, but Marie couldn't make out what he said. Then he tightened his grip on the woman's face until the pressure of it ached over Marie's cheekbones, and just when the pressure was unbearable, he twisted. There was a snap of bone and cartilage, a zinging charge of electricity up her spine then sudden darkness.

And Marie Warren found herself upright in the middle of her bed, drenched in sweat, screaming her throat raw. She switched on the bedside lamp, nearly tipping it over in her effort to drive back the darkness that suddenly seemed unbearable.

It was the banging of the shutters that brought her fully back into the waking world, trembling, teeth chattering. An icy wind blew through the window that she had left open to combat the unseasonable heat, but now she was freezing. Shivering hard, she got up and jammed the window shut, cursing under her breath.

Tim's Land Rover was now parked next to his farm house. He'd been called away by Keswick Mountain Rescue, for which he volunteered. Some tourist was lost around Raven Crag. By bedtime he still wasn't home.

The relief at seeing he was back froze in her chest. The fine hair on the tops of her bare arms prickled. In the pale amber light of the lamp, her image was reflected clearly in the dark glass of the window pane.

But she wasn't alone.

It was a reflection of a reflection she saw. Her night-shirted back was clearly visible in the free-standing mirror next to the closet, but through the patina of mist on the surface from the unusual chill, a dark image stood behind her, heavy arms folded across a broad chest, something coiled in his hand. For a split second she could almost swear she heard his heavy breath. It wasn't possible, and yet there he was, the man from her dream, standing on the other side of the mirror smiling out at her. 'You dreamed their dream,' his voice was a deep rumbling between her hip bones. 'What a clever girl you are, invading dreams that don't belong to you. Rather rude in reality, but then I suppose no one can really blame such an innocent, someone who doesn't know any better.' She could swear she felt his hot breath against the back of her neck. 'Perhaps you'd like to share my dreams as well. I'd welcome you with open arms, my lovely.' He raised his hand in a swift upward motion, palm spread wide facing the sky and suddenly the fire in her pelvic girdle leaped upward to a blinding flash behind her eyes.

Images flew at her like a driving storm. There was a sailing ship tossing in an angry sea with Tara standing on the prow chanting words Marie couldn't hear. There was water and fire and people drowning in both. There was a pale woman with golden hair sinking lifelessly beneath the waves. There was another woman tumbling backward off a precipice and falling endlessly. There were screams from the leaping flames, there was the crack of a whip, the brittle snapping of bones and Tara wandering the fells raging at the darkened sky. There was pain and suffering and sorrow deeper than anything Marie had ever felt before. And Tara Stone was at the centre of it all. The unbearable lot of it pressed down so hard on Marie that she cried out and doubled over as the man's voice exploded inside her head. 'Shall I now show you your own death? Would you like to see that too, my beauty, or perhaps you'd find Tim Meriwether's death more interesting?'

For a split second she felt Tara's rage, and it exploded up through her and outward in all directions, like no anger, no pain she had ever felt before. Then somehow, from somewhere, it was suddenly her own rage that shoved its way to the surface, as she forced herself upright. A tingle and a sharp burst of heat rushed back down to her belly where it settled in a tight embrace, and she was blessedly free of the man in the mirror.

She stumbled toward her bed just as the pale shape of Anderson wavered then appeared. He rose from where he sat, walked quickly to the mirror and with a hand that seemed to take shape as he moved made an arching swipe across the misted glass. For a second Marie felt a wave of nausea, but only for a second, then she found herself stumbling drunkenly, barely able to stand. 'Anderson? Anderson, what the hell's going on?'

He literally materialised around her, and it was a good thing. She wouldn't have made it back to the bed without his solid support. At first he felt like cold marble, but the hard muscle of his embrace warmed almost instantly to body temperature.

'What the hell are you doing here? Who was that?' She slapped his hands away once she was settled onto the bed. 'You think just because you're a ghost you have the right to come and go as you please and materialise when you want and make things cold and scare me and, and, and fuck me.' She bit back an angry sob.

He pulled away slightly and folded his hands in his lap, sitting there on the edge of the bed like he was the fucking king of the universe. 'I apologise for all of those offensive behaviours. I can certainly see how they would not be tolerated in polite society. Though I cannot take credit for the chill, I am sorry you had to endure it. As for the fucking you, however,' he held her gaze. 'I cannot apologise for something I did not instigate, but neither am I sorry that fucking you did take place. Are you?'

'Well I … I mean. I … No, but I might not –'

'You might not have fucked me if you had known I was a ghost? Yes I am aware of that.' He leaned forward so close that she could feel his warm breath, very disconcerting coming from a ghost. 'However you were not intended to see me at all. I was sent to guide you down off High Spy without being seen.'

She blinked. 'You can do that?'

'I could have, yes, but you saw me.'

'Of course I saw you. Even in the fog, I saw you! You were

right there in plain view.' Christ, her voice was starting to sound hysterical again and the burning dance and tingle in her pelvic girdle felt like it would burst into flame. Involuntarily, she clutched at her stomach.

'I can assure you, my dear Marie, I was in plain view to no one but you, a fact of which I was unaware until it was too late.' His eyes followed her hand. 'You must relax into the feel of my presence.'

'What?'

He nodded to her stomach. 'You are a rider. The sensation you are experiencing low in your abdomen will always alert you to the presence of spirits, whether in the flesh or not. It is nothing to be feared.'

'A rider? What the hell is a rider? And who was that man in the mirror? Another horny ghost? A friend of yours?'

'No friend of mine, Marie, I assure you, nor is he yours.' He reached for her hand but she jerked it away. 'I am deeply saddened by any behaviour on my part that was untoward, but now that you have seen me again, and after recent events,' he nodded toward the mirror, which still contained the swipe mark of his large hand, 'I must ask that you please accompany me back to Elemental Cottage. There, all shall be explained to you and you will be ...'

'What? I'll be what?'

'In good company. And now that my state of existence has been made known to you, I sincerely hope not to be offensive to you again.' He stood and straightened his dark jacket. 'I will wait in the parlour for you to dress – that is if you will condescend to go with me.'

'Damn right, I'll go with you. I want an explanation, and I bloody well expect to get one.' Plus she was scared shitless. But if there was one thing she'd learned in her old life, it was how to bluff.

As he left the room, he turned and offered her a wry smile. 'We will have to take your vehicle, Marie, as I have no mode of transport.' His lips curled into a delicious bow that she would have liked to have kissed off his face in spite of the fact that she was angry at him. 'After all, I am a ghost and seldom find myself in need of transport.'

Tim woke with a raging, nearly painful, hard-on. He groaned and fumbled with the sticky towel that half tented his erection beneath the duvet. The night's wank fest with Lisette came back to him in a rush of guilt. Stupid really. There was nothing to feel guilty about. It didn't happen often, and what did the taunting and the egging on of someone long-dead have to do with him, anyway? He never asked for any of this. None of it was his fault. He shuddered as he gripped his cock, and his whole body tensed with the weight of arousal way too heavy for someone who had just come so hard such a short time ago. He opened one eye and squinted around the darkened room. Lisette was nowhere to be found and neither were any of the usuals who were likely to be hanging about his room after dark hoping to catch him masturbating. Bunch of voyeuristic bastards, he thought. Still it was strange that no one was there.

The thought was barely formed before the scent of sex shoved in around him from all sides with oppressive intensity. OK, he'd always had a vivid imagination, but the clarity with which the vision struck him was startling. Marie lay writhing on a bed of cushions and the Elementals were touching her, exploring her, eating her out. But then she was back in her own bed dreaming sex just like he was dreaming sex. He gasped and pressed his thumb to the underside of his cock to keep from coming. Jesus, they were all over her in his imagination! And it was so real! And it was the hottest thing he'd ever seen. He more than saw it, he felt it, almost like he was there, almost like his hands were on her, on them, kneading rounded breasts, teasing gaping slick pussy lips apart, raking stiff nipples and clits with impatient fingers.

And there was someone else, a man. He was surely imagining the man Marie had described to him earlier, the ghost, though he didn't look very ghostly. He was in a cave, half dressed with his fly open, and Marie was on his lap naked, positioning herself, lowering herself so that her gaping pussy was right above the man's cock. He lifted her effortlessly and with a grunt slipped up inside her. Tim could feel her tight grip, as surely as if she were mounting him. He could feel her skin, glistening with the heat of lust, he could feel the grudging yield of her hole to the man's thickness, which felt like his own thickness.

Then the smell of sex surrounded him again, closed in on him, and my God, he'd never had such a vivid fantasy! They were all over each other, all over him. He could nearly feel heated flesh against his own fevered skin. He, like the man in his fantasy, struggled to hold back just a little longer, just a tiny bit more, knowing that the orgasm they were all about to have would be shattering, wanting it to be, wanting it to build until it blew him apart into ecstatic little pieces tiny enough to float away on the night breeze off over Robinson and High Spy, out across Derwent Water, dissipating onto the breeze above the Sharp Edge of Blencathera and vanishing deliciously, blissfully, like he'd never been.

Then he was back in his body and his cock would be controlled no more. He arched up, heels digging into the mattress, spine bowing, buttocks clenching, flooding the towel with his lust. Behind his tightly closed eyelids pinpricks of light burst into a photo-negative image of the space where Marie and the witches and the dark haired man writhed out their own lust, then he was in Marie's room watching her rise from her bed, practically floating to the window. And just before he slipped into unconsciousness, he could have sworn that in the mirror standing at the foot of her bed he saw the image of a deep-chested man with a bullwhip curled in his hand.

Chapter Six

MARIE WAS SURPRISED AT just how close Elemental Cottage was to Lacewing Farm. It was only a quarter of a mile up the main road, then off down a narrow tree-lined lane. The night had cleared and the moon was bright. She found herself in front of a lovely farm cottage, which was considerably larger than either hers or Tim's. Even in the moonlight she could see that the front garden was beautifully done with climbing roses and wisteria in bloom early because of this spring's heat. The whole garden grew in managed wild profusion, creating a shield of privacy from the outside world. It was an appropriate home for witches specialising in sex magic, she thought.

Anderson didn't knock. He simply opened the door and stepped aside for her. She was instantly engulfed in Tara's embrace. 'Oh thank Goddess you're safe, Marie!' She gave Anderson an affectionate kiss on the mouth, then returned her gaze to Marie. Her eyes were darker than Marie remembered them and Marie couldn't keep from feeling that they were hiding something, in spite of her warm smile. Her skin was as pale as porcelain, and the bright patches of colour on her cheeks along with the moist glow caressing her face told Marie whatever the woman had been doing, it was enough for her to break a sweat. She wore a black robe of raw silk tied carelessly about her waist.

'Come on. We're all in the kitchen making something to eat.' She grabbed Marie's hand and practically dragged her through the Victorian parlour. 'Fiori and Sky are dying to meet you after all they've heard. We were planning to invite you over for dinner, but after what happened, now seemed like a better time. Fiori, Sky, look who's here.'

She propelled Marie into the kitchen straight into the arms of the red-head, the one whose neck had been snapped in her dream. And suddenly the heat in Marie's pelvic girdle felt like a blast from a kiln, too hot to be contained. It crackled up her spine to the base of her skull, taking her breath away as it went. She cried out and stumbled backward, nearly knocking a coffee mug off the counter. The blonde, who scurried around sorting cutlery and pouring juice, stepped forward to steady her. At her touch, the sensation leapt as though someone had poured petrol on the flames. Marie yelped and pushed her away, shoving back until the edge of the granite island in the middle of the kitchen bit into her hip. Dark spots danced in front of her eyes. The dream flashed through her head, the snapping of Fiori's neck, the tossing of the ship, the fire, the man with the bullwhip. It was as though the bottom had dropped out of the universe.

'You're ghosts,' she managed. Goose flesh erupted up her arms and cold sweat broke on her forehead and between her breasts. 'You're both ghosts.' She forced the words up through her constricted throat, words she barely heard over the pounding of her pulse in her ears.

It was Anderson who stepped forward and offered her his calm dark gaze. 'You must relax into the sensation, my love. Relax into their presence as you did mine and the feeling will dissipate, will even become rather pleasant, if you allow it.'

She dropped onto a stool and waited for the usual heart palpitations and the shortness of breath while the three ghosts and Tara watched her. Nothing happened. Tara moved between the frozen tableau that could have passed as a sculpture in its stillness. She handed Marie one of the glasses of juice that Sky had poured. Marie took it and sipped. No panic attack, even though if there was ever a time for one she would have thought this would be it. She handed the glass back to Tara. 'You're the only one who's not a ghost?'

Tara nodded.

'Does Tim know?' She asked Fiori.

'No,' the redhead said. 'I wasn't dead when Tim Meriwether and I had sex.'

'You had sex with him? He didn't tell me that.'

Fiori offered a wry smile. 'You can hardly expect him to talk about the woman he fucked with the woman he hopes to fuck. Besides,' colour rose up her pale cheeks, 'I'm not welcome at Lacewing Farm any more. None of us is.'

'I'm sorry to hear that,' Marie said, 'Really, I am, but I need an explanation.'

'And you'll get one,' Tara said, 'after you eat. After we all eat.' Before Marie could protest, Tara raised her hand. 'Magic demands a lot of energy; therefore it's always followed by food. It's not optional, especially not after what you've been through. End of discussion.'

As much as Marie wanted to be stubborn about it, her stomach growled, and her mouth watered as Sky began cooking bacon.

By the time everyone had eaten their fill and Fiori had topped off coffee and teacups again, all the polite questions about how Marie liked the Lake District had been asked, and all of the suggestions for great fell walks she wouldn't want to miss had been made. She had been assured that yes, ghosts in the flesh did enjoy a good fry-up now and then. She had been given a full description of the herbal shop the Elementals ran in town, even though Sky and Fiori were both dead, a fact Marie couldn't quite get her head around.

'Tim says that ghosts have no flesh without the Love Spell, and yet here you all are.'

Fiori smiled. 'Sky and I were both riders in life. We knew the spell. It's no more effort for us to do on ourselves.'

'Riders? That's what you call yourselves?'

Sky sniggered over her teacup. 'Ghost riders. It's Fiori's little joke about what we do, and well, it stuck.'

'And Anderson?'

'I'm a bit of an exception.' He offered a self-deprecating smile.

'Anderson came by enfleshment a different route, a route most ghosts can't access,' Tara said. 'He comes from a long line of witches who walked in the Ether. The Ether is neither

58

the place for the living or the dead, so to them, it didn't much matter.'

Marie shifted on the camelback sofa, suddenly feeling the weight of a reality that logically shouldn't exist, and yet did. 'I don't understand how any of this could happen. Why me?'

Anderson moved to take her hand, but she pulled it away. 'Don't touch me. I don't trust you. I don't trust any of you at the moment.'

'But you're scared,' Tara said. 'And there's no one else you can turn to but us.'

The area below her navel burned and tingled and made her feel wrong-footed. When Sky refilled her teacup, a particularly strong burn had her grabbing her belly.

'If you let us we can teach you to control the power surges and channel them,' Fiori said.

Anderson shot her a warning glance.

'Who was the man in the mirror?' Marie asked still clutching at her stomach, wondering about the nasty knot that tightened in her chest when she thought of him. 'In the dream, he killed you,' she said to Fiori, fighting a sudden wave of vertigo at the memory.

Fiori nodded. 'Sadly that bit wasn't a dream, and he takes great pleasure in reminding us all of it. He wheedled his way into our dream magic, just like you did, and then, he decided to visit you too.'

'We hadn't counted on this,' Tara said. 'We didn't suspect, though I suppose we should have.'

'What should you have suspected?' Marie asked.

'You. After what you did to Anderson, it should have been obvious. It was you. You unleashed him. You unleashed Deacon on us,' Tara said, holding her gaze.

Suddenly Marie realised they were all staring at her. 'What? I don't understand? I haven't done anything. What are you talking about?'

For a long time the darkness was like warm velvet against cool flesh, and Tim could almost feel his bare feet slipping along it as he walked, walked with no destination, no intention, no forethought.

At some point, he really couldn't remember when it happened, he noticed there were shadows swaying in the darkness. Strange that before he noticed the shadows were actually people, he could hear their breath, at first just barely, then like a ragged wind beating a rocky coast. That was the moment he realised just how many of them there were. That was the moment he felt his skin prickle, felt his stomach lurch. Then the people became sharply defined, and he wondered how he could have possibly walked all this way and not seen the horror of them. A woman reached out to him. Her eyes were bruised, her nose was bloodied. She clutched a torn dress over her breasts. There were deep, raw gashes along her bare back. Opposite her a woman writhed in a circle of leaping flames. Her terrified eyes bulged from raw sockets; her teeth gleamed from a lipless mouth. The stench of smoke and burning flesh filled the air.

Tim would have turned to run, but it was as though he were suddenly rooted to the ground. Shards of ice ran up his spine as the smoky shadows parted and Deacon stood before him, arms folded across his chest, bullwhip curled in his hand.

'You did this.' Tim choked out the words.

But the man shook his head and smiled sadly. 'No, my dear boy I did not do this. Tara Stone did this. She is responsible for all of this, as was her mother before her. She is a witch, deception in the frail flesh of a woman.' He took a step closer, and Tim stepped back. 'She's the one who killed your dear Fiori, though I am sure she blamed it on me, did she not?'

'That's a lie! You broke her neck. I saw it. I see it in my dreams over and over again. Did you think I didn't know? Did you think I wouldn't see?' Tim's throat burned from the acrid smoke, but the tightness he felt there had nothing to do with the flames.

The man took another step closer, and Tim forced himself to hold his ground even as everything in him burned with the urge to run.

'She has power over the dream world, Mr Meriwether. Guardian of the North our Tara is. She knows the dark places

60

of the soul, and she knows how to use them to her advantage. Do you really think she couldn't wheedle her way into your dreams and make you see what she wants you to see?' He chuckled. 'Oh, my dear Mr Meriwether, you are naïve.' He took another step forward.

This time Tim did step back. 'You snapped her neck. I saw it. And the next time I saw her she was dead. She thinks I don't know. They all think I don't know.'

Deacon grabbed Tim by the shoulder with an enormous hand and Tim's whole body felt as though it would explode from the touch. 'Watch, Mr Meriwether. Watch what really happened.'

With an upward sweep of his hand, the flames erupted around them. In front of him through the haze of smoke, he saw the scene he'd watched a hundred times before, Fiori kneeling naked and Deacon looming over her, a heavy hand on her cheek, another moving over her body. Tim couldn't hear what he was saying because it was Tara's voice he now heard. Chanting something about life may flee but the flesh will return at will and the power will be retained. Then with a wave of her hand, for the briefest of seconds, it was she who stood behind Fiori. And it was her hands that closed around the woman's face giving the sharp quick twist, snapping the connection, that delicate wisp of a connection that animates the flesh to live and move and breathe. Instantly, Fiori's breath caught and her eyes went dark. Then Deacon erupted in almost the same space Tara occupied and with a powerful backhand sent her flying across the dark expanse of the dreamscape.

Fear prickled up Tim's spine and the urge to run was both overwhelming and useless. He couldn't move. Deacon, once again, stood next to him, so close Tim could feel his hot breath against his cheek. 'I didn't want Fiori dead. Fiori was nothing but kind to me. I still dream of how she made love to me, how she took care of me. And that is the very thing our Tara could not tolerate.'

'It's a lie,' Tim whispered, feeling as though he wanted to vomit, but not even being afforded that luxury in his paralysed state.

'No, Mr Meriwether. It is the absolute truth. It was Tara, not I who snapped our beloved Fiori's neck, who took the life from one so lovely, so delightful.' He stepped forward until his face filled Tim's field of vision. 'Your sweet Marie is with Tara Stone and her minions even now, and in who knows how much danger.'

Tim struggled with all his might, but he couldn't move even one single muscle. 'It's a lie, it's a filthy lie!'

Deacon spoke against his ear. 'Ask her. Ask Tara to tell you the truth.' His voice trailed off in a hiss of icy wind.

Tim shoved his way out from under the duvet. He was halfway to the window before he was fully back in the waking world. He threw open the curtains and the bottom dropped out of his stomach. Marie's car was gone. Her house was dark. He was still shoving his way into his clothes, as he grabbed the keys to the Land Rover and dashed out the door, heart racing, skin slicked with the sweat of fear.

Chapter Seven

'TELL ME WHAT I have to do with any of this,' Marie said. 'How is this mess my fault?'

For a long moment no one responded. Everyone looked a bit embarrassed including Anderson, but Tara didn't budge. Still holding Marie's gaze, Tara spoke. 'Anderson, show her.'

The ghost shifted in his seat. The colour in his face darkened and the clench of the muscles along his exquisite jaw looked granite hard. When he spoke, his voice was tightly controlled. 'Tara, my darling, perhaps this is not the ideal way to –'

'Do it,' Tara cut him off with a sudden raise of her hand and a swish of the wide silk of her sleeve that snapped almost like a sail in the wind. The tension in the room rose another notch. Sky and Fiori shot each other a surreptitious glance that even Marie could tell was not one of comfort and ease.

Anderson's spine stiffened. All emotion disappeared from his face, but his voice was suddenly icy. 'Very well, as you wish, Madame.' He bowed his head briefly in acquiescence, then lifted his dark eyes to Marie. His gaze softened as did his voice. 'My dear Marie, I am truly sorry for what I am about to do.' Then instantly he was gone, vanished into thin air.

The startled gasp that pushed its way past her lips was followed by another tight sting and tug low in her belly. 'What happened?' she asked when she regained her equilibrium, 'Why did you send him away?'

Tara sat back in her chair and rested both hands against the arms. She looked suddenly regal. 'I've not sent him anywhere. He hasn't moved.' She nodded to the sofa where Anderson had been sitting next to Marie.

Before she could think about the implications, she reached out her hand to the space where he had been. There was a collective gasp among the witches, herself and Anderson as her fingers touched the marble cold of his arm that instantly began to warm beneath her touch. Anderson's heavy intake of breath vibrated through her hand and up her own arm, then down in her belly where the fireworks were, and suddenly he was there again. His eyelids fluttered and his lips parted, and everything in her wanted him with an ache that was almost unbearable.

She cried out and pulled her hand back, not from fear, not from surprise, but from the embarrassment at just how close she was to coming, and just how badly she wanted to. And as surely as he was sitting there again, she knew by his own deep-chested groan that he was riding the edge with her, that his need was as great as her own.

Tara nodded to Anderson, who then leaned forward toward Marie. 'With your permission, my love.'

It felt like it was supposed to happen. It felt like nothing else could possibly happen. With lips parted, he took her mouth. There was little more than a feather's flick of his tongue and a brush of his breath against her lips. His hand cupped her cheek, then moved along her nape to the back of her neck cradling her close to his breath, his delicious warm, superfluous breath.

And she came, trembling and grasping and pulling him to her, whispering his name into his mouth, oblivious to the three witches watching. And as she returned his kiss with her own, she heard his grunt, felt him convulse and tremble against her, sharing in her lust and her release, and suddenly she wasn't embarrassed at all. Suddenly she felt freer than she could remember ever feeling before. It was exhilarating, wild, totally mad, and she never wanted the feeling to end.

But it did end, and it ended with an icy flash of the man snapping Fiori's neck in the cave. They both felt it, she could tell by the shudder down Anderson's spine followed immediately by the protective way he tightened his embrace around her as though he were steadying her.

Then she was shoving and pushing her way up from the

sofa babbling hysterically about wanting to know what was going on and wanting to know right now. The businesswoman in her stood back and shook her head disgustedly while the rest of her dissolved into a puddle of hysteria until Tara took her face between her hands and said calmly. 'Stop it. If you want the truth then behave like you can handle it.'

Marie wasn't sure what it was about the witch's touch but it was calming. She sat back on the sofa and wiped frantically at her eyes, embarrassed that she'd let this experience shatter her façade, but then again, nothing in the banking world had prepared her for this. She sniffed, wiped her nose on the back of her hand and squared her shoulders. 'OK, tell me what just happened,' she blushed, 'Other than the obvious.' This time she didn't shove him away when Anderson took her hand.

'You have the power of enfleshment without the Love Spell. That's what just happened,' Tara said. 'I don't know how. I don't know why. My mother speculated that such power existed, but she never saw it, and neither have I until now.' She nodded to Anderson. 'Anderson is, even now, being held in the flesh by your power. If you wish it, you can will him out of the flesh just as easily.'

Involuntarily, Marie tightened her grip on Anderson's hand. The very thought made her skin crawl. 'Why? Why can I do that?'

'Because you're a rider,' Fiori broke her silence, 'a rider who doesn't need the spell. I assume Tim Meriwether has told you all about it.'

Marie nodded, feeling like it was just the thin layer of her own skin holding her together, keeping her from flying apart with all of this information she didn't want. 'And you're saying I unleashed this … this …'

'Deacon,' Sky said. 'He calls himself Deacon.'

'You're saying I unleashed this Deacon in the same way my touch can enflesh Anderson?'

'That's the only explanation,' Sky replied. 'We bound him securely after the incident with Tim Meriwether three months ago. We were very careful to make sure he had no avenues into the flesh, then you show up, and suddenly he's shoving his way in again.'

'But I didn't do anything. I would never want someone like that free. I mean it was different with Anderson, but this man is a murderer, and he's …' She found herself suddenly at a loss for words, suddenly fighting tears again.

'Oh, it's not your fault,' Tara said. 'Deacon is clever. He would have been aware of everything that has anything to do with me, and the people I care about.' She looked down at her hands folded now in her lap. 'And until you came along, the only other person walking among the living I had reason to protect was Tim Meriwether, though I had to do it very stealthily and with the help of the spirits. Deacon knew the minute you arrived, as did we, that there was something extraordinary about you. We knew up on the fells that you could see Anderson. We knew that you were a rider. But we didn't know until you enfleshed him without even being aware of what you were doing just how much power you wielded, and just how dangerous that could be to all of us.'

'And my getting lost? Was that a part of your little plan? Me losing my compass?'

This time it was Anderson who replied. 'The loss of your compass was none of our doing.'

And once again Marie remembered the dark figure she had seen before Anderson came to her in the mist. 'It was him.'

They all nodded in unison, and her skin crawled at the thought of how close she had been to danger.

'We sent Anderson because we thought he could guide you down safely without revealing himself, and protect you. We still didn't know the extent of your powers,' Tara said. 'Not until you were in the cave with him did we realise what was happening.'

Thoughts of her time in the cave with Anderson made the heat in her stomach dance in a much nicer way. 'And the … the way it makes me feel?' Marie found herself blushing.

'It is your lust, your passion, my dear,' Anderson said. 'It is the power that drives every rider, the power that activates the magic. The uncomfortable heat you feel is a build-up of unchannelled sexual energy stimulated by the presence of a ghost. Never underestimate the power of human sexuality.'

'OK, I can understand that with you, Anderson, but I certainly wasn't turned on by this Deacon guy.' Marie shivered at the thought.

A meaningful glance passed between the rest of those present in the room, meaning that was lost on Marie. Fiori heaved a sigh and spoke. 'Everyone is turned on by Deacon, Marie. Don't doubt his appeal for one moment, or it may cost you dearly.'

Marie ran a hand through her hair and closed her eyes. When she opened them four pairs of eyes were looking back at her. 'I feel like I've been dumped in the middle of a horror film. I'm just getting bits and pieces of what's going on and none of it makes any sense.'

Tara's gaze was like fire against her, burning her almost like the heat low in her belly that she was strangely beginning to get used to. 'What? What is it?'

Tara took a deep breath and released it slowly. Her gaze was still locked on Marie's. 'I kept Tim Meriwether out of the loop, and it cost Fiori her life.' She raised her hand to prevent Fiori's response, 'And now every day we fear for him as well. Deacon has had the upper hand long enough. We've got to stop fighting a defensive battle.' She slid off the chair and knelt in front of Marie, taking her hands in hers. 'Marie, if you're willing, we can show you everything, we can help you understand.' She squeezed her hands hard. 'But it won't be easy for you. It may be the hardest thing you've ever done.'

'Understanding would be a good start.' The hammering of Marie's heart in her throat felt like it would suffocate her.

'You have already dreamed with us and thus inadvertently participated in our magic,' Anderson said, moving still closer to her. 'One can only imagine how confusing that must have been with you having no context for such an experience.'

For the first time, the fire in her pelvic girdle calmed to an even spread of warmth. 'This isn't going to go away, is it? What's happening to me, what I've become?'

'No,' Anderson whispered.

And Tara shook her head, her eyes dark and sympathetic.

'And afterwards?' The words pressed themselves up her throat.

Tara released a long sigh. 'Afterwards, once you understand, then we'll teach you how to cope. We'll teach you how to use your magic. We'll teach you what's good and wonderful about becoming what you are, what we all are.'

Marie closed her eyes and swallowed hard, then looked around at everyone, they all seemed slightly out of focus, but before she could respond, Anderson spoke.

'Tara, my love, you realise the risk you will be taking, I have no doubt. But do you not think it wise to inform Marie of the risk she will be taking?'

Tara turned to Marie, whose hands she still held. 'You might die, or worse.'

There was a collective intake of breath in the room, all ghostly. Marie found herself calmer than she could remember being in months, maybe years.

'And if I don't do this magic with you? If I go home and try to ignore you like Tim has?'

'You might die, or worse,' Tara repeated.

'And this Deacon guy, will he leave me alone?'

Tara's eyes darkened and the emotions that flooded her face were too many and too fast for Marie to read, but for the tiniest of seconds she caught a glimpse of sorrow so deep that it left her breathless. Then Tara's mask was once again firmly in place. She shook her head. 'Never, not as long as I'm alive he won't.'

The answer really came as no surprise, though the fact that it didn't, the fact that it didn't shake her resolve surprised her a lot. She held Tara's gaze. 'Then I don't really see that I have a choice, do I?'

Into the charged atmosphere, the doorbell rang, repeatedly accompanied by a heavy pounding. Only Marie jumped.

A knowing look passed between Tara and Anderson, and the ghost rose to answer the door.

Before Tara could continue with what she had been saying there was a loud commotion in the hallway, a sound of something heavy crashing on the floor, and Tim Meriwether burst into the room with Anderson right behind him. 'Where is she?' He was shouting, breathing like he'd just ran a marathon. 'Where's Marie?'

He stopped at the door with Anderson nearly ploughing into him and took in the scene, Sky and Fiori were seated in wing backed chairs to one side and Tara still knelt on the floor with Marie's hands in hers.

The clench of his jaw, the tension along his neck muscles combined with his uncombed hair and untucked shirt caused a different kind of tingle at Marie's centre. His icy gaze fell on Tara. 'Get away from her.' His voice was little more than a low growl.

'Tim, what the fuck is the matter with you,' Marie began. 'You can't just walk in –'

'It's all right,' Tara interrupted. Her voice was calm and suddenly very remote. She gave Marie's hands another reassuring squeeze and moved back to her chair. Tim stormed in and grabbed Marie by the arm, but she jerked away. 'What the hell's going on, who do you think you are –'

'Did she tell you it was her? She didn't, did she?' He cut her off and threw a venomous glance at Tara. Anderson bristled, but Tara calmed him, calmed them all with a quick look. All except for Tim Meriwether.

'Tim, what the hell are you on about?' The anger and irritation at Tim's bad behaviour gave way to something a little more frightening as his gaze came to rest on Fiori, and his eyes darkened.

Then he addressed Tara again. 'If you don't tell her, I will.' He grabbed Marie by the arm and manhandled her from her seat. 'We're leaving, Marie, now, while we still can.'

'I'm not going anywhere, damn it!' she jerked back so hard that she lost her balance and toppled back onto the sofa. 'What the hell's wrong with you? Tell me what?'

'Tara didn't tell you that she's the one who killed Fiori, did she? That she's actually the one who snapped Fiori's neck.' Before anyone could respond he shot another glance at Fiori. 'Did you think I couldn't tell? Did you think I wouldn't know? And yet here you sit like her lap dog after what she did. Is that how she controls you? Did she do it to you too?' He nodded to Sky, who bristled, then calmed at Tara's glance.

'Where the hell did you get that idea,' Marie slapped at him as he grabbed for her again. 'That's not what happened. I saw what happened. It was Deacon. Deacon killed Fiori, and who the hell do you think you are waltzing in here and –'

'I know what you saw. I saw it too,' Tim interrupted, running a heavy hand through his hair. 'Jesus, I've seen it every night in my dreams since it happened, but don't you see? It's what she wants us to see.' He gave a vicious nod to Tara. 'What she wants us to believe.'

'That's ridiculous. You're totally mad, why would she do that?'

'I don't know, to control them, to control us? I don't know. But it's true, ask her. Just ask her.'

Anderson grabbed for Tim, but he shrugged free and pulled Marie forcefully up off the sofa again with her fighting and clawing and kicking, as the room erupted in chaos. Her foot landed hard on the inside of Tim's calf just as Anderson wrestled Tim away from Marie, but not before getting an elbow in the stomach. The two men were like wild animals in a cage, knocking over a chair and smashing two cups onto the Turkish carpet. Sky and Fiori were both shouting at once, Sky grabbing for Anderson and Fiori for Tim. And all the while Marie's stomach burned like fire.

'Stop it! Stop it now!' Tara's voice rose above the din. 'I'll have no more of this violence in my home. Enough.' A deafening silence fell over the room, one that Marie wasn't entirely sure might not have been magically enforced. Everyone froze, no one breathed. Even the ghosts held their breath. Tara still sat unmoving in her chair as though none of this had anything to do with her.

Then Marie shoved her way out from between Anderson and Tim and moved to stand in front of Tara. 'Is it true? Is what Tim says true?'

'You don't understand. You don't understand how it happened, what it was like,' Fiori began, but Tara silenced her with a glance that could have almost been a caress. The

70

redhead leaned forward in her chair and her eyes welled with tears. 'But they need to know. They need to understand.' Sky reached out to her and took her hand.

Then Tara turned her attention back to Marie. For a long time she said nothing. Anderson said something under his breath in what Marie thought might have been Italian. The knot of fire in her stomach suddenly felt more like ice. 'Is it true?' she asked again. She made no attempt to hide the tremor in her voice. Even with her skills at the negotiating table, she couldn't have if she'd wanted to.

'It's true,' Tara's voice was soft, barely more than a whisper. 'It's true I killed Fiori. Tim is right.'

Both Fiori and Anderson started to speak. She silenced them with a glance, and Marie stumbled backwards, steadied herself on the edge of the upturned chair, and gave Tim a hard shove when he reached for her.

There was chaos again, arguing and shouting, but she was outside of it all, moving in a different dimension, watching it all from a cold grey place. She watched herself run out of Elemental Cottage. She heard Tara tell Anderson to let her go. She watched Tim come after her, yelling something about her safety something about her not being alone right now. She watched herself get into her car and drive away, screeching her tyres on the driveway. She watched herself turn away from the road that led to Lacewing Farm and keep driving.

She didn't know how long she had driven aimlessly. When she came back to herself, it felt like she had been somewhere else for ages, maybe even for years. It took her a little while to realise she was driving over the Kirkstone Pass in the greying dawn. With a start, she recalled that she might not be alone, but there was no burning sensation between her hip bones, and when she called out Anderson's name, there was no response. As for the possibility that she might with equal ease conjure up Deacon, well she didn't even want to think about that.

As she descended from the pass and drove along the shore of Ullswater, she thought she might just drive for ever. Something about driving gave her a sense of security, albeit a false one. She was certain of that, as the memories of the past

48 hours lapped at her in waves not unlike those on the windy shore of the lake. In the end, she circled back on to the A66 as the sun turned the saddle of Blencathera pink. There was no place else to go but Lacewing Farm. It was now the only home she had, and there was no going back to Portland. She had burned her bridges even if she did want to return, and she didn't. Like it or not she would have to face Tim. She would need him. They would need each other. This was not the time to be without allies.

Chapter Eight

TIM WAS IN THE stable with the mare when she arrived. She could see his broad back through the open door. A sudden eruption of butterflies in her stomach made her skittish like the mare had been, was it only yesterday morning? It made her not want to face him, not just yet. As she watched him moving about the stable, heard him talking softly to the horse, the ache she felt was a very human one, one that sprang from being alive and not wanting to be alone and all the other things that living entailed. It was not the fiery burn that accompanied the presence of spirits. It felt cleaner somehow, more sane. But on some deeper level, it felt at least as frightening, so she swallowed hard and turned quietly toward her cottage.

She was half way up the porch steps when she changed her mind, squared her shoulders and headed for the stables.

When he saw her, he surprised her by scooping her into his arms, holding her tight, so tight she could barely catch her breath. A sense of relief rushed over her, a feeling that she wasn't in this alone, and she held him tight right back.

'I was so scared,' he spoke against her ear, his voice thick with emotions. 'I didn't know what they'd do to you, if they'd follow you, and I didn't know where you'd gone or where to look for you. I couldn't bear the thought of it happening to you. What happened to Fiori.'

She said nothing; she wasn't sure she could speak without blubbering.

'I'm sorry,' he whispered against her hair. 'This is not how I wanted it to be. This is not what I wanted you to know about me.'

'What?' She pulled away enough to look up into his eyes,

'Tim I don't blame you for any of this. I still don't know what to think about it all. I don't know …' Her voice drifted off. 'Do you think we should go to the police?'

'And tell them what?' he said stepping back. 'We're the only ones who know. We're the only ones who can tell they're dead. To anyone else Fiori and Sky look as real and alive as you and I do, as real as that Anderson bloke you let plough you. He must have been impressed, the way he fought me.'

This time the clench in her stomach was anger. 'You son of a bitch!' She shoved him with the flat of her hand and he yielded, perhaps too shocked to do anything else. She shoved him again. 'What the hell business is it of yours who I let plough me anyway, and for your information, yeah, he liked it just fine. Like you care.' She shoved him again, and the mare looked up from munching her breakfast. 'Lest we forget that you ploughed Fiori. Oh that's right, I forgot that was different. She wasn't dead when you fucked her, so that makes it all right.'

She saw his face darken, and in her own mind's eye, she saw the woman's tragic death, and for a split second she wished she hadn't said anything, but damn it, he was such a bastard. 'First you treat me like I don't exist, then you go all big brother on me like I'm too delicate and soft-brained to take care of myself. Well I have news for you, Tim Meriwether, I was taking care of myself for a long time before you decided I needed looking after.' She shoved again, and this time he grabbed her with such force that she felt the bones in her neck pop.

With her forward momentum, he stumbled over an uneven paving stone, lost his footing and went over backward into a manger full of fresh hay, pulling her on top of him.

Before she could shove and claw her way to her feet, He grabbed her around the waist and rolled, pinning her beneath the weight of his body. He gave her no time to think about it, but pulled her into a bruising kiss, forcing her lips apart, probing her hard pallet with his dexterous tongue, biting her lower lip before he came up fighting for the breath to speak. 'I think about you a lot, Marie,' His chest rose and fell in hungry

74

gasps. 'But I promise you, none of those thoughts were even remotely brotherly.'

She bucked underneath him and clawed at his shirt. 'Then do something about it, damn it, and stop toying with me.' Several buttons popped and flew across the stable floor. He forced her legs apart with his knee, moving it up to rub against the crotch of her jeans. She shoved his shirt open and arched up to him as he pushed her T-shirt up and manoeuvred and tugged, forcing her breasts free from her bra into his splayed hands and hungry lips.

She fumbled with the fly of his jeans, sliding an anxious hand into his boxers. He huffed a breathless grunt, and the muscles low in his stomach tensed as she closed her fingers around his engorged penis and began to stroke.

He had just began the anxious efforts with her own fly when suddenly the stable door slammed shut, and the light bulb overhead exploded in a shower of fine glass plunging the two into total darkness.

Marie yelped, and Tim cursed. As they fought their way to their feet, the mare screamed, and they could hear her struggling.

Tim vaulted over the manger's edge seconds before Marie, calling back to her. 'Get the door. Get it open.'

Struggling to secure her jeans with one hand, Marie felt her way along the perimeter of the stable toward the door. The relief was short-lived when her fingers closed around the handle, and it wouldn't budge.

'It's locked,' she shouted above the desperate cries of the mare.

'What do you mean, it's locked,' Tim shouted back. 'It doesn't have a lock. It can't be locked.'

'I'm telling you it won't open,' she yelled back, feeling an icy chill blasting her from behind. With one final tug, the door gave and she tumbled backward on her arse. The sharp knife-edge of light that shot through the darkness was blinding, like a flashbulb going off, leaving a deep bruised after image dancing in front of her face, an after image of Deacon.

She cried out and crab walked backwards, as he stepped

toward her, unfurling his bullwhip, in what seemed like endless slow motion.

Then from somewhere beyond the blinding light, Tim grabbed her beneath the arm pits and hauled her to her feet, pulling her protectively to him, manhandling her until his back took the brunt of the whip's lash, as it cracked like thunder even above the horse's terrified screams.

Marie felt his body tense, jerk and go rigid, felt his heavy pull of oxygen.

Then the air was suddenly warm again and filled with birdsong, and the mare was instantly calm. The light from the sun filtered through the open stable door sliding down the dust motes as though nothing had happened. With a sob of relief, Marie wriggled free of Tim's arms and shoved at his shirt. 'Get it off! Get it off. Let me see.'

'I'm all right,' Tim said.

'Let me see!' Marie shoved and tugged at his shirt, then turned him so his back was to her.

'I'm all right,' he repeated. 'Honest. It wasn't real. It only seemed that way.'

And sure enough Tim's broad muscular back was smooth and supple with no sign of the damage a whip would have made on tender flesh.

'But you felt it,' she breathed incredulously. 'I felt it. I felt the wind of it as it snapped by.'

'Marie,' he turned to face her and took her by the shoulders. 'It wasn't real.'

She felt the tension ease from the back of her neck. The mare munched her oats as though nothing had happened. The heat of the heavy morning once again settled around them like a thick blanket. Marie nodded up to the shattered light bulb. 'Parts of it were pretty real, I'd say.'

'So what are we going to do?' Marie said, pacing the floor in front of the kitchen table ignoring the cup of tea she'd just poured for herself. 'I don't have any knowledge of magic and the paranormal, and we just found out the only person who might have been able to help us is a killer. Any suggestions?'

76

Tim sipped his tea and ran a hand through his hair. 'They can't be the only woo woo folks in Cumbria, Marie. There must be someone else who could help us out.'

'Woo woo is one thing, Tim. I have no problem with people who want to dye their hair red and dance naked in the full moon, they're harmless. They're innocuous, but we're not dealing with woo woo. We're dealing with a poltergeist or a demon or something, and he's real, and he wants to destroy us because of our association with Tara Stone.'

He raised an eyebrow. 'Is that what she told you, that it was all because of her? Well what the hell did you expect her to tell you, Marie?'

She turned to face him, hands on her hips. 'She hasn't tried to hurt me, Tim, and she's had plenty of opportunity. In fact, I don't know what would have happened if Anderson hadn't shown up when he did last night, or on the fells the day before for that matter.'

Tim cursed under his breath at the mention of Anderson's name. 'I don't know why they do what they do, but I do know that Fiori is dead and she's dead at Tara's hand. Of that much I'm certain.'

She dropped into her chair and glared across the table at him. 'How did you know that Tara killed Fiori?' Even now, she found it hard to believe, even after Tara had admitted it, and something definitely didn't add up when Fiori stood right by her and fought like a trooper.

'I know.' Tim was suddenly very interested in the spoon in the sugar bowl.

She reached across the table and grabbed his hand. 'Tim, I need to know how you know. Who told you? Was it the bum bashers?'

He shook his head, still avoiding her gaze.

'Then who?'

A fine tinge of pink rose above his collar and onto his neck and cheeks, and with an icy knot of certainty she knew. 'Jesus, Tim, Deacon told you, didn't he? And you believed him?'

'I didn't have to believe him, did I? She confirmed it.'

'But you believed him when you came in. You believed him

77

enough to barge into a house that didn't belong to you like a rampaging bull. I saw it in your eyes. How could you believe him? How could you possibly trust him at all?'

Tim pushed the chair back from the table with a loud screech. 'I don't trust him, and I don't doubt for a minute that he would lie to me if it would get him what he wants. But this is a truth he likes. This is a truth he wants made known. It serves his purpose.' Then he added quickly. 'That doesn't make Tara Stone any less of a killer, does it?'

'So that brings us right back to where we started.' She watched him pace. 'What do we do? Especially if what they say is true about me.'

That got his attention, and he eased back into the chair. 'What did they say?'

She told him about her ability to enflesh ghosts without the spell, without even realizing what she was doing. She told him that they all believed she was responsible for Deacon's unbinding. All the while she spoke, the lines along Tim's jaw got harder, straighter. Several times he cursed under his breath. By the time she had finished, he sat with his arms defiantly folded across his chest. 'So you conjured this Anderson bloke, and Deacon? That's what they're telling you?'

She nodded.

'And do you believe them?'

She released a slow breath, and squared her shoulders. 'After what's happened to me the past 48 hours, I don't know what to believe. I can see how I could have conjured Anderson. I saw him with Tara. I had opportunity. As for Deacon, I can't imagine how I could have conjured him. But I do know that knowledge is power, and without the Elementals, we had better be for finding another source of knowledge really quickly because I have a feeling we're gonna need all the power we can get.'

He worried his lip with his bottom teeth, then nodded to her laptop where it sat on the end of the table in a pile of newspapers and unopened mail. 'You any good at research on that thing?'

'Not bad. You?'

He disappeared out the door and returned in a couple of minutes with a bright red netbook. 'OK, let's do this then. Let's find us some knowledge.'

She grabbed the mocha maker from the cupboard. 'We're gonna need coffee.' At least they were doing something, and she was amazed at how much consolation she took in such a small thing.

Serena Ravenmoor was startled out of her meditation by the ghost watching her at the water's edge. She loved it when he watched her. She loved it that he found her so fascinating. A gifted witch, he had called her that first night before he made love to her, before he made her come like she'd never come before. Just thinking about it made her heart race. And thinking about him, like always, summoned him to her side.

He helped her to her feet. 'I hope I didn't disturb you, my darling. But I just couldn't stay away from you any longer.' He raised a hand with a flourish in front of her chest and offered a wicked smile as her nipples hardened beneath her blouse without so much as a touch. She gave a little whimper of delight at what she felt far south of her nipples. He chuckled softly. 'This place is much too public for me to pleasure you as I desire.' He rubbed the thick pad of his thumb against his index finger and dropped his gaze to her crotch for the briefest of seconds. And her whimper became a little cry, which escaped before she could cover her mouth.

A man sitting on a nearby park bench looked up from his newspaper. But he only saw what he might have thought was a silly woman probably yelping at the sight of a spider or some such. He had no idea that the orgasm she was in the midst of would have rendered it impossible for her to stand if not for the support of her ghost, her lovely, strong, virile ghost, which the man, like the rest of the people enjoying the sunshine around Derwent Water, couldn't see.

As her Deacon moved to support her, he guided her hand against the bulge threatening the crotch of his leather trousers. He spoke against her ear. 'That was only just a foretaste of what I will do to you if you take me home.'

She had conjured him at the psychic fair, was it only three days ago? It was on the green, down by Derwent Water across from the Theatre by the Lake. Stupidly, she'd brought her new scrying mirror with her, rather than the cheap plastic one she usually used for such events. She was good at scrying, and she thought the sight of her lovely mirror would be more likely to draw clients. Besides it was such a beautiful mirror, with its exquisite inlay of silver, tooled in the image of a circle of women dancing naked beneath a canopy of oak trees. She couldn't bear to leave it at home.

She was certain it was very old when she'd seen it at the car boot sale, and when she'd felt its vibrations, its energy, she'd known she was supposed to have it. She'd left it unguarded on the table for only a second, but it was long enough. The stupid American chick had picked it up, handled it like it was any of the other cheap rip-off charms and potions being sold at the fair. Oh the woman had been very apologetic when Serena had jerked it away from her and practically screamed at her that one does not touch the magical tools of a witch. She had been furious, mostly at herself for leaving it in harm's way. It had taken her weeks to cleanse it and purify it and meditate with it until it truly was attuned to her energy, and now she would have to start over again because it had been polluted by the touch of another.

That's what she'd been thinking about when suddenly, out of nowhere, he had been there, looking a little confused at first, his gaze following the American as she disappeared among the crowds. He was frightening and lovely and dark, and he carried a bullwhip, which she found rather sexy in a BDSM sort of way. What mattered, though, was that he was a ghost, the first ghost who had ever contacted her, and he had revealed himself to no one but her.

She had always known she possessed the gift. She had always believed that eventually she would make contact with the other side, but she never imagined it would be with anyone so powerful.

That night he made her feel things she never imagined she could feel, like she was flying, like she was timeless, like the whole realms of the living and the dead and even the Ether were hers to command. He said she was just coming into her power. He said she would do greater things that she could imagine and he would help her. In fact, he said, just as it had been intended that she should have the mirror, it had also been intended that he should be sent from the other side to serve her.

And, Goddess, how he served her! That night he had made her come more times than she would have imagined possible, and yet he held his sexual energy, never coming himself. It made his magic stronger, he'd said. And pleasuring her would strengthen both of them. Afterward, when he lay next to her naked and still hard, he whispered against her ear, 'the American. Do you know her?'

She shook her head. 'Why?'

'She troubles me,' he replied. 'She troubles my dreams.'

Up until that point, Serena had no idea ghosts dreamed.

Fortunately, she didn't live far from the lake, because her Deacon was insatiable and had given her two more orgasms before she managed to throw herself through the front door of her flat and slam it shut behind them. Then he scooped her into his arms and carried her to the bed, shoving her skirt up over her hips, lifting her arse and running a heavy finger along the wet gusset of her panties, laughing wickedly as she squirmed. Then he slipped them off over her hips. Straddling her so that the bulge in his trousers was only inches from her mouth, he tied her wrists to the headboard with her knickers. Then he ran his hands down over her breasts and scooted back, forcing her legs apart with his knees.

'Shall you be my sacrifice, my lovely?' He pinched her clit and she yelped and wet herself further 'Shall you be my offering to your beloved goddess?' Then he took his bullwhip and raked the coil of it between her drenched pout. 'Oh yes,' he breathed. 'Such a succulent juicy sacrifice you would be.' His eyes were wild, dark. His pupils dilated and his jaw set hard. With his free hand, he opened the flap of his trousers and released his always heavy dark cock.

'I think your goddess would be very pleased with such a

81

sacrifice, don't you?'

The tiniest frisson of fear crawled up her spine, but was quickly forgotten when he pushed into her and began to thrust.

Later, so many orgasms later that she was barely conscious, he curled around her and gently kissed her raw nipples. Then he whispered next to her ear. 'The American will come to you with a young man, a sheep farmer by trade. They will desire you to help them with sex magic' He pinched her nipple hard and she yelped. 'Pay attention my lovely. This is very important.' He pushed the damp hair away from her ear and whispered. 'Here is what I want you to do.'

Chapter Nine

TARA DIDN'T KNOW HOW long she had been wandering the fells before she realised she wasn't alone. It miffed her a bit. Most ghosts knew that when she took to walking the fells alone at night, it meant she didn't want company. There was only one ghost bold enough to follow her anyway.

The moon was still full enough to reflect silver off the sheen of Derwent Water, which sparkled up the reflection of the lights of Keswick around its North Eastern shore. She stood for a long moment taking in the view from the top of Latrigg, then heaved a sigh and wiped sweat from her forehead. 'Anderson, I know you're here. What I'm wondering is why you're here.'

For a second a shadow appeared and shimmered next to her, and suddenly the ghost, fully enfleshed, stood next to her. 'My dear Tara, I think you know the answer to that query as well as I do.'

'I don't want company, Anderson.'

He folded his arms across his chest and stepped closer to her, and she was reminded again of just how substantial he was when he was in the flesh. 'I suppose, as my high priestess, you could order me to leave, but we are not, at the moment, about coven business, nor are we performing any acts of high magic, therefore, I do believe I am as free to wander about on the fells at night as you are.'

She turned on her heels and continued to walk as though he were not there. He followed, keeping her impressive pace.

'I don't need a babysitter.'

'A fact that relieves me greatly, my love, as I have no gift with children.'

She walked on. 'You're a smart arse sometimes, you know

that?'

'So I have been informed.'

For a few moments they walked on in companionable silence, the view disappearing as they walked the shadowy path under the trees.

'They are both safe and unharmed.' Anderson said, at last.

She stopped suddenly and he nearly ran into her. 'You stayed with her?'

'Of course I stayed with her. In her distress she was not able to call me forth into the flesh as efficiently as she otherwise would have been. I assumed that would be the situation, though it was a bit of a risk.'

'A bit of a risk. Right.'

An owl trilled and they both glanced out into the trees toward the sound. Then the ghost added, 'Of course it would have made no difference if she had been able to force me into the flesh. I am quite capable of enduring her wrath if I must.'

Tara grunted a chuckle. 'I have no doubt of that.'

The ghost stepped forward and slid a warm hand onto Tara's shoulder. 'If you would but let me talk to Marie, I am sure I could make her understand.'

Tara shook her head. 'I'm not happy with the way things have gone either, Anderson, but holding them too closely may only put them more at risk.'

They walked on with the moonlight glinting in and out of the thicket of trees. At last Anderson spoke again. 'No doubt you know Deacon paid them a visit this morning? At a most inconvenient time, as he is wont to do. They were about to engage in intercourse.'

Tara nodded. 'Yes, I know. Deacon provided a very powerful distraction. But no one was hurt.'

'At the moment he is just toying with them, and with you.' Anderson spoke to the back of her head. 'At the moment.'

'Don't badger me about this, Anderson.' She turned on him. 'Don't you think I'm racking my brain trying to figure out how to protect them, how to get them back to where they're safe.' She forced a laugh that sounded more like a sob. 'If there even is such place.' She raised a hand before he could speak. 'I

84

knew this would come up, I knew I would have to talk about it, about …' She swallowed hard. 'About what really happened. That's why I wanted the time with Marie, I wanted her to understand on a deeper level than just me telling her that I killed Fiori.' She forced the last words back in a gulp of breath that made the delicate bones of her throat contract tightly and ache, words she hated, a truth she hated, a vision that would be for ever burned into her memories. 'And now she'll never understand beyond the taint of the act.'

This time, Anderson didn't allow her to push him away. He took her into his arms and pressed her close to his chest, close to the beat of his heart. 'I think it is you, my dearest Tara, who cannot see past the taint of that act to the mercy and tenderness it yielded up.'

For a few seconds, she let him hold her, took comfort in the one who had been with her the longest, the one who knew her best, the one Deacon could not take away from her. Then she squared her shoulders, pulled away and continued walking, him amiably now at her side.

'They are both very aware that they need help, that they cannot face Deacon alone. And they, at least now understand they will have to face him. They are seeking out the help of other witches,' he said at last.

'Other witches,' Tara snorted. 'What other witches?'

'I am only telling you what they are doing,' he said. 'I am hoping that the futility of their quest will at least allow me to talk to Marie. I think she is more inclined to listen to reason than Tim, and in some ways she is more practical, more objective.'

'That's because she hasn't lost someone she cares about yet. She can still afford to be practical and objective.'

Anderson stopped, took a deep breath of night air and released it slowly. 'Perhaps that is true, but if no acceptable solution to our dilemma is found soon, I will go to her, and I will make her understand.' Then he moved on, his eyes on the dark hulk of Blencathera silhouetted against the sky. 'I would much prefer to do so with your approval, my love.'

Tara offered a grunt. 'As if I've ever had any control over

you, Anderson.'

He gave her a disappointed pout. 'My darling, Tara, if you had no control over me, I would have left all of this madness you have so cunningly involved me in, long ago.'

'You're kidding? Right?' Marie looked over Tim's shoulder at a website called *Magical Solutions*. 'It sounds like a cheap interior decorator. And Serena Ravenmoor, can you get any more woo-woo than that?'

Tim sat back in his chair and stretched. 'Her name keeps coming up as someone who knows what she's doing.' He pulled up the 'about' page on her website with its picture of a wraith of a woman weighted down beneath a tumble of red hair. She was dressed in a black beaded gypsy skirt and a bustier layered in blue-black feathers that offered up the round tops of breasts the size and colour of ripe peaches, breasts nearly lost in a cascade of jewellery – all sorts of crystals surrounding an enormous silver pentacle encrusted with what looked like moonstones. In one ring-cluttered hand, she held a silver chalice that looked like it could have come straight from a Renaissance fair, and in the other she held a bone handled knife with a straight, ornately carved blade.

Beneath the photo was the name, Serena Ravenmoor, specialist in sex magic.

'You're kidding? Right?' Marie said again.

'You didn't seem to doubt Tara Stone when she gave you her card that said she practiced sex magic.'

'Of course I doubted Tara Stone. I thought she was full of shit. And that was even after I'd seen what she and Anderson were capable of.' She sighed. 'At least Tara wasn't a twit.'

Tim glared up at her. 'No, Tara's a murderer. I'll take my chances with the twit. Besides,' he added. 'I don't see that we have much choice. Her CV seems better than anyone else's we've read and the stuff on her website sound like … well …'

'Sounds like woo-woo squared, Tim. My God, none of it makes any sense. It's rubbish, all of it, just new age rubbish. Besides, I've met her. The chick's a nutter.'

'You've met her?' Tim folded his arms across his chest and

leaned back in his seat. 'Tell me just how did you meet her?'

Marie pulled her chair up next to his and told him about her unpleasant encounter with this Serena chick at the psychic fair. 'I'd been walking around town, and the fair was free, so I was curious. She went ballistic when I picked up her damned mirror. If she didn't want it touched, she shouldn't have left it lying on the table with all of the other woo-woo stuff people were poking through. How was I supposed to know?'

In spite of himself, Tim's lips twitched into a smile. 'So you're afraid of her, that's what you're saying.'

'No! That's not it. I thought she was a nutter then and I think she's a nutter now, but,' she chafed her arms and shivered. 'There was something very creepy about that damned mirror.' She forced a laugh and glanced up at him. 'Now I'm sounding like a nutter.'

Tim leaned forward in his chair. 'Why? Why was it creepy? I can't imagine anyone as sceptical as you feeling vibes off of something or feeling the energy of the past owner.' He made swirly motions with his hands.'

'It wasn't anything like that. It made me feel, I don't know, sort of sick to my stomach, sort of like I feel when I'm around ghosts only maybe with a touch of food poisoning thrown in for good measure.' She shrugged. 'This Serena chick didn't need to worry about me fondling the mirror. I put it down fast and couldn't wait to get away from there.'

'It's common knowledge not to touch another witch's tools,' Tim said. 'I'm not surprised you felt ill.'

She studied him for a moment. 'Fiori tell you that?'

His jaw tightened. His eyelids fluttered slightly, and he nodded.

'Bet Fiori didn't leave her tools out on display at a psychic fair where someone could pick them up, did she?' Before he could reply, she added. 'This is the kind of chick you think can help us? I just want to know why. Give me one good reason why.'

He scooted his chair back up to the table and began to flip through pages on his computer. 'First of all, she has quite a web presence. She's fairly googleable, as googleable as any witch in Cumbria is.' Marie looked over his shoulder. Sure enough the woman had spoken at lots of psychic fairs and woo-woo shops. She'd had articles published in several new-age papers, magazines, and websites. Her topic of preference seemed to be ghosts and sex. That was certainly in their favour – if she actually knew anything about either, and from what could be gleaned online, Marie felt the jury was still out.

Tim scratched at the stubble now gracing his chin. 'You got a better idea? I'm listening.'

'All right.' Marie stood and stretched, then plugged in the kettle. 'Call Ms Raven Britches then, and we'll see.'

With a fresh pot of tea, they settled in at the table just as the moon peeked in the kitchen window. Tim placed the call putting his mobile on speakerphone. Neither of them gave a thought to how late it was.

Three rings, then four. On the sixth ring, just as Tim reached to turn off the phone, there was a breathless female voice on the other end of the line. 'I was on my way out, when I realised this had to be an important call,' the woman said, sultriness replacing breathlessness.

Marie rolled her eyes, and Tim glared at her.

Marie sat with her arms crossed below her breasts feeling more and more uncomfortable as Tim told Serena Ravenmoor a whole lot more about their situation than she wished he would.

'I see,' Serena was saying. 'And you're plagued by ghosts who want to have sex with you.'

Could anything sound more stupid? Marie thought . Even woo-woo chick had to be practically wetting herself to keep from laughing. Either that or she would send the padded van their direction as soon as she hung up.

But Serena seemed nonplussed. 'You see, Tim, we who walk among the living consider our flesh a weakness. It's always getting ill or getting injured and ultimately it ages and dies. But to those who have no flesh it's a treasure beyond price. And one of the deepest pleasures of the flesh is, of course, sex. I don't find it surprising at all that the spirits would long for flesh so that they could have intercourse with you.'

Marie bit her lip to keep from giggling at the blush that crawled up Tim's throat at the mention of intercourse with him.

Serena's voice and grown warmer and more honeyed the longer she had spoken with Tim, and just when Marie was expecting the phone sex to begin, Serena's voice changed, became more distant, more ethereal. Good job, Marie thought.

'Tim, I can help you. And your friend.'

Before Tim could finish his sigh of relief, she added. 'But you must come tonight. The veil between the worlds is thinnest tonight while we still linger in the Moon's power. You must come tonight.'

'Tonight.' They spoke at the same time and looked at each other.

'You mean you can't help us any other night,' Marie said, sounding every bit as sceptical as she felt.

'Of course I can help you on another night, but your chances for success will be much better tonight. Besides,' the witch added quickly, 'it's not practical to think one session will be enough when I'll need to be with you intimately, first of all, to assess the situation more fully.'

'Hold it!' Marie ignored Tim's glare and hand motions for her to be quiet. 'Intimate, what do you mean intimate?'

The woman's voice suddenly dripped condescension through the speaker. 'It's sex magic, dear. Some level of sexual intimacy will have to occur between Tim and me for it to work. I'll accept cash only, as you must understand, and if that's a problem, I'm sure you can find a cash machine.'

Marie cursed under her breath. They could get a similar deal on some of the back streets in Portland any time they wanted it, and no doubt in London too, she thought, but it was called something different.

She was about to say just that to Tim when Tim surprised her by saying, 'Ms Ravenmoor, look this is a huge decision. We'll need to think about it at least overnight, no matter how good the convergences and stuff are.'

'Of course you will, Tim. I understand. But I'd be lapse in my duty to my sacred oath if I didn't warn you not to wait too long.'

He thanked her and had barely got the phone turned off before Marie let go. 'Total bullshit. Surely you can see that? She wants to have sex with you, and make you pay for it. There's another name for that where I come from.' She scrubbed her hands over her face. 'I need a shower.'

He waved her away. 'Go. You need a break. I'll keep looking.' He turned his attention back to the computer.

She pulled the bedroom door to and left a trail of clothing across the floor feeling desperately wilted and exhausted. She'd feel better after a shower. Then a nice pot of coffee, maybe they'd scrounge a snack and ... Her tummy did a tight little quiver as she thought of what almost happened between her and Tim in the manger. She forced herself not to think about why they hadn't followed through. He was here with her now, had been most of the day, and she was sure neither of them wanted to be alone tonight.

She cranked the shower and adjusted the temperature, all the while thinking about the feel of him on top of her, the lovely thick length of his cock in her hand, which was easily thicker than her favourite vibe. Her pussy tensed at the thought. She closed her eyes and lifted her face to the spray, thinking about his delicious scent, all leather and dusty male sweat with just the right base note of super-charged pheromones. Even thinking about it made her giddy, made her slightly dizzy, slightly disoriented. The delicious feel of warmth in her pussy migrated up inside her, higher, deeper, to rest between her hip bones where it blossomed to heat, then burst like a flash fire raging up through her abdomen. Before she could double over from the intensity of it, a thick arm caught her around the middle and a large hand clamped her mouth before she could cry out.

'Hello, my lovely.' She felt Deacon's voice more like a low rumble mixing with the heat. He tisk-tisked. 'If our dear Mr Meriwether won't help you with those hard to reach places, then I'm happy to do the honours.' He shifted his hips and she felt his thick cock high against the crack of her arse. He stroked her face with a large hand, cupping and caressing his way over the thin skin along her trachea. 'Such lovely, delicate, flesh.'

He enunciated each word carefully, fully, deeply. As he caressed his way along the exposed path of her neck, even with her eyes open there were flashes of him in nearly the same intimate position with Fiori before she died. Marie tried to swallow, but he held her with just enough pressure at the throat to make it difficult. Suddenly, with a deep surge of empathy in the pit of her stomach, she understood completely why Tara had killed Fiori, and why the other witch would have welcomed death at her hand rather than Deacon's.

Deacon released her throat and moved his fingers down over her breasts. 'I'm hurt, my darling Marie. You think I can't be gentle, don't you? You think I can't pleasure a woman until she writhes and moans and begs for more.'

With the slightest movement of his hand and a catch of his own breath, the heat in her abdomen combusted to nearly unbearable lust. He chuckled again, aware of what she felt. 'I can offer you so very much more than le petit mort, my dear Marie. Oh such ecstasy. You'll never want me to stop.'

But there was something else rising too, something else deep in her ribcage just below her heart. Anderson, she wanted Anderson, but she'd told him to leave her alone, and Tara, Tara could protect her, Tara was a match for this bastard. He pinched her nipples to tender swollen points and her pussy felt gaping enough to swallow up the universe. But he had killed Fiori, as surely as he stood there, and Sky, and the other woman, the one who sank beneath the deep waters in her dreams. He wasn't offering pleasure. He only wanted to hurt Tara, and he wanted to use her to do it. What rose beneath her ribcage and felt as though it would explode out of her whole body was white hot rage. She had spent the last ten years of her life being used to make other bastards rich. She would not be used by another one.

Afterward, she was never really certain if she had actually screamed the words, 'get out,' or if they had just filled every cell of her brain until there was room for nothing else. Whatever had happened, in an instant, he was gone, and the next thing she knew, she was falling on her knees in the shower just as a wild-eyed Tim pulled the door open and dragged her out. But for a split second, wavering in and out of consciousness, gasping for breath, she though she saw Anderson standing behind Tim.

Then there was just the two of them. Tim had wrapped her in her heavy terry robe, then in the duvet he'd dragged from her bed. He sat with her pulled against his chest on the bathroom floor, taking her pulse, checking her pupils, checking for symptoms of shock while she caught her breath. 'He was there, in the shower,' she rasped. 'I swear he was there.'

'I know,' Tim said. 'I knew from the beginning, but I couldn't get in. I went wild. I kept yelling and banging on the door, yelling for you, but you didn't answer.'

She squeezed his hand. 'Tim, I couldn't hear you. I couldn't hear anything but him.'

His fingers white knuckled around hers, and he nodded. 'I suspected that. At least I hoped that was all it was. He wanted me to see. He wanted me to watch while he hurt you.' He moved her hand away from her throat and swallowed hard.

'There are bruises?' She asked.

He bit his lip and nodded.

'I thought there might be.'

'Bloody bastard,' he said. 'What happened, why did he leave?' He touched her throat tenderly. 'From the looks of that, he wasn't intending to play nice.'

'I told him to leave. I told him to get the fuck out. I told him that he was never going to hurt me or the people I love again, I told him ...' she caught her breath when she saw the look of concern on Tim's face. Then she grabbed his arm. 'That's it, don't you see? I told him to leave.'

Tim forced a laugh. 'Oh, like he'd listen.'

'He didn't have any choice. Tara told me that same power I have to hold ghosts in the flesh I can also use to kick their asses out if I need to. That's what happened, I know it is. I felt it.' She shook her head. 'I don't know how I did it, but I know there was rage, horrible rage, so hot that it made the burn in my belly feel non-existent.'

'Are you all right to get dressed, or shall I stay with you?'

She shook her head. 'I'm fine now. He won't be back

tonight.'

He studied her for a minute. 'How do you know that?'

'I just know.'

When she returned to the kitchen dressed, he was eating a turkey sandwich, and he nodded to one waiting for her on the table along with a glass of juice. 'I hope you don't mind, but I raided the fridge. We both need to eat, especially you after your encounter. Fiori told me magical encounters require lots of energy, and I was always hungry after ...' He looked away and shrugged. 'Anyway, you need to eat.'

She ate the offered sandwich and another before he dropped the bomb shell. 'I called Serena. Get your jacket. We're going.'

She bit back her protests. Even though she didn't believe for one minute it would do any good. He certainly seemed to. And maybe he was right. Maybe her vision was coloured by the fact that in times of crisis it had been Anderson and Tara who had rescued her. Her encounter with Deacon made her more certain than ever that she didn't have all the facts, and the only place she would get them was from Elemental Cottage. She would go with Tim tonight and get the woo-woo out of the way, but then she was going back to Elemental Cottage, with or without him. She had gotten lucky with Deacon this time, but the next time she might not be so lucky, and what if the next time it was Tim he went after? Did he have her gift? The Elementals hadn't mentioned it if he did. At any rate, she wanted answers, and the only place to find them, she was now certain, was with the Elementals. The thought of seeing Anderson again made her feel giddy, and there was a warm spot that was way higher than her hip bones at the thought that he had come to her rescue, that he would have broken every rule to get to her. She knew that. She didn't know how she knew it, but she did.

Chapter Ten

ANDERSON MATERIALISED INTO THE middle of the circle the other three witches had cast in the Room of Reflection. It was an unorthodox entrance, but then his leaving had been no less so. All three witches broke their meditations and rushed to his side.

For a long moment he stood in the centre of the circle soaking in the magic, still shaken by what he had just witnessed.

'Well?' Tara demanded.

He looked up at the women and felt his heart surge with pride. 'She cast him out.'

'What?' Fiori grabbed his arm in such a bruising grip that for the moment he wished either one or the other of them weren't flesh and bone. 'How can that be? No one's taught her.'

'Nevertheless, that is what she has done. I arrived at the very instant when her rage was brighter than anything I have ever witnessed. I do not know what he did to kindle such a rage in her, but she was formidable, nay, she was terrifying.' His lips curled in a smile as he remembered her naked and wet from the shower, at the moment when one should be afforded the least dignity, and yet she was like a goddess blazing in her fury. He remembered the three witches standing around him. 'I left when I was certain she was all right. And I am equally certain he will not attack her again tonight.'

'So they're safe for the moment then,' Sky said.

'It is a small reprieve, yes,' Anderson answered.

'But? What is it,' Tara reached out and stroked his arm. 'What's troubling you, Anderson, you never were very good at

94

subterfuge, at least not with me.'

He held her gaze. 'I fear that this time there was physical injury to her person.'

'Fuck.' Fiori cursed out loud, something she rarely did. She chafed her arms and her face lost its colour. 'What did he do to her?'

'Only a bit of bruising,' Anderson said, feeling it more politic not to say where those bruises were. 'But that he can now cause physical damage must be a warning that our situation has most definitely worsened.'

All three witches nodded their agreement. Sky heaved a sigh. 'Well at least they're safe for the night.'

'Not quite, though I don't perceive any real threat coming in the form of one Serena Ravenmoor,' Anderson said.

'What does that woman have to do with any of this?' Tara asked.

Anderson felt himself heartily blushing. Serena Ravenmoor had worked for Tara at the herbal shop. He didn't know the details. He only knew that powerful herbs were taken from the shop without authorisation resulting in the near hospitalisation of one of the woman's so-called clients. Needless to say, Tara did not hold Serena Ravenmoor in high esteem.

'She is where their research has led them, I fear.'

'Oh for fuck sake,' Tara cursed. 'How can such a powerful couple behave so stupidly? The woman's a quack, completely barmy. Plus she's dangerous.'

'I think our Marie would agree with you, but as you have often said of those of my sex, it is not always our brain that dictates the choices we make.'

'Rubbish,' Fiori said. 'Tim Meriwether is one of the most level-headed men I've ever known.'

Anderson shrugged his deference. 'In truth, I think it is more likely that even for him it is an act of desperation. But of our lovely Marie, I am not mistaken in that she called out for me in her time of need. I do believe she will swiftly be returning to us.' That she had called out for him, that she had wanted him made him feel things he hadn't felt in a very long time, but that much he would keep to himself, as he was not, as

Tara would call it, a navel gazer.

Tara cursed again, this time under her breath. 'Now, if we can just keep Ravenmoor from poking someone's eye out with a lit candle or poisoning them.'

Anderson struggled to curtail his smile. 'Forgive my eavesdropping, but I did feel it necessary at such a time, I think her plans are for Tim Meriwether and his athame, unless I am mistaken.'

Sky snickered behind her fingers, then bit her lip to keep from laughing.

'I can understand why she might want the use of his athame,' Fiori said.

Tara sighed. 'In the meantime, we wait. Anderson don't leave their side. Stay hidden if at all possible, but if they need you, then do whatever you have to.'

Anderson found this command from his high priestess to be no hardship.

They met Serena Ravenmoor at the car park on the flank of Raven Crag. She was dressed in an ornate black gown with a tightly cinched bodice barely concealing her nipples. She was heavily made-up, and her wild red hair had been sprayed so that it sparkled in the moonlight. Only the lightweight walking boots she wore were even remotely practical. She pressed a tight hug against Tim and kissed him on the mouth, then she glared over at Marie. 'I thought I told you not to bring her. Her lack of belief is disturbing to me.'

'And I told you I'm not leaving her.' Tim's voice was infinitely patient.

'What?' Marie shoved her hands against her hips. 'You don't want me here? She doesn't want me here? Why didn't you tell me she didn't want me here?'

'Because I wasn't going to leave you, that's why.' His focus was still on Serena. 'Now, we can do this with her here, or I can leave now and take my two hundred quid with me.'

'Two hundred quid? She's charging you two hundred quid to fuck you. Hell, I would have done it for free.'

'Shut up, Marie.' Tim's voice was still the epitome of

patience. 'We'll talk about this when we get home. Now, Ms Ravenmoor, Serena, she doesn't have to be involved in the ritual ...' He raised his hand before Marie could protest further. '... She just has to be in my sight at all times. Is that acceptable?'

The woman huffed out a displeased breath. 'I don't see that I have any choice, then do I? But I can't guarantee results with her here.'

Marie raised both hands and backed away. 'Hey, lady, if you can guarantee results, I'll happily take the Land Rover back to the house, have a bit of a snooze and come back later when you're done with him.'

'Marie.' There was a slight edge of warning in Tim's voice this time.

'Of course I can't make guarantees.'

'I didn't think so.'

'Marie, could you just please give it a rest.'

'I've had a bad night, Tim. You'll have to excuse me if I don't much like being invited to a party and then being told I can't dance.'

'I didn't invite you to this party,' the witch retorted.

'Shut up, both of you.' Tim raised his voice this time, but only enough to make the warning in it very noticeable. 'Now, I'm sorry about this, Marie. I know it won't be much fun for you, but if you'll just cooperate, we can get on with it and be home in time for breakfast.'

Suddenly Marie remembered Anderson standing there behind Tim, and reminded herself that tomorrow she would go to him, tomorrow she would get some answers, and tomorrow maybe it would be her getting laid rather than being the spectator. 'Sorry.' She tried to force a smile. 'Just do what you have to do.'

They followed the witch up a winding path into the woods and for a while the woodland was too thick for the moonlight to penetrate. They stumbled in darkness until Tim pulled out a torch. The witch already had one. He settled back to walk next to Marie. He tried to take her arm, but she pulled away. 'You can't believe I'm doing this because I want to, Marie.' He spoke between barely parted lips.

'It's none of my business who you fuck.'

'Jesus! Do you think that's what this is all about? Do you think I'd even be considering this if we had other options?'

'That doesn't make this any less stupid nor her any less a quack.' She raised both her hands realising to her dismay that she was doing it again. 'I'm sorry. I promised I wouldn't do this. I promised. Of course you're right. Our options are thin on the ground at best.' She was sure he would like her plan to go back to the Elementals even less than she liked his, but hers made a lot more sense.

This time she didn't pull away when he took her arm. He spoke very close to her ear. 'Are you jealous? Because there's no need for you to be, though I'd be kind of flattered if you were.'

Before there was time for anything more than Marie's heart to do a little quiver, they found themselves in a clearing, and Serena turned to them. 'This is where the ritual will be. 'Tim and I will be there.' She took his arm, and pointed to a grassy spot open to the moonlight. 'I don't care where you are as long as you remain outside the circle, is that clear.'

'Crystal.'

'Right then. Shall we get on with it? First, I need the money.'

Marie bit her tongue to keep from making a comment as Tim handed Serena cash and she stuck it into a small bag that hung around her neck. That done, she smiled up at him. 'Whenever you're ready then.' She turned and headed into the clearing.

Tim walked hand in hand with Marie to the edge, then he folded her in his arms. 'I'm really sorry about this, but if it helps, it'll be worth it.'

'Then don't be sorry. Desperate times call for desperate measures.'

He surprised her by taking her mouth in a hungry kiss, deep enough to make her knees weak as he lowered her to sit on the ground just outside the circle. 'We have unfinished business. Remember? He brushed his fingertips along her cheek, settled another light kiss on her lips then followed Serena into the circle.

It was a testament to just how tired she was. And really, she hadn't had a decent night's rest since after the walk on Maiden Moor. When she had the chance to be a voyeur and have a little wank on the side, she promptly fell asleep, dreaming that Anderson and Tim, together were doing their best to make her feel really good, and that involved a little guy on guy fun as well. She didn't know how much time had passed, but just when the dream was getting really good, Tim shook her awake. 'Come on Marie,' he said breathlessly in her ear. 'We're leaving.'

'What? What happened?' she asked, scrabbling to her feet. She could just make out the back side of Serena Ravenmoor moving down the path out of the clearing at breakneck speed.

'Nothing happened,' he said, pulling her to her feet. 'Just like you said. Nothing happened.' The tight pinch in his voice told her something was wrong.

'Tim, what's the matter? What? Was it Deacon?'

'No. It wasn't Deacon. Would you mind just being quiet for a little while, OK, just don't talk to me.' This time the warning in his voice was not even slightly veiled.

They made it to the car park just in time to see Serena Ravenmoor's car screech out onto the road.

'She's upset,' Marie commented, trying to keep her voice calm.

'That's right. She's upset.'

She waited for it.

He helped her into the Land Rover, then slammed the door behind her and got into the driver's seat. 'She's fucking upset because I wouldn't give her two hundred quid more for a bunch of lame-arsed herbs and crystals and potions.'

'Jesus!' Marie braced herself as he did his own version of screeching out of the car park.

For the next few miles, he said nothing else. And when the silence became thicker than lamb stew, she spoke, 'Are you going to tell me what happened?'

99

'I already told you. Nothing happened. She was a quack just like you said. I would have thought you would have at least stayed awake to gloat.'

She bit back the retort at the end of her tongue because clearly something was bothering him.

But he kept talking. 'It was as good for you as it was for me then, so good that you fell asleep.'

'Sorry. I didn't plan to. I just haven't slept in a while, and since I wasn't participating, well, nature took its course.'

'Yep, nature took its course. I could have used some support.'

She felt herself bristle. 'What? Did you want me to stand on the side lines and be your cheerleader while you porked woo-woo girl? Fuck her again, fuck her again, harder, harder.'

'Shut up, Marie.'

This time she more than bristled. 'If you tell me to shut up one more time, I promise it'll be painful for you.'

'Goddamn it, Marie!' He slammed his open palm against the steering wheel, hard. 'I didn't fuck her, OK? Now can we just drop it, please.'

The rest of the trip passed in prickly silence. By the time they drove up in front of Lacewing Cottage, dawn was breaking. It was pouring with rain, and the fells had all disappeared into the mist. He pulled to a stop in front of her cottage and followed her up the steps. When she turned questioning eyes, he said, 'I'm not leaving you alone.'

Not figuring it was a great time for the "I can take care of myself" argument and not real keen on being alone either, she opened the door and motioned him in behind her. Inside, he kicked off his shoes, shucked his jacket on the peg by the door and moved toward the couch. 'We both need some sleep,' he said, settling in. 'If you could just find me a pillow and an extra blanket, that would be great.'

She brought a pillow and an ageing quilt and handed them to him. 'I'm sorry,' she said softly.

'So am I,' he replied, avoiding her gaze. 'Now get some sleep. I know you're exhausted.'

*　　*　　*

'It wasn't my fault,' Serena sobbed against Deacon's broad chest. 'It must have been him. It had to have been him.'

'Oh come now, my dear Serena.' Still breathing heavily, Deacon rolled off of her, and she felt suddenly deeply empty as he pushed away from her. 'I can promise you Mr Meriwether has never had any problems getting his cock stiff, nor is he lacking skill when it comes to using it.' He glanced down at his own heavy cock still wet from the merciless pounding he'd given her, then he began to stroke himself absently, the very act of which made her ache for him all the more.

'I have to say, my darling, I must call into question your abilities as a practitioner of sex magic if you cannot make one man of above average virility stiff.'

Serena couldn't help but notice that Deacon stroked the upward curve of his erection in much the same way he stroked the leather of his bullwhip before he unfurled it. She shuddered at the thought, and yet in spite of it, she slid a hand down in an effort to ease the fire in her pussy, but he slapped her hand away. 'I don't think your slut hole has earned relief tonight, loveliness.'

She cried out and writhed against the mattress. 'I'm telling you there was something else going on, some other form of magic, powerful magic. I felt it. I tried to warn him about it, but he wouldn't listen.'

'Liar!' The sudden raise of his voice made her jump and cringe. 'You tried to sell him your hocus pocus rubbish, didn't you? Didn't you?'

She blinked back tears and nodded. 'I didn't know what else to do. I'm sorry. I'm so sorry.'

His face softened. 'Of course you are, my darling.' He pulled her close to him, his strong arms settling her on top of him, but he held her so no amount of wriggling would allow her to impale herself back on his desperately-needed cock. He caressed her cheeks and breasts. Everywhere his hand touched felt like he had ignited lust until every pore of her body trembled with need. 'Perhaps I demanded too much of you too soon. Perhaps you're just not as ready as I thought you were, my lovely. Perhaps it was foolish of me to send you, so untried as you are, to do such an important task. But I must confess, I really thought you were ready.'

'Please, darling,' she let the tears slide down her cheeks. 'I am ready. I really am. You must believe me, there were powers at work, other powers. Maybe that horrible American he was with, maybe she was doing something behind my back, maybe she had done something to him before they arrived. I asked him not to bring her, demanded it even, just like you said.'

He held her in a disappointed gaze. 'My dear Serena, Marie Warren did nothing to Mr Meriwether before his arrival at Raven Crag, I promise you. And as for her time at the site, well she slept through your debacle. Since you could not keep her away, I made sure of that myself. I assure you she had nothing to do with Tim's unfortunate lack of interest in you. Oh come, come, my dearest. Don't fret so.' He pinched her nipples until she winced in pain that somehow still felt like enflamed desire. 'I suppose it is possible that there was other magic at work, just as you say. After all, you are a powerful witch. You would certainly know these things, wouldn't you?' He pinched again and moved so his cock rubbed agonizingly at the edge of her raw pout.

Suddenly she was aware of how hard she was trembling. How many times had he made her come? It had to be magic that had allowed her to drive the car and arrive home safely. He was on her before she cleared the woodland. She couldn't see him, but dear Goddess, her body felt him like a fast moving fever threatening to burn her up. At least he had waited until she was out of sight of Tim Meriwether and his woman, at least he'd spared her that humiliation. Beyond that, he had left her little pride, and as mindless with lust as she was, it didn't matter. It didn't matter if she died in the throes of the ecstasy he could offer. She could only take what he gave her and whimper for more as her desire built rather than dissipated. It was only as he dragged her from the car and pushed her down on the bed in her flat that she fully realised the extent of his rage. He never unfurled the bullwhip. He didn't need to. He offered a far more exquisite punishment.

She bit back a sob. 'It wouldn't have taken much power to

realise there was strong magic on him.'

'Of course not, my darling, of course not.' He held her so her aching gape was pressed up tight and begging against the blunt head of his cock. 'And we shall get to the bottom of that powerful magic together. Now that I have seen more clearly the situation, there is yet a better way that you may serve me, but first, my sweetheart, let me ease the rage of your need.'

With that he pushed into her so hard and so deep that it took her breath, and yet she sobbed with relief as he began to jack hammer with bone breaking force. Whatever it took. She could endure little more without some real relief.

Chapter Eleven

THE AFTERNOON SHADOWS WERE lengthening across her bedroom floor when Marie finally woke up. For a second she wasn't sure where she was, for a second there was a lingering tingle low in her belly and she thought of Anderson, but then he'd said she would feel that tingle when any spirit was close. She shivered remembering the events of the past 24 hours, then groaned. 'It just gets more insane all the time,' she spoke into the silence.

Then she remembered Tim sleeping on her sofa. She dressed quickly, noticing once again with an icy shiver the bruise marks along her neck where Deacon had held her. She brushed her hair down over them, then shuffled into the lounge.

Tim was gone, but the ripple of fear that clawed at her insides eased off when she saw the quilt folded neatly at the foot of the sofa with the pillow stacked on top of it. A cup had been used, washed, and placed neatly in the draining rack, and the kettle, which Marie always forgot to refill, was full. He had a farm to run, she reminded herself. He didn't get the luxury of sleeping till he was rested. She wondered if he'd found something to eat. She wondered if he was OK.

She felt a surge of guilt at her bad behaviour last night. Whatever had happened with Serena, she should have been there for him, even if it meant having to watch the bitch fuck him. The strangeness of it all suddenly hit full force. There was no way in hell she could have slept if Tim were fucking Woo-woo Woman. The barb of jealousy aside, he was doing it for very serious, very important reasons, and the raunchy little voyeur in her would have relished a good look at Tim's junk and how he used it. The wank potential was too hot to be ignored, let alone the danger he had actually put himself in. That sharpened the bite of guilt, but also made her wonder what else had been going on. Surely Serena Ravenmoor didn't have the power to cause her to sleep while she had her way with Tim. And what had she actually done to him to make him so upset?

Before the thought was completely out of her head, she was halfway down the steps. It wasn't hard to find Tim. He was unloading hefty bags of grain from the back of a flatbed into the barn. The day had dried and warmed to a steamy Cumbrian greenhouse, a condition that seemed to be the order of the day for the past week and a half. It had been enough to cause Tim to take off his shirt, and the sight of him naked to the waist nearly took her breath away. No. She was absolutely certain she could not have slept through that.

'You all right?' He called, wiping a gloved hand over his sweaty brow.

'Not so bad. You?'

'Better now. A little hard work's always good for what ails you.' She thought she saw a pained look cross his face, but it passed so quickly that it could have just been the play of light and shadows.

'You must be famished,' she called up to him. 'I know I am. I've got everything for a fry-up if you're interested.'

'I wouldn't say no.' He offered her that boyish smile that had made her knickers wet the first day she met him, when he handed over the keys. After that, he'd not smiled very much. Now she knew why that was. He looked down at the patina of sweat and dust covering his broad chest. 'Give me time to clean up.'

She fought back the urge to ask him if he needed help with that. Instead, she glanced down at her watch. 'You've got 30 minutes, then I eat it all myself. Consider yourself warned.'

'It smells great,' he said, as he stepped into the kitchen all clean and freshly scrubbed. 'I didn't think an American could do a proper fry-up.'

She smiled up from her efforts at the stove. 'My mother was

a Brit, and if there was one thing she taught me it was to do a fry-up.'

'And to make good coffee,' he said as he took up the cup she offered.

'My dad taught me that. He was a real coffee snob.'

'Ah,' he said, leaning up against the counter next to her, the angular lines of his body making the heat in the kitchen a lot more intense. 'The best of both worlds.'

'You?' She asked, turning her wandering attention back to the eggs before they burned.

'Cumbrian born and bred,' he said. 'I lived in London a good bit of my life, so sadly I lost the accent.' She saw the blush crawl up his throat. 'Now I wish I hadn't. Maybe with time, I'll earn the right to claim it back.'

She settled food onto the plates and nodded to the table. 'Is that what the farming is all about, earning it back?'

'Sort of, I guess.' He pulled her chair out, then settled in next to her. 'Though it's not a hardship earning it back in this place in this way.' He smiled at her look of disbelief. 'I mean it's hard work, but that's not the same as a hardship, is it?'

She shook her head, remembering the work she'd left.

They finished the meal in light, getting-to-know-each-other, conversation – the type one might have experienced on a first date, the type that kept what was really on their minds enough at bay for sanity to prevail a little while longer. Afterwards, they did the washing up side by side in companionable silence. They had settled in for another pot of coffee when she approached the subject of the night past.

'Tim, I'm sorry for my terrible behaviour, and the falling asleep.' She found it hard to meet his gaze. 'That wasn't me. I would never have been able to sleep under such circumstances.' She lifted her eyes. 'I was afraid for you, and to be honest, I was afraid for the Ravenmoor woman too. One minute I was watching with my heart pounding in my chest while she cast the circle and the next you were waking me up.'

She could see the tension along his shoulders that hadn't been there before, and the hard line of his mouth reminded her of the Cumbrian stone walls always marking the boundaries

106

not to be trespassed upon.

'I thought of that afterwards,' he said, seeming to find it equally difficult to meet her gaze. 'After I'd added my own dose of bad behaviour to the evening.' He forced a grunt. 'Mind you, it was just as well you weren't watching.'

'Tim?' She reached over and took his hand. For a second, she thought he would pull away, but instead, he wrapped his fingers around hers. 'Tim, what happened?'

The blush that rose from the open collar of his shirt up over his cheeks was dark crimson. The muscles of his jaw twitched, and his shoulders got even stiffer. 'Nothing happened, Marie.'

'Look Tim I really am sorry that I wasn't awake to be there for you and that I was so rude to Serena but really ...' Then she got it. 'Oh. Nothing?'

He shook his head and glared into his coffee cup. 'I mean she was doing sex magic, for fuck sake, and I'm not shy, but I couldn't ... I tried.' His hand twitched beneath hers. 'That's when she started trying to sell me all her stupid crystals and potions to help my fucking libido. Marie, I swear, nothing like that has ever happened to me before.'

'Tim, look at me.' When his eyes met hers, she continued, 'You've felt sex magic before just like I have, and how hard was it to get turned on?'

He huffed out a breath, and raked a hand through his hair. 'It wasn't getting turned on that was the problem, it was trying to keep from ripping off my jeans and fucking everything in sight. That was the problem.' His hand suddenly went low to his belly. Marie couldn't help noticing that even the thought of what the ghosts made him feel, what the Elementals made him feel caused an instant bulge against his fly. She forced her attention back to his face, but not before she remembered the silky hard feel of his cock in her hand there in the manger, and her pussy was most definitely sympathetic.

He continued. 'And that burn, you know what I mean. At first it hurts like hell until you get used to it. Then it twists and turns and rearranges itself until, I swear, Marie, it feels so damn good, and ...' His voice drifted off. 'I didn't feel that. I didn't feel that at all.' For a second the two sat in silence as

Tim contemplated his observation, then he spoke softly, 'OK, so there was no magic. You did warn me that she was a quack, but still, the woman wasn't exactly unattractive, was she? If I'd met her at a pub and we'd spent an evening together over a few drinks ...'

Marie's hand mirrored Tim's resting low on her belly, remembering. 'There was magic, Tim. I remember now. I remember feeling it just before I fell asleep, the burn, and I remember thinking maybe Anderson had come. But then I knew it wasn't him.' This time it was her turn to blush. 'Then I don't remember anything else until you woke me up.' She shuddered at the memory of how desolate she felt when she realised it wasn't Anderson.'

Holding her breath, she leaned forward and laid her hand on the bulge at his crotch, and he sucked air. 'Tim, if there is magic that makes us horny, don't you think maybe there could also be magic that makes us, you know, not able to. Maybe magic that's there for our own protection?'

He placed his hand on hers, and rocked his hips forwards into her touch, and his eyelids fluttered. 'I think it's a theory worth investigating, and we do have unfinished business, don't we?'

She lowered herself to the floor onto her knees in front of him and the room was awash in heavy breathing as she undid his fly, a bit more awkwardly than she intended. Before the zipper was down, the heavy weight of his erection shoved forward into her hand. She offered a throaty chuckle. 'Tim Meriwether, a commando boy, who'da thought.'

'Missed laundry day,' he breathed. 'You know with everything going on.'

'Makes it easier for me,' she sighed, leaning forward to take him into her mouth.'

'Oh God,' he gasped and curled his fingers in her hair. 'Oh God, Marie.'

For a deliciously endless moment, the only sound other than her wet ministerings to his cock was their heavy breathing and the slight protests of the wooden chair as Tim braced and ground against it. The tightly controlled shifting of Tim's hips made deep-throating him a pleasure, so much so, in fact, that she fumbled with her own fly and slid her fingers down inside the cut-offs, bucking against her hand with the first shiver of delight as she parted her wet folds.

'You can't keep that to yourself,' Tim managed between laboured breaths. 'I want to see. I want to taste.'

She ploughed two fingers deep into her slick hole, then eased them free, glistening and creamy with her juices. Shifting only enough that she could see his face well, she lifted her fingers to his mouth.

His cock surged as he pulled them between his lips with a hungry slurp. He made almost the same kind of sound he'd made over the breakfast she'd cooked, only deeper, so deep she could feel the vibration of his moans down his body clear into his cock. And his tongue, my God what the man could do with his tongue, even just on her fingers, made her gasp, made her pussy let down a fresh flood.

'You can't keep such sweetness from me, woman.' He pulled away from her. 'Now that I've tasted you, I want all of you.' With the same animal power he had used to heft the bags of grain into the barn, he lifted her until her arse rested firmly on the oak table, then he pushed her back with one hand, kissing his way over her still-clothed breasts and down her belly to where the humid heat of his lips and tongue conspired with his nimble fingers, pushing and pressing and rootling until her shorts and knickers were down over her hips. As she lifted her bottom so he could shimmy them off, his mouth kept on target right down over her mons to linger for a tonguing and a suckling of her clit, which caused her to make sounds not unlike the contented grunts of Tim's mare.

Then he went deep, as though he were searching for buried treasure and he knew exactly where to look. Cupping her buttocks to him, he tongued and slurped and suckled her swollen lips, returning to the nib of her clit to stoke the flames that had become a full-fledged inferno. Then the middle finger of one hand sought out her anus, already wet from the delicious mix of her juices and his saliva dripping down over her perineum. He plunged it deep, judging perfectly the results, which with just the right nip on her clit, sent her writhing into orgasm.

Then he pulled away, face dewed with her heat. With one shove of his hand, his jeans were around his knees, and he pushed into her grudging pussy with a growl so feral that she gushed again and responded with her own growls and grunts. She wrapped her legs around him, locking her ankles until he was bear-hugged between her thighs. She met him thrust for frenzied thrust, until the whole world and every conscious thought that existed in it centred around his cock in her cunt. Nothing else existed, nothing else mattered.

She screamed her next orgasm until her throat was raw, just as he grunted next to her ear. 'Jesus, Marie, I have to come. Now!' And he did. She felt him, felt the core of him as he emptied himself into her over and over again there on the kitchen table.

They managed to make it to the bed for round two, which was long and lingering and playful. At some point, Marie lost track of how many times she'd come, and even the slightest doubt about the working order of Tim's junk was replaced with heated, naughty admiration. She drifted off to sleep in a spoon position, his cock still happily nestled inside her, his hand cupped possessively around her breast.

No problems had been solved. They would wake up with Deacon still looming over them like a bilious plague, but at least for the moment they could pretend that all was well with the world.

The room was deep in shadow when Tim woke up with Marie wrapped in his arms. The sight of her, the memory of what had led him to be in this enviable position made his cock tense again, but he ignored his desire to wake her for another good fuck. He was used to the craziness. He'd lived with it for three months now, but she was not, so he opted to let her sleep while he took care of his evening chores.

She moaned softly and shifted on the pillow, as he carefully disentangled himself from her, but she didn't wake up. He dressed quietly, resisting the urge to linger and watch her sleep.

On his way out the front door, he grabbed a piece of cold bacon left over from the fry-up and wolfed it before pulling the door quietly to behind him. Hopefully he'd be back before she woke up, and he smiled at all the wonderful ways he might tease her into the waking world.

It was the painful heat rising from between her hip bones that woke Marie, woke her with the unnerving sensation of falling.

She knew before she heard his voice that he was there. Despite the heat in her groin, the cold feel of him was like no one else. Instantly, she was wide awake, pushing terror to a remote corner for another time when she could collapse into a heap. If she survived that long. She couldn't afford terror at the moment. As her eyes searched the gloom, he spoke in words that vibrated up through her spine. 'Did you think I would stay away, Marie? I'm quite hurt that you and Mr Meriwether had such a delicious party and did not invite me.'

At the sudden realisation that Tim was gone, her stomach clenched and she bolted upright in bed, pulling the duvet to her breasts.

She heard his chuckle before she felt the pressure of his body sitting on the bed next to her. 'Oh don't worry, my lovely. Mr Meriwether is unharmed. At the moment it is not he who interests me, but you, my darling.' He ran a thick finger down the side of her cheek, and instead of the shudder she expected, she felt a warm tingle. 'Your uniqueness intrigues me. Of all Tara Stone's menagerie of witches and sluts and curiosities, you are the most interesting in a very long time, a very long time indeed.' He heaved a sigh as though he were taking in the view at the top of his favourite fell. 'So invigorating to have such an interesting creature at my disposal again after all this time.'

She pulled away. 'I'm not at your disposal.'

'Oh but you are, my darling, of course you are. It is a game of cat and mouse, and one you have no chance of winning,' he shrugged, 'though I wager the sport shall offer me great exhilaration, much more so than with any of Tara's other pets. I cannot begin to tell you how that excites me.' He shifted just right so she had no trouble seeing the heavy bulge in his leather trousers.

'Where's Tim?'.

'He's been called away on a rescue mission, nothing to concern you, and nothing a stalwart member of the Keswick Mountain Rescue team can't handle, I assure you.'

'What do you want from me?' Her voice sounded a hell of a lot more calm than she felt, she wondered how much she could bluff with Deacon.

'I want the pleasure of watching you embarrass yourself. I want the pleasure of making you beg for it, even when I hurt you, and I promise you that I shall ... hurt you. I want the pleasure of knowing that even in your agony, you lust for me.' He leaned forward and kissed her ear and the shocking heat of it made her pussy clench and gush. She offered up a startled gasp and the duvet slipped from between her fingers to reveal the painfully hard rise of her nipples.

He tisk-tisked, then leaned forward and sniffed. 'You are like all the others, a slut who always stinks of the rut. Perhaps I was wrong. Perhaps you are no different at all. Perhaps you will offer little sport.' He took her face in one large hand forcing her to look at him, squeezing until the pressure along her jawbone was nearly unbearable, and still her pussy clenched, and she cried out her frustration.

He reached down and stroked the coiled leather of his bullwhip the way most men stroke their cocks. 'You see, Marie, I don't have to wine you and dine you and seduce you and preen in front of you.' Then the stroke of the leather seemed to be happening between her pussy lips. She crabbed walked backward on the bed and tumbled off onto the floor, unable to think, unable to concentrate beyond the sudden desperate need to come. 'I already have complete control of your flesh, and I can offer you pleasure that you can never get enough of, or pain beyond bearing, and in the end, you will beg me for either indifferently.'

With her back to the wall, she stumbled to her feet, glancing desperately around for something, anything, but Jesus, she needed to come!

He stroked the curve of the bullwhip with the pad of his thumb, and her clit marbled and thrummed, and she cursed her frustration. 'Shall I make you come, Marie? Would you like that? I think that you would. I think that I would particularly enjoy pleasuring you to the point you can take no more and yet you beg for it still.' He unfurled the bullwhip in a long, easy movement, 'And then, I shall show you how equally adept I am at offering up pain, and you will like that just as much and beg for it just as hard until I have flayed the flesh from your bones and let the ravens peck at your lovely breasts, and still you will beg for more.'

She made a run for the door, but he was instantly on her, pulling her back almost gently, running his hands tenderly over the curves of her breasts. 'Oh don't worry, I won't end it all tonight. I am one who believes very much in foreplay, and when I finally bring you that very last time, I will insist upon a little voyeurism from my dear Tara Stone.'

He pulled her close and kissed her nape. 'But in the meantime, when we are finished tonight, when Tim returns from his fool's errand, I promise you, no other man but me shall ever be able to satisfy your hunger again.'

'Tim?' The voice over his mobile uttered a heart rending sob. 'Oh thank goddess, Tim! I was so afraid you wouldn't answer, so afraid you wouldn't understand, and you'd be too angry.'

He had thought it was Marie calling, so sure had he been that he answered it without looking to see.

It wasn't.

'Who is this?' He was just about to call it a prank and hang up when the caller begged.

'Oh goddess, Tim, please don't hang up, please listen to me. You have to listen to me. It's Serena Ravenmoor, Tim, and I'm so sorry. I never thought this would happen. I never meant to hurt you.'

'Serena? What the hell's going on? Where are you?'

There was more sobbing, and he heard her snuffle hard. Behind her he could hear the wind. 'Raven Crag. I'm at Raven Crag.'

113

He felt a surge of anger. 'Look, no hard feelings, and keep the two hundred quid, but I'm not interested in trying again, honestly, I think we just –'

'I'll jump, Tim.'

The irritation expanding in Tim's chest suddenly felt cut through with ice.

Serena continued, 'You have to come to me. I need you to understand what he'll do to me if you don't, and I can't bear that, so I swear I'll jump. I swear I will.'

Tim's gut clenched. Just what he didn't need right now another fucking bastard, who thinks it's his manly right to hit and abuse a woman. 'Serena listen very carefully, no one has the right to hurt you. We can protect you. We can find you a safe place and make sure this bloke can't hurt you ever again.'

She was crying flat out now. 'He said he was here for me. He said he would do what I wanted him to do, what I needed him to do, and then.' There was more hard sobbing. 'Tim, I'm so scared.'

'All right, Serena, don't move, don't do anything. Just wait for me I'll be there as soon as I can. Can you do that?'

More sobbing. 'Oh dear goddess, thank you Tim,' she hiccupped. 'And Tim, you have to come alone. Don't bring that woman, don't bring your mountain rescue team, don't bring anyone or I'll be dead when you get here. He'll see to it, I swear.' More sobbing. 'I know you think I'm a fake. I know you think I don't know anything, but I swear if you bring anyone, or tell anyone, I'm not the only one who'll suffer.' Then the phone went dead.

There was a finality in the message, and a terrifying certainty of impending danger, that made Tim shiver as he shoved the phone in his pocket and spun around, nearly running through Lisette.

'Christ, Lisette, I don't have time for this. I have to go, and I have to leave Marie alone and … Fuck.'

She stepped aside and moved effortlessly next to him as he raced toward the Land Rover.

'You need help, Tim Meriwether,' Lisette said softly, watching as he checked his climbing gear and first aid supplies in the back of the Land Rover. 'Shall I get help?'

He turned on her with every intension of telling her to fuck off, but something in her eyes stopped him, gave him pause for the tiniest of seconds, and calmed him. He took a deep breath and nodded. 'Yeah, Lisette. If you could get help, I'd appreciate it, and …'

'Yes I know, Tim. I'll tell your Marie and see that she isn't left alone.'

He jumped in the Land Rover and sped away from Lacewing farm. For the first time in the past three months he hoped desperately that the ghosts who had plagued him all these weeks really could help him. Though he wondered why they should, after his bad behaviour toward them.

Chapter Twelve

SOMETHING DIDN'T FEEL RIGHT from the moment Tim got out of the Land Rover and headed up the trail into the thick wooded darkness of Raven Crag. Raven Crag was a fell he'd been on so many times with Mountain Rescue that he could have found his way around blindfolded, and yet he felt strangely disoriented. The skin along the back of his neck prickled as he walked through the thicker patches of woodland hearing the night sounds that he'd heard a thousand times before, but suddenly he wasn't certain of any of them.

This is what happens when you're under slept and over stressed, he told himself. How many times in the past few weeks had he considered quitting the Mountain Rescue because he feared the stress and the lack of sleep would make him a liability rather than an asset. And now here he was doing something that went against all of his training, striking out on his own, not only striking out on his own, but doing it with no one knowing where he was.

Lisette knew, he told himself, and she had promised she would tell Marie. She certainly didn't owe him any kindness considering how he had treated her, and yet there had been no subterfuge in her face when she had approached him. She had promised she would get help. Even if that meant calling on this Anderson bloke, he reckoned he could easily live with that, if it would keep Marie safe.

It seemed that Deacon had definitely set his sights on her, and that frightened him more than anything else he could imagine. Each time Deacon upped his game and got to Marie, he found it more and more difficult not to think about what had happened to Fiori, not to draw parallels. But Marie was nothing like Fiori, he told himself. She was totally different, and yet it had been Marie who had unleashed Deacon back into the land of the living where he could do damage. Jesus, his head hurt just thinking about it all.

As he drew closer to the summit of Raven Crag, he walked more quietly, though he tried not to lessen his pace, but he needed to listen. He knew where the most likely place for a suicide attempt was, and he knew that Serena would also know that. But he hoped perhaps she had pulled back to safety once she knew he was coming. She could have found some more sheltered spot than the sheer rock drop that overlooked Thirlmere with a dramatic cliff that belied the rest of the fell's forested flank.

But he was practically on the precipice before he heard quiet sobbing. He felt a surge of adrenaline.

'Serena? It's Tim. Serena, where are you?'

'I'm here,' came the weak reply from below, and when he looked over the edge, his heart nearly stopped.

'Bloody hell, Serena! How did you get down there?'

'I can't get to her,' Lisette said, frantically pacing the parlour in Elemental Cottage, worrying the long string of pearls that hung knotted between her breasts. 'She's in there, I know she is, but I can't get to her. Tiggs, Finney, Michael, we've all tried. It's like there's a horrible dark blanket wrapped around her cottage. And I promised Tim I'd see to her, see that she wasn't left alone.'

Anderson would have already been there if Tara hadn't held him in a firm grip.

'It's as we feared,' the coven leader said. 'Deacon's separated them. What else did you hear, Lisette.'

'It was some woman named Serena on the phone. Threatening suicide. Stupid woman,' she interjected. 'And he went alone. She made him promise. She kept saying if he didn't she would kill herself because she couldn't bear facing *him* again.' The little flapper blushed hard. 'I eavesdropped. I assumed Tim knew it was Deacon she spoke of. Now I'm not so sure.'

'How long ago?' Tara asked.

She stopped her pacing and stroked at the pearls in concentration. 'It couldn't have been more than a minute. I'm sorry for the delay, but we tried everything. And Tara, I couldn't contact Tim either. That same feeling, that same dark sinister blanket kept me from him, and you know how I home in on Tim. I'm frightened for him. Do you think we should call Mountain Rescue?'

'There's nothing Mountain Rescue can do, hon,' Tara replied. 'I'm sure Deacon will have made it so that a normal person would never know anything was wrong. Go back to Lacewing Cottage and stay close, Tiggs, Finney, Michael, all of you, in case Anderson needs you. We'll bring Tim back safe, I promise you.'

The little ghost nodded and was gone in an instant.

'Tara, you must let me go to her, now.' Anderson pleaded. 'We have a bond, I can help her.'

Tara turned to Anderson who was positively bristling, and kissed him. 'Be careful.'

He returned her kiss. 'You too, my darling, all of you, and I will see you soon with Marie safe in tow.' With that he vanished.

Tara turned her attention to her sisters. 'We three will go to Raven Crag.' She nodded to Fiori and Sky, 'Go on ahead and do what you can. I'll be there as soon as I can with the Land Rover and the climbing equipment.'

When Marie was able to focus on more than the fire of her need, she was relieved that Deacon was in no hurry. He was toying with her. He didn't consider her a threat. And that could be to her advantage, if the son of a bitch were only wrong. She fought back another wave of arousal. He wasn't touching her. In fact, he was barely paying attention to her. He wanted her to believe none of this mattered to him, that she was as nothing to him. At least that was something. He was arrogant. That was a weakness, a weakness any good investment banker should be able to exploit.

Her finger nails had drawn blood in her palms in an effort to keep her hands away from her cunt. She wouldn't give the bastard the satisfaction, but Jesus it was hard! 'Why do you hate Tara Stone so much?' She forced her mind to think of Tara because for some reason that helped focus her attention on something other than the terrible, painful need to come.

Her question seemed to surprise him. 'Oh I don't hate Tara Stone. In another lifetime Tara Stone and I might have easily been friends, lovers even. It is her mother I hate, but her mother is dead, long dead, and I will have my revenge.'

The shiver of revulsion was piggybacked on another wave of lust. 'What did her mother do to deserve such perverse hatred that you would visit it on the innocent?' she asked, struggling to keep her mind focused.

His surprising burst of laughter caused her to jump, not a good move. Her pussy clenched desperately and she dug her nails deeper into her fisted palms. 'I should think that would be obvious to anyone of average intelligence.' He stood and turned slowly around, and as he did so, he faded to nothing, then back to solid form again. 'Her slut of a mother is responsible for my untimely death.' He waved his hand dismissively. 'Everyone must die, and I have never feared death, but I expected my power to increase in death, not diminish. I was not ready, and her little gift to me in the back alley of Concord, well let us just say it was not a part of my plan.' With that, he took the flat palm of his hand and ran it lightly between her breasts and down over her stomach. Her response was not dignified.

'Son of a bitch! Oh shit!' she screamed, her eyes watering with the pain that rode the sharp edge of nausea, converting to lust as he drew his fingers down to rest just above her pubic curls.

He clucked his tongue. 'Such filthy language. When I lived in the Americas, a lady would have never spoken so, nay, even a roughened sailor would not have used such invectives.'

The pain had come earlier than she had expected, and it did nothing whatsoever to diminish the lust. In spite of the hatred that rose in her chest for the monster standing before her, she wanted desperately for him to fuck her, and that made her furious.

He chuckled. 'That was a bit naughty of me when I have been so careful and tender in our foreplay up until now, but I find a little pain invigorating, as I'm sure you will. It sharpens the senses, makes the release all that more exquisite when it comes. And it will come, I promise you.'

His gaze softened to near sympathy. 'Please believe me, Marie, darling, I am not ungrateful to you, after all you brought me here.' He smiled at her and nodded. 'Oh yes I know. I know who invited me back into the world of the living. Granted I didn't at first. I was curious about you. As you know, anyone who interests Tara Stone interests me, but I didn't know just how much you interested me until you opened the way through that silly charlatan's scrying mirror at the psychic fair. You didn't know that, did you?' His voice became mocking. 'That's how you so kindly set me free by touching the daft woman's tools.'

'Makes as much sense as anything,' she replied.

'It is because I am for ever in your debt, my dear Marie, that I intend to give you a release fit for a goddess, a release you shall never forget, a release that will bond us so deliciously that I shudder in anticipation. And here is the beauty of it, my love. I do not believe in, what is it you call it? Ah yes, non-consensual sex. Oh no, my sweet. You will want me as you have never wanted any man before.' He laughed softly. 'I can already see your lust for me building. And when that time comes, when you are ready and begging me for it, I promise I will not deny you.'

He moved to pace in front of her and with a slight flick of one thick wrist, her nipples, which were already erect beyond painful, felt like electrical charges had been passed through them, electrical charges connected to her cunt. She grunted and closed her eyes, riding out the wave of pained arousal. The more it built the more it hurt, the more she needed release, and yet everything in her was certain that to give in would be fatal. She sucked breath and struggled to focus.

'Oh don't think that because you inadvertently freed me you have some power over me, girl.' He was now so close she

120

could feel the energy practically rippling off his body, and she wondered that his cock didn't burst completely through the restraining leather, and yet he seemed to ignore his own arousal completely.

'I think that if I were you, I'd be a bit concerned that I could just as inadvertently return you to your bonds if I were distressed enough, and you're certainly pushing me in that direction.'

'Not true at all, my dear. Not true at all. All I want is to pleasure you, to give you a release, a magical release that will be so delicious.' For emphasis, he pinched a swollen nipple, and chuckled as though she amused him when she bit back another curse.

'That your … distress could possibly return me to my previous state of bondage, my lovely, is a chance that I shall have to take.' He shrugged dismissively. 'To be honest, my dear, you are so much less of a challenge than I expected. Already you disappoint me. I don't even need to summon my full power to hold you enthral. While I watch you writhe and lust, I send your dear Tim on a fool's errand. It was not mountain rescue that called him away, I fear, but my dear, foolish Serena, threatening suicide if he doesn't come to her rescue and come alone. And for me, she would do it happily if he doesn't do exactly as she asks.' He shrugged, 'Perhaps not happily, but one must expect a bit of, what is that term used so often these days? Ah yes, collateral damage.' He drew within a kiss's breadth from her lips and brushed his words against them like a fine coating of dust … Like a fine coating of dust … dust from something long-dead, dust from something no longer significant.

A bright spark burst in her head and her attention was suddenly riveted to the mirror at the foot of her bed, as the scene in it shifted and brightened to something other than her own bedraggled reflection and that of the monster who held her captive. She saw reflected back at her a man strangled with his own bullwhip behind a brothel, where he had been taking his pleasure. The prostitute cowered and sobbed against the dirty brick.

He was a self-fashioned preacher, of sorts, a practitioner of arts so dark and evil that Marie shuddered to think. A dark-haired woman stood over him chanting words, weaving a spell, a complicated spell. A tall blonde stood next to her holding a length of bloodied lead pipe in a white knuckled grip. As the whip tightened around his neck and the last words of the spell wove into an equally tight strangle-hold, with the very last ounce of life, with a tremendous effort, he spoke. 'I make this sacrifice for power you can't imagine, witch.' Then he grabbed the pipe from the blonde and shoved it hard up his own arse. The resulting ejaculation spattered the dirty brick wall in front of him. As the breath left him, the blonde shouted, 'There is no power left for you to grab at, preacher. Fuck yourself if you must. But my sisters who have suffered at your hand will be avenged.'

As though the blonde's anger were transferred into her own soul, as though she were heaving aside a garment too tightly fitting, too constraining, everything in Marie's consciousness exploded outward with rage far older than what threatened to burst her own chest. The room flashed blindingly bright, Deacon roared, cursed and was gone. Marie fell to the floor as though someone had punched her in the stomach, punched the breath out of her.

Bent double and shuddering, it took her a few seconds to realise the heat between her hip bones was suddenly clean, suddenly invigorating, suddenly familiar. Then Anderson lifted her carefully into his arms and carried her to the bed.

She watched as he undid his trousers nearly ripping them in his efforts. 'My love, Deacon is gone. You have banished him.' He yanked his trousers down enough to release his cock and stroked it rapidly. 'This is not how I would choose to make love to you, my darling, but you must have relief or I fear for your life.'

She heard his words from a long way off. Already she'd opened her legs to him and arched up to meet him as he positioned himself. 'Please,' she begged. 'Anderson, please help me.'

'I am sorry, my love. But when next I enter you, I promise it shall be truly for pleasure.' He sank his cock into her with one swift thrust, and she screamed like a mountain lion before the world exploded into blessed relief and she lost consciousness.

'Oh please, Tim, hurry. I'm so scared.' There was no disguising the high pitched hysteria in Serena's voice. Seeing where she was and that she wore only a thin nightie, Tim knew that speed was of the essence.

'Serena, are you hurt?' he asked.

'No. I'm not hurt, please hurry!' She burst into more sobs.

'Listen very carefully, Serena,' he said as he tightened the climbing harness and clipped onto the rope he had secured to a nearby tree. 'I need you to relax for me and stay calm. I'm coming to get you. Just stay calm and hang on.'

He could have scrambled down to her without roping up, but he could never get a terrified woman, with, as far as he knew, no climbing skills, safely to the ground below.

The closer he got, the more audible her sobs became. 'You said you served me,' she sobbed. 'You told me that you were here for me. Why did you tell me that? Why?' Then she gasped. 'No, please don't. Please. I did as you asked me. Please don't.'

Tim approached from her blind side, thinking that perhaps she was hallucinating. Maybe that's what had got her in this position in the first place. Some of the herbs she had offered him last night were just barely legal. And then he froze on the tiny footholds of rock just out of her view.

She was not hallucinating.

There next to her with the bare wedge of the moon visible through his transparent body, standing effortlessly on nothing, was Deacon. While Serena sobbed, he turned a warm smile to Tim, as though he were welcoming him to his house for tea.

'You are very punctual, indeed, Mr Meriwether, just as I knew you would be. Are you surprised to see me? Certainly your Marie was. And she was quite upset when I told her I had sent you off here to save a damsel in distress.' He gave an unsympathetic nod in Serena's direction and she flinched. Then he returned his attention to Tim. 'Of course, you understand, timing is everything, isn't it? And contrary to popular belief, we who are not among the living have a much more finely honed sense of that. Oh yes, Mr Meriwether, we are very aware, often painfully aware of every passing fraction of a second.' He knotted his hand into a tight fist and the woman on the ledge cried out and doubled around herself sobbing. 'Every breath concerns us, Mr Meriwether, every opening of every single pore.' He heaved a happy sigh and looked down again at Serena. 'So, as you can imagine, I knew exactly how much time I would need with our dear Marie before I should return my attention to you. In all honesty, it took much less time than I had expected. Pathetically weak really. I was sorely disappointed with her.'

'If you've hurt her, so help me I'll –'

Suddenly Deacon stood nose to nose with him nearly unbalancing him. 'You'll what, Mr Meriwether? You'll what?'

With his eyes still on Tim, he reached behind him toward Serena and made another fist, and suddenly she convulsed and writhed in hysterics.' Tim let out a loud yell and half jumped, half dived through the transparent Deacon. He felt like shards of ice had passed through his whole body, just before he landed on the lip of the ledge, grabbing Serena around the waist as she shuddered dangerously close to the precipice. With his back to the cliff wall, he sat down hard and hugged her tightly against his body, taking all the strength he had to keep them from both going over. 'Stop it!' He shouted breathlessly. 'Stop it, you bastard. She's done nothing to you.'

Immediately the convulsions stopped and Serena went limp in Tim's arms. 'You're right, of course. She hasn't.' Deacon sighed. 'But she's weak and thick and not very interesting really. Surely there are others more deserving of life than she.' He shrugged. 'Either you or your Marie, Mr Meriwether. Both are worth much more than this breathing carcass. Hardly worth the risk of one such as yourself, certainly not in the larger picture, as you say.'

Tim slipped the rope around Serena and secured it, fearing that Deacon would cause her to convulse again, and not at all sure he could hold her in such a tight space.

Deacon offered a deep sigh that Tim felt like ground glass low between his hip bones. 'Of course you can save her, Mr Meriwether, I'm certain those of you who find it rewarding to give your time to rescuing unfortunates off the fells must possess among you some ridiculous code of honour, something about the sanctity of life. So of course I won't prevent you from rescuing poor unfortunate Serena. However ...' Suddenly he loomed over Tim and Serena larger than life, roiling like heavy smoke. '... You must choose whom you shall save. Shall it be this worthless lump ...?' With the flick of a finger, Serena cried out in terror and scrabbled desperately closer to Tim, tightening her arms around his neck to a near stranglehold. Deacon shook his head in disgust. '... Or your lovely, vibrant Marie, whose pleasure I can still smell on your body. You may have the life of one or the other, Mr Meriwether, but I cannot allow you both.'

'Please, please! Don't let him hurt me any more,' Serena keened, tightening her grip.

As the horror of the situation settled around Tim, Deacon gave another flourish of his hand, and a howling wind rose buffeting the two from the side, threatening to blow them off the ledge.

Deacon looked around at the miniature storm he'd created and smiled. 'Not gale force, not yet, my dear Mr Meriwether, but soon, very soon. If I were you, I would make my decision quickly.'

'And if I don't choose?' Tim shouted into the wind, pulling Serena closer to him.

Another twisting of Deacon's hand had Serena choking for breath she could no longer get. 'I don't need the wind nor the cliff for this one's demise, Mr Meriwether, and your Marie is only a split second away for me. As for you, well, I'll be ever so careful to keep you safe so that you will live with the guilt of two deaths on your hands rather than one.'

Serena was now desperately clutching at her throat, eyes bulging and Tim could barely hold them both on the cliff face. 'Stop it!' he shouted. And instantly Serena could breathe again. 'You son of a bitch, Tara was right about you. You're a

125

coward, always happy to hurt people weaker than you.'

Suddenly the image Deacon had projected wavered and he roared. 'That woman knows nothing. She is the coward. She is weak, unable to protect those she loves.' The image of Deacon wavered, then disappeared, then stabilized again. For a second he looked frantically around him before slowly unfurling his bullwhip, then the air crackled with static, and the smell of ozone made Tim's eyes water. For a second the wind calmed and he shot into action.

'Get on my back, get on my back!' he shouted to Serena. He was suddenly thankful that she was so bird-boned. 'Be as still as you can and hang on. The rope's secure, just hang on.' Dear God, he hoped his instinct wasn't wrong, but his gut told him Deacon was having a bit more trouble than he had anticipated, and there wouldn't be another chance.

All he needed was time to abseil down to where the fell flattened out. It wouldn't take long, seconds if he were reckless, and he couldn't afford not to be at this point. He had swung into position when the burn in his gut nearly made him lose his footing. Goose flesh prickled along his neck and he looked up to see Deacon standing above him, the shiny blade of a very large knife glistening in the moonlight.

'I won't make it that easy for you, Mr Meriwether.' He spoke between laboured breaths. 'I have informed you of my demands. They have not changed. As you see, I hold the upper hand.' He lifted the blade so that it caught the reflecting light of the moon. 'A fraction of a second, Mr Meriwether. A fraction of a second is all I need to assure a swift death for that one.' He nodded to Serena, who whimpered against Tim's back. 'And a very painful death for your Marie.' He stroked the flat of his blade with a thick finger. 'You see, to your sweet Marie, I will make that fraction of a second seem like a thousand years, and I promise visions of her suffering will haunt you in your dreams for as long as you walk among the living. It's simple, really. All you need do, Mr Meriwether, is take your own blade, cut the charlatan free and give a tiny shrug. Then you will be relieved of your burden. I will allow you to descend to safety and return home to fuck your Marie, and no one will ever be the wiser.' He nodded to Serena, who whimpered on his back but didn't move. 'At some point someone will find a decomposing corpse, and when the coroner's report comes back, the conclusion will, of course, be suicide. Suicides happen all the time, after all, a tragic part of the human condition. Make your decision, Mr Meriwether. My patience grows thin.'

Tim would have doubled over with the pain between his hip bones had he not been pressed tight against the rock. He didn't waste breath cursing, though he felt like it. What he needed was a clear head, what he needed was a way out, a way to assure Marie's safety. But a split second for him was only that, a split second. Once again, the image of Tara snapping Fiori's neck flashed through his head followed quickly by Fiori, Sky and Anderson fiercely flanking Tara Stone in her defence in spite of the truth she did not deny, a thousand years of suffering, Deacon had said. A thousand years of agony at his hand, played out in a split second. And suddenly, Tim understood completely. With every ounce of strength he could muster, he mentally shouted and screamed and begged for Tara, for Anderson, for the Elementals. And in his mind's eye, he pictured Marie safely folded in Anderson's strong arms. Dear God in heaven, please let it be so!

'Your time is up, Mr Meriwether.' Deacon raised the knife. 'Indecision is such a weakness in a man.'

The reflection of the blade in moonlight flashed blindingly bright. In the blue-black after images that paraded across his retinas, Tim saw Tara Stone flanked by Sky and Fiori, drawing a blade of her own, long, thin, and desperately sharp, a blade that hissed and crackled with old magic. He didn't know how he knew that, but he did. Tara's voice carried on the wind. 'It's your time that's up, Deacon. You will go, and you will leave me and mine alone. There will be no more sacrificial lambs, but bared swords and sharpened daggers waiting for you. There will be no more meek for you to trample upon. I will live to see my mother and my husband and my sisters and all of those you have stolen from me avenged. And you will be returned to the dust, forgotten as though you never existed.' Lightening

127

crackled, heat sizzled, and with a wide, sweeping arc, Tara Stone brought the blade upward and rent Deacon from groin to shoulder with a deafening crack of thunder.

And just like that, he was gone.

Chapter Thirteen

MARIE WOKE, BURNING UP. She clawed off the duvet and sat bolt upright as terror knotted her stomach. Then she realised she wasn't at home. Other than the pale moonlight shining through the window, the room was dark. She was sitting naked in the middle of a very large four-poster bed, and Anderson was sitting next to her.

'Everything is all right now, my darling.' He placed a cool hand on her cheek, then her forehead. You are safe at Elemental Cottage.' He didn't wait for her to ask. 'Tim Meriwether is also safe and resting under the watchful care of Fiori. He asked to return to Lacewing Farm. As is the case with most of my sex, he is very protective of his territory. Tara and Sky have taken Serena Ravenmoor to a safe place.'

The events of the night came crashing in on her in a wave of nausea. She braced herself and closed her eyes until her insides righted and she was certain she wouldn't be sick. 'I need a shower,' she forced herself to sound calm. 'I'm sweaty, and … I feel really dirty.'

'A cleansing ritual of some fashion after what you have been through, my dear, is not only recommended, it is essential. But are you sure you are recovered enough?'

It was only when she stood by the bathroom door and saw the shower looming in front of her like a gaping mouth that she balked, as memories of Deacon's shower visit flooded back to her. Anderson, who was standing next to her with a reassuring hand on her arm, brushed the damp hair away from her ear. 'I will stay with you, if you wish it.'

'Thank you.' Her voice was breathy and thin, like it too might belong to a ghost. Perhaps she was a ghost. Perhaps

Deacon had killed her, and she just hadn't realised it yet.

With Anderson's comforting form fully visible through the safety glass of the shower, she took her time, scrubbed herself hard, and let the tears slide down her cheeks. How was she ever going to survive what she now faced? And even worse, how would Tim survive when it was clear Deacon planned to use them each to the detriment of the other. And worst of all, as the water stimulated her skin to a rosy pink, she realised the desires Deacon had kindled were still there, and in spite of herself, she wondered what it would have felt like if she had given in, if she had let him pleasure her to release.

She cranked the water to cold and stood in the sluice of it until her teeth chattered, and still it was as though a million tiny pinpricks were alive just beneath the surface of her skin, as though he were still reminding every single pore in her body how desperately she needed to come.

She was shivering uncontrollably when Anderson opened the shower door and shut off the water, ignoring the splash on his pristine white shirt. 'It is enough, my love. I cannot allow you to catch your death.' He bundled her into a huge blue towel and began to dry her goose fleshed skin vigorously. He tisk-tisked. 'My dear, even I am warmer than you when I first take the flesh. This will never do.'

She tried not to writhe beneath his touch, but the misery of her need was overwhelming. Her lip trembled, and in spite of her best effort her eyes misted. 'I wanted him, Anderson. Dear God, how could I want him?'

He lifted her open palms and placed a kiss on each where her nails had pierced her hands. 'You have no idea what you have done, do you, my sweet Marie? Of course you wanted him. That is his magic, to make himself the most desired of all beings, to make his victims feel in their bodies hunger and lust for him like they have never imagined. Even Fiori, who is a powerful witch, not to be trifled with, gave in. But you did not. You banished him twice and remained free.'

'Then why do I feel this way if I'm so special? I feel like I'm on fire, I feel like I'll explode if I don't … if I don't get some relief. It disgusts me that it's because of him, and yet still

130

I want.'

'Shhh!' Anderson stopped her words with a light kiss. 'My darling Marie ...' He wiped a single tear from her cheek and lifted her chin so that she met his dark gaze. '... There are many elements, many facets to sex magic. And that with which Deacon has afflicted you, he cannot now take back from you. It is now yours. And what is now yours, you may freely give to me, you may allow me to ease your need, as you did earlier when the situation was more desperate. In doing so, we may, together, transform it to pleasure and even something more powerful still.' He kissed her palms again. 'If you will permit me?'

'Permit you? I beg you, Anderson.'

'My love, it would never in a hundred lifetimes be necessary for you to beg love from me.' He took her mouth deeply, tongue plundering, teeth nipping, lips insisting. He lifted her in his arms and carried her to the bedroom, where the bed had been mysteriously, perhaps magically, made up. There, he pulled back the duvet, kissing and coaxing her down onto the soft mattress.

His body was shades of silver and shadow in the moonlight, teasing her eyes with glimpses of the hard plain of his belly and the tight half domes of his buttocks. As he shrugged out of his clothes, the shape of him still remained vague and mysterious but exquisitely solid, substantial as he moved onto the bed next to her, his anxious cock leading the way. He dropped a wet, suckling kiss on each of her heavy nipples, and she arched her back and ground her arse against the clean sheets.

'I think we must first give you some much-needed relief.' He brushed a thumb solicitously against her bulging clitoris, and she whimpered and shifted her hips against his touch. 'The seat of your pleasure is ripe with your desire,' he said. 'And I have such a fondness for ripe fruit.' Still stroking the swell of her with his thumb, he slipped two fingers between her pouting labia and the catch of his breath mirrored hers as he gently probed and withdrew and probed again until he found her g-spot and she soaked his hand and nearly bucked off the bed.

He released a deep sigh. 'You are as wet as the fells in

heavy dew, and the feel of you makes my own need almost more than I can contain.'

'Please,' she moaned. 'Please ...'

He lifted her on top of him and carefully positioned her, stroking her pussy lips, then parting them. She felt the press of the head of his penis against her pout. His hands on her hips guided her downward, and she cried out at the exquisite pleasure of him pushing into her grudging tightness, then yielding, then pushing again until she had completely accommodated the fullness of his erection. And suddenly her thoughts were as filled with Anderson as her body was with his substantial cock. Then he began to move inside her, shifting his hips in such a way that with each thrust he raked against the swell of her clit, sending shock waves of delight up through her body as she thrust back.

'I think we shall not linger long this first time,' he gasped between barely parted lips. 'Your need is too great, and mine is little less so. Once we have achieved some measure of relief, there will be all the time we need for pleasuring, and I think we shall need a lot.'

She thought he might be right.

He cupped the bounce of her breasts with skilled hands and stroked and tweaked her nipples until they were bullet tight, and every sensation seemed hardwired into her clit and her grasping, gripping cunt. Each time he thrust, she felt him deeper and deeper, and each time she tightened her grip, she felt his penis surge inside her.

As they grunted and pushed, the sound of their lust filled the air, and urgency grew. It was as though they were suspended in the infinite moment before the explosion. They shoved in and out, grasping and clenching and desperately needing until at last the room exploded in bursts of light as they gasped for breath and bore down against each other, overcome by their respective orgasms. With each spasm of pleasure, Marie could feel the surging of Anderson's penis as he emptied himself into her. And with each spasm, each emptying she felt cleansed of Deacon's influence. Even more, she felt in her mind's eye as if she, with Anderson's help, was bending and twisting and transforming Deacon's dark magic into something flash-fire bright and razor sharp. They were creating a tool for her own use, as surely as Serena had spoken of her scrying mirror. A tool no one could touch without her permission.

For a terrifying, ecstatic moment, she was above her body looking down at the two lovers in the throes of their passion. She feared she might be dying. She couldn't breathe, she couldn't think, but it hardly mattered. Then she was back inside herself convulsing with the aftershocks, trying to get still closer to the man, the ghost, who had given her such pleasure, who now crushed her to him with strong arms and covered her face with kisses.

'Most often ghosts quickly forget the needs of the flesh, and pass on effortlessly to other realms,' Anderson said as he fed Marie mushroom pâté on toast from a silver platter, which had mysteriously appeared on a cart outside their room. He had retrieved the feast and insisted that she eat. She should have done upon his arrival at Lacewing Farm, but he agreed, offering her his delicious dark smile, that under the circumstances, there had been more pressing matters to be dealt with. However he apologised heartily for not seeing to her sustenance before he engaged her in sexual congress for the second time in her weakened condition. Sexual congress! That remark was nearly enough to make her throw him down on the bed and mount him all over again.

He wiped the corner of her mouth with the edge of a finger that smelled like her pussy and continued, 'For some ghosts, however, the needs of the flesh intensify when there is no flesh for the satisfaction. The need grows beyond all proportion until the poor ghost is desperate for relief. The necessary relief, however, can only come in the flesh. That is why the work of my dear Tara and the Elemental Coven is so important.'

'Is that how it is with you?' She spoke around a grape he had just popped between her lips.

'It is different with me,' he said, flicking his tongue over the pâté that had dropped from the toast onto his finger. 'My family practised Ethereal magic. Being out of the body was a

133

common experience, and therefore returning to the body after working high magic in the Ether was always a time of powerful hunger in the flesh, every variety of hunger. 'I am descended from a long line of witches. My grandmother was burnt at the stake. You see, I am the grandson of a martyr.'

'Then you knew the spell when you died?'

'It is more accurate to say that I was born with the spell as a part of my being. Wandering the Ether is not so different from wandering the realm of the living as a ghost. Both my mother and my grandmother walked often with the living after their deaths. As a child, it was long before I realised my grandmother was no longer numbered among those who drew breath. Both she and my mother took many lovers after their deaths. They were women of boundless passion.

'And I am my mother's son.' He sipped the heavy red wine that had come with the feast, then he took her mouth, drizzling the heady liquid onto her tongue until she suckled at his lips with hunger for something far more than wine.

He guided her back down onto the bed, fingering open the sash at the waist of her robe, shoving aside the fabric and kissing the outside of her knee and her thigh just above it.

She squirmed at the warmth of his mouth and reached out to run her fingers through his dark hair. 'And your need is never diminished?'

He looked up at her with lust in his eyes. 'Not in the 38 years before my death, and not in the 150 since.'

'Anderson,' she breathed, halting his progress up her thigh. 'I want to see you. I mean really see you.'

He rose over her, kissed her on the mouth, then lay down next to her, chest heaving with desire. 'As you wish, my love. I am at your command.' He nodded down to the sash of his own robe, losing the battle for containment. One dark nipple peeked out at full attention and the heavy folds of terry cloth mounded precariously around his growing erection, then fell open to reveal the straight line of one hip and the hard muscles of his thigh.

With her heart racing, she eased herself up on to her haunches and undid the sash to reveal the broad expanse of hard muscled chest, surprisingly smooth and lacking in hair. She ran her hand down over the mounds of his pectoral muscles, and his areole tensed and puckered at her touch until he squirmed beneath her. Just above his left hip was a white scar rising like a ribbon atop his smooth, olive skin. She traced it with her finger. 'What happened?'

'A dual. Over a woman.'

'You lost?'

His hand came to rest on top of hers, pressing it to his flesh. He held her gaze. 'I won.'

'Then this is not how you …'

'How I died, no. I lived a long time after this; long enough to have many more lovers and fight several more duals.'

'Then how?'

'I fell from a cliff trying to rescue a friend. Not far from here. Perhaps some day we may go there together.'

'And the friend?'

'He lived to sire many children and named his eldest son after me.'

'You were a good friend.'

'I did only what had to be done, Marie, as we all must.'

His body was a map of his life. There were other scars in other places, and yet the centre of that map lay fully erect against his belly, springing from its cushion of soft brown curls. 'You're beautiful,' she whispered.

'It gives me great satisfaction that the sight of me pleases you,' His breathing had become more laboured, and he now struggled to lie still for her explorations.

'Turn over,' she commanded. 'I want to see all of you.' He did as she asked, holding his cock tight against his belly as he rolled, exposing first the straight lines of his hip, then the elongated mounds of his buttocks, which she stroked and kneaded and separated until she could view the knotted grip of his anus, which tightened and relaxed as she fondled his bottom.

He glanced over his shoulder at her, one hand now stroking the length of his cock. 'Shall you play with my nether hole then? That would please me very much.' Without waiting for

135

an answer, he pulled her hand to his lips and suckled her index finger. Then, holding her gaze, he guided her to his dark hole and pressed back against it until the tightness yielded and her finger slipped inside. He shuddered and his cock surged against his hand, but she slapped his hand away and took him into her mouth, carefully at first. He was big and swollen and tasted of her pussy. Surely he must have wanted to thrust, but he held very still allowing her time to get used to the heft of him. All the while his anus gripped and released, gripped and released her finger.

She ran her tongue along the underside of his penis and he gave a deep-throated groan, and curled his fingers in her hair. Then she shifted to straddle his leg, shoving aside her own robe to rub her wet swell against his bare thigh.

'Oh, my dear woman,' Anderson grunted. 'You will surely be my undoing.'

Rubbing against him until her pussy felt as swollen as his cock, she moaned and suckled and whimpered. With each move she dug her finger deeper into his back hole, then, awkwardly, she slipped another one in next to it.

With a thick groan, he pushed her away. 'My darling, as much as it would please me to take my release in your lovely mouth while you caress my nether hole, shall we perhaps linger a little more in our pleasure this time?' It was hard to argue as he nibbled his way down between her breasts and over her belly to her pussy. There he pushed her legs apart and buried his face in her slippery snatch. He reciprocated by slipping a thick finger into her back hole. Then he mounted her thrumming pout and she wrapped her legs around him, arching up to meet him as he thrust.

As she was about to burst with orgasm, he pulled out, turned her over so that her arse was in the air then probed her anus with his hot tongue, followed by the return of a finger, then another in quick succession. She knew what was coming, and in a second of fear, struggled to get away from him. But he held her. 'I will stop if you desire it, my love,' he whispered against her arse, nibbling her buttocks just enough to make it sting. 'But I promise if you trust me the experience will be very pleasurable.'

When she relaxed and nodded her consent, he reached over her with his free hand, found a bottle of lube in the nightstand and generously applied it, first to the fingers stretching her arsehole, then to his straining cock With each stroke and thrust of his fingers, she lifted her arse closer to him, longing for more, and yet feeling the nerves tighten in her belly. He pulled his fingers out of her, splaying her hole as wide as he could. 'You are ready now, my darling,' he breathed. 'Your lovely nether hole begs to be filled, and I am wont to oblige. Relax now and push out as I push in.'

She did as he commanded, and suddenly she felt as though she was about to be split in two as he eased into her. 'There now, my love, do not fret. I am almost there. Only relax a tiny big longer. There now. There.' His voice was tight with exquisite control.

The brief cry of pain that accompanied the final push, gave way to the pleasure of fullness she had never imagined. As her anus yielded to accommodate and he found his rhythm, he kneaded and tweaked first her breasts, then her clit. Then from the still-open drawer of the night stand, he produced a thick dildo and buried it to the hilt in her pussy, and she could take no more. She growled like a wild animal, bucking and thrashing and quivering as orgasm avalanched over her in wave after wave until he wrapped his arms around her waist to hold her, until his own orgasm burst up from his balls, and she thought he would strangle her in his bear hug.

At last, as they collapsed onto the bed, he whispered against the back of her neck. 'You truly are the Fourth Element, my dear Marie. And now the circle is complete, Earth, Air, Fire and Water. You will be an excellent ghost rider.' She didn't know what the hell he was talking about, but she figured she'd ask him after she regained consciousness.

Chapter Fourteen

FOR A LONG, DELICIOUS moment, Tim neither remembered where he was nor who. That suited him just fine. Though that disconcerting sensation did occasionally plague him when he was overly tired, this time it seemed more a blessing than a plague, and he understood why when reality came rushing back to him. He groaned out loud and threw an arm over his face.

'Welcome back to the land of the living, Tim Meriwether.' He opened one eye to see Lisette sittingdemurely on the chair at the foot of the bed, the one buried in clothes that were not quite dirty enough to be laundered yet, but neither could he be arsed to hang them back in the closet.

'I'm not dead then?'

'No. You are very much alive or of what interest would you be to me?' She offered him a smile that, for some stupid-arsed reason, made him feel better.

'If you had any real interest in me, you'd bring me coffee.'

'If I had flesh, I would bring you coffee, and anything else you might like.'

He started to sit up but thought better of it when the room spun out of control and the pain in his ribs took his breath away.

Lisette shook her head. 'Nothing's broken, Fiori says, But you'll hurt for a while. You're damn lucky.'

Tim didn't remember much of the drive home, mostly because he wasn't driving, and exhaustion had taken its toll. He'd been reassured that Marie was fine and that in fact it was her feistiness that had weakened Deacon and sent him raging to take out his anger on Tim.

That Marie was now at Elemental Cottage in the tender care

of Anderson made Tim feel strange things low in his belly, things he would have probably taken more time to contemplate if he hadn't been so exhausted and so relieved, and if it hadn't been Fiori next to him, behind the wheel of his Land Rover.

Fiori. The thought of the red haired witch made his heart flutter, made him feel things much lower than his heart, made him ache with thoughts of how things had turned out. 'Is she still here, Fiori?' he asked Lisette.

'She's here all right,' came a response from the door, and there she was like he remembered her three months ago, standing in the doorway, hair mussed, wearing only his shirt and carrying two mugs of coffee. But this time, though her hair was mussed, she was fully dressed, and she carried a tray.

She offered an irritated huff. 'Breakfast is ugly, I'm afraid. Your larder is, well you don't really have one, do you? I certainly pride myself in being creative in the kitchen, but … well you get a Marmite and cheese sandwich and a cup of tea with milk I stole from Marie's cottage. I figured she wouldn't mind.'

'What?' He raised an eyebrow. At least that much didn't hurt. 'You couldn't have stolen some bacon and eggs too while you were at it?'

'Could have done,' she said setting the tray on the nightstand and coming to help him into a sitting position. 'But watching you eat a marmite and cheese sandwich will be much more satisfying. A bit like penance for a bare larder.' For a fabulous cook like Fiori, he reckoned an empty larder was deserving of penance.

As he struggled to ease himself into a comfortable position, Lisette paced at the side of the bed, making mother hen sounds that he might have found irritating had he not owed the little ghost his life and the life of people he cared about.

Once he was as comfortable as he was likely to get around the bruises and abrasions, he grabbed a quarter of the daintily cut sandwich and shoved it whole into his mouth. 'Mmmm good,' he said, holding Fiori's gaze. And he was right. It tasted fantastic.

'There are two. I'll make you another one if that's not

enough. I tried to get you to eat last night before I got you in bed, but you were too far gone. This morning, however, I will force feed you the mare's oats if I have to. Food after magic, always. Essential rule number one.' Before she finished her lecture, he had already downed one sandwich and half the mug of tea.

As though intuiting the need for private conversation, Lisette vanished and Fiori took her own mug of tea from the tray and sat on the chair where the little ghost had been. She sipped thoughtfully for a few seconds, then she spoke without preamble. 'I died without pain. I died with dignity and I died quickly.' Her eyes misted for a minute and she took another sip of tea as though it calmed her. 'You have no idea how grateful I am to Tara for that, and I hope that if the tables had been turned I would have had the courage to do the same for her.'

He laid the sandwich he'd been about to stuff into his mouth down on the plate and studied her, his heart racing in his chest like it wanted to escape, like it didn't want to know. '

She continued, 'I'm the guardian of the South in the Sacred Circle.' She waved a dismissive hand. 'You'll be learning about that soon enough. The Guardian of the South is the Guardian of Fire. Deacon takes perverse pleasure in using the elements against us. 'Sky, he pushed her from a cliff, well that's a simplification of what actually happened, and it was a long time ago, but she's the Guardian of the East and of Air. And Rayna, may she rest in the arms of peace, Rayna's no longer with us, she was the Guardian of the West and of Water. He drowned her.' She shivered and chafed her arms. 'Deacon is a master of fire himself. He's burned stronger witches than me at the stake. He knew how to make the flames just hot enough for optimal pain while prolonging the life of the victim as long as possible.' She swallowed hard and looked up at him. 'But in later times. Well let's just say he got a lot more creative with his use of fire.'

Tim remembered Deacon saying he would cause Marie's suffering to feel like it lasted a thousand years, and he suddenly lost his appetite. 'I'm sorry. I didn't know.' He wanted to say so much more, but it seemed like too little too late.

Fiori blushed hard and looked away. 'Deacon knew you didn't know. He took advantage, that's all.'

Tim took the teacup between his palms needing the warmth of it. He studied her for a minute feeling the burn low in his belly that caused his cock to stir now, caused him to feel heat for her differently than he felt when she was alive. There was so much he wanted to say to her, so much he wanted to ask her, but somehow he felt he was trespassing in pain he couldn't begin to understand. And yet he had nearly died, he reminded himself, and so had Marie. He had a right to know. He started to take a deep breath and thought better of it as the pain hitched in his ribs. 'Deacon. He's not like the rest of you, is he?'

The blush that rose to Fiori's face this time was rage barely contained. 'He's nothing like we are, Tim, nothing!' She caught her breath and struggled to gather her thoughts, white-knuckling her mug. At last she spoke. 'Deacon was originally a powerful witch in Tara's mother's coven. She banished him when he began to dabble in the dark arts. Too late, she realised he'd done a helluva lot more than just dabble. Immediately upon his banishment, he joined a group of puritans, religious nutters is really what they were, extreme even by the standards of the day. Hiding behind the skirts of the church, he offered his rabidly pious brethren witches to be burnt, all for the glory of God. And of course, being a witch himself, he knew where to find them, didn't he?'

'Jesus!' Tim felt suddenly dizzy.

'Eat,' Fiori commanded when she saw the sweat break on his forehead. 'You're still weak. The truth is easier to handle when you're at full-strength.' She watched until he forced another bite of sandwich down, then she continued. 'Deacon added to his atrocities by taking to the allies behind the brothels. There he'd catch unsuspecting women and use his bullwhip on them.' She held his gaze. 'As you can imagine, there was a close association between the Stone Witches and the women in the brothels. They knew about ghost riders, and though they weren't riders themselves, they were sympathetic.' Fiori seemed suddenly embarrassed, and she downed the rest of her tea and looked away. 'Tara should be sharing these things with you, not me. It's hers to tell.'

'Fiori, I need to know what I'm up against. Both Marie and I do. You know that.'

She sucked a deep breath and wiped sweaty palms on her jeans. 'Deacon made some kind of arrangement with a demon, some dark spirit whose name there's no record of, as far as we can tell. There are accounts of events, incidents that, in retrospect, we think were probably the acts of this demon. At first, all the lives were sacrifices to the demon. But Deacon wanted more than just to be the demon's minion, Deacon wanted to be the vessel for this demon. LaRayna Stone couldn't have known that when she killed him, nor do any of us really know what binds him to the demon.' She looked down at her hands, clenching and unclenching around the empty cup. 'If we ever hope to defeat him, then we have to find that out. We have to find out how to separate Deacon from the demon and destroy the demon if any of us is to survive.'

All the while Tim had been listening to Fiori's story, something had niggled at the back of his mind, and it was suddenly clear to him. 'Fiori ...' he tried to reposition himself to get more comfortable. '... There haven't been burnings of witches in a very long time, and yet you say Deacon and Tara's mother were contemporaries. How can that be?'

Fiori held his gaze. 'Barring accidents or other misfortunes, ghost riders are very long lived, Tim.'

'How long?'

'LaRayna Stone was one hundred and fifty when she died in a riding accident. Tara was born in Colonial America, and I was born just after the second Jacobite rebellion.'

'I see.' The fact that he took this information in as though she had just given him the weather report for the fells was a testament to just how much he had been forced to take on board in the last few months. He wondered what it would take to shock him now. But then he was certain he really didn't want to know. 'And Marie and me, will we also age slowly?'

She nodded. 'All riders do. They age slowly, and there are very few new ones born. Tara's mother is the only rider I know of to ever birth another rider. It's seldom inherited.'

142

For a long moment they both sat in silence lost in their own thoughts. At last Tim looked up at her and forced another painful breath. 'If I'm a rider, then I'm one of you. You won't shut me out this time?'

She shook her head. 'That was a very foolish mistake meant to protect you.' She nodded to his bruised ribs. 'Obviously, we can no longer afford to keep you in the dark.'

'You'll train me, show me what I need to know?'

She held his gaze. 'We would have always trained you if you would have let us.' She looked down at her watch. 'Now, if you're up for it, get cleaned up and we'll meet the others over at Elemental Cottage. This time, I promise there'll be no more secrets.'

'I'm up for it. But I need to do the chores first, the farm won't run itself.'

Her mouth became a thin line and she folded her arms across her chest. 'Obviously you're not fit to do the chores Tim. Tiggs and Finny are taking care of it. They are farmers, after all. And Michael is helping out with the mare. He was quite the equestrian when he was alive.'

He cursed under his breath. 'And just how the hell are they going to do that? They're ghosts.'

The flash of fire in Fiori's eyes made him instantly regret his outburst. 'I enfleshed them, Tim.' Her voice was suddenly cold. 'They'll stay in the flesh as long as I remain awake, and since I now happen to be a ghost too, that'll be for as long as I need them, and as long as I'm needed. That is if it wouldn't be too degrading for you to have ghosts working your precious farm. Now get a shower. We have work to do.' She grabbed up the tray and spun on her heels. Then turned back to face him. 'I didn't make you what you are, Tim Meriwether, and I didn't want to die, but we get what we get, don't we?' Then she disappeared into the kitchen and Tim hobbled to the shower feeling worse things than bruises and abrasions.

Marie had had another shower, this time with Anderson, and it had taken a very long time to get around to actually bathing. She was now dressed in a flounce-skirted sundress which she had borrowed from Sky. It felt very naughty and barely there. Anderson, wearing his usual dark trousers and jacket, had watched her dress with lustful eyes. In spite of just having had more orgasms than she could count, his hungry gaze had left her with wet knickers, something there would be no time to do anything about before they met the others downstairs. But when Anderson moved in from behind, folded his arms around her and slid his hands inside the come-hither bodice to cup her braless breasts, she held him to her and sighed. 'We'll have to wait or we'll be late. Maybe tonight.'

'Sadly, not tonight, my love. Tonight Tim Meriwether will need you in his bed, I think.'

Her heart gave a little flutter. 'He may not want me in his bed knowing that I've shared yours.' She leaned back against the ghost. 'That doesn't bother you? Me sharing both your beds.'

He dropped a kiss on her neck. 'I would like it better if I were also invited to share Tim Meriwether's bed.' He heaved a Gallic sigh. 'But then again, in his weakened condition the addition of my sexual demands into the equation might be more than can be expected of the man at the moment.' He nodded as though he had come to a very important decision which involved the stroking and tweaking of her nipples, 'Yes, I think the man will do well to survive your tender ministerings, let alone those of the two of us combined.'

The thought of the three of them in the same bed did nothing to ease the dampened condition of Marie's knickers. 'You'd like that, would you? To have sex with Tim, I mean?'

'Of course I would like that.' He relocated a hand to slide up her thigh and into the front of her panties. 'And the excited condition of your womanhood suggests that you might also find such an arrangement pleasing.'

He scissored two fingers into her sticky pout while the rough pad of his thumb went to work on her clit. She tensed and shifted and rubbed her scantily-clad arse back against the bulge threatening the integrity of Anderson's immaculate trousers. Her skirt had ridden up until only her knickers separated her undulating arse from his fly, and he responded by

144

matching her, undulation for undulation. 'Shall you make me come in my trousers, Marie?' he grunted. 'It seems unavoidable under our present circumstances.' The last words were barely forced between his lips before he convulsed and uttered what might have been a stream of foreign expletives. It might have been the day's grocery list for all Marie cared as she rode his dancing fingers to her own shuddering orgasm.

'Leave it,' Anderson said when she shoved away toward the bathroom for a quick clean-up. He held her gaze. 'Sadly, I'm sure you must have noticed the one thing I am incapable of in the flesh is a scent of my own. It is the part of my condition I regret the most. I had a very virile scent.' He licked her juices from his fingers. 'But it is sex magic that is practised in this household, and with what we are to face, the ambrosial smell of your sex is powerful magic, the scent of the ultimate creative force in the world.' He rested a hand low against her belly. 'Never underestimate that force, my dear Marie.'

'Oh, and my love, perhaps you would like to know,' Anderson turned her to face him. 'Tim Meriwether's impassioned cry for me to go to your aid nearly split the Ether in twain last night. There were others upon whom he could have called, but he did not. It is possible he does not dislike me too terribly, nor is he completely opposed to me taking my sexual pleasure with you.'

She felt a shiver of tenderness beneath her rib cage. 'I didn't know.'

Before they could continue the intriguing conversation, there was a soft knock on the door and Sky poked her head inside. 'Tim and Fiori have just arrived.'

Only a few hours ago, Tim would have never imagined that he would be returning to Elemental Cottage as an invited guest rather than a gate-crasher, and with Fiori on his arm. Well, actually he was on her arm, which made walking a whole lot less painful. A little while before they left, she had given him some kind of herbal draft that tasted like something she'd had Michael shovel out of the mare's stable. She might have done just that, as angry as she had been at him earlier, but whatever

145

it was, it had taken the edge off the pain and made him feel quite mellow, which was a good thing considering where he was and what was about to happen.

Flanked by tall and willowy Sky, Tara greeted her reluctant guest with a smile that seemed warm enough, warmer than he deserved, he was sure. She wore a thin summer wraparound dress with a flowing skirt and a deep-cut bodice. Her hair was done in a loose knot on the top of her head with a single red rose resting in the nest of shiny dark curls. Though she looked the epitome of feminine beauty and grace, for an instant, he saw in his mind's eye the woman on the fell top, who wielded expertly a bad-arse, magical sword. The thought stirred him more than he would have thought possible, made him blush, tightened his nipples and forced him to readjust his stance so his cock sat more comfortably in his jeans.

'Welcome to Elemental Cottage, Tim Meriwether.' Her voice drew his attention back to the gracious woman standing in front of him, the 250-year-old woman standing in front of him, he reminded himself.

He had just mumbled some sort of greeting, and Tara had turned to embrace Fiori when he found himself nearly nose to nose with the cool, elegant Anderson, hand in hand with Marie, whose clothing did little to ease the growing weight of his cock.

Before he could say anything, Marie came into his arms, a little less gently than was comfortable on his aching body, but balm for the soul to the rest of him. 'I'm so glad you're safe,' she breathed against his ear. 'I was so worried.' Then, as though it didn't matter at all who saw, she lifted her lips to his and kissed him hard, reacquainting her tongue with his. The feel of her, the smell of her overrode caution. Ignoring the pain in his ribs, he pulled her tighter and returned her kiss. When he pulled away, nearly passing out from the pain of it, it was Anderson who steadied him.

'I am told you fought courageously, Tim Meriwether, though I am not surprised.' He offered Tim his hand.

Tim shook it. 'Thank you for taking care of Marie.'

Anderson offered a smile that seemed to turn slightly

inward. 'Taking care of our Marie is no hardship, as you know.'

Tim felt a different kind of heat between his hip bones, not unpleasant at all, and rather intriguing that the two of them might share Marie amicably and that she would be OK with that. He held the ghosts gaze and offered a slight nod. 'No. No hardship at all.'

Tara led everyone into the lounge, which now showed no evidence of the destruction Tim had brought on Tara Stone's home. It pained him terribly now to think what he had done. But when the woman sat him on the sofa with Marie seated next to him and Anderson on the other side of her, he got the impression that perhaps Tara had a wicked sense of humour.

When tea had been poured and all politeness dealt with, Tara placed her cup down on the carved wood coffee table and sat silently for a moment. Her head was bowed, her hands were folded in her lap, as though she were collecting her thoughts.

At last she spoke. 'Marie, Tim, I'm sorry that you've been dragged into our nightmare. Believe me there's nothing in my power I wouldn't have done to prevent it. But it's happened. You are a part of it now, both of you, and like it or not, you're fighting for your lives.'

The woman's bluntness was a bit shocking at first, but Tim had to admit he liked it. He liked that she didn't try to soft pedal the truth.

She glanced first at Anderson then at Fiori. 'I know you two well enough to know that most of what I would now say you've already regaled our new friends with.' She waved aside their slightly embarrassed looks.

'It's just as well. That means we can get on with what really matters, and that is, first of all to train the two of you so there'll be no more unnecessary surprises, so that you're connected to the coven and can use your own magic effectively as well as the collective magic we share. We're stronger together that we are alone. And if we're to hold any chance of defeating Deacon and getting our lives back then we'll need all the strength we can get.'

'Then we do plan to fight him?' Tim asked quietly,

suddenly finding himself the centre of attention.

Tara's grey eyes bore into him with heat much deeper than what the ghosts made him feel. 'Yes, Tim. We plan to fight him, and we plan to defeat him and take back what's ours. It won't be easy for the two of you.'

Tim found himself gripping the arm of the sofa as though he were afraid he'd be ejected. 'It hasn't been easy in a while.'

Marie laced her fingers through his and gave them a reassuring squeeze. 'How soon can we get started, then? We know what we're up against, now I'd like to know what our weapons are and how we use them.'

'You don't know what you're up against, Marie.' Tara's voice was calm. 'If you think you've seen the monster at his worst, then it'll be your undoing.'

Anderson bristled, and gripped Marie's other hand. But before he could say anything, Tara continued, 'Deacon will test and probe and push, but never use more energy than he needs until he has you complacent. And each time your guard's down, he'll be studying you, observing you, getting to know you even better than you know yourself. And he'll keep it up until at last he discovers the perfect way to hurt you the most, to do the most damage to you, to all of those you love, and,' her voice softened, 'to me.'

Marie's face was suddenly porcelain pale. Tim was instantly on alert, remembering the way she had hyperventilated that first morning in her kitchen, the morning she had discovered she could see ghosts. Had it been such a short time ago?

But when Marie spoke, her voice was firm. She held Tara's gaze. 'Then perhaps that's our strongest weapon, knowing what he really wants.'

Tara nodded slowly. 'And making damn sure he doesn't get it this time.'

'This training we'll receive,' Tim said. 'What does it involve and how soon can we get started?'

'Now would be good,' Tara replied. 'Tim you'll need to stay at Elemental Cottage tonight. Fiori tells me she's made arrangements for your farm to be seen to.'

'I understand,' Tim replied.

'Good.' She turned to Sky. 'Is the Room of Reflection ready?'

Sky nodded

'There's little time to waste, since we don't know how long it'll take Deacon to regain his strength, or if he even needs to regain his strength. It may be that he's just toying with us. But the more magic we generate, the stronger we make ourselves, so it's to our advantage to bring the two of you into the coven as soon as possible, teach you the basic Love Spell and train you as best we can to do magical battle with a demon.' Tara forced a smile. 'And all that before breakfast in the morning.'

'Shall we, then?' Sky stood and motioned for them to follow.

Chapter Fifteen

SKY LED THEM DOWN the hall past an antique mirror that Tim had nearly shoved Anderson through when he'd barged his way in the other night. But now, as the sun glowed low on the horizon, the mirror seemed strangely dark and cloudy. It was only then that he realised Sky was alone with the two of them; the others had somehow vanished.

Sky led them past a study, with tall bookshelves rising out of the deepening shadows, to where a large wooden staircase curved upward into darkness. The flame of a large candle quivered ensconced at the foot of the stairs in a free-standing pedestal. She took a tapir from a basket on the floor, lit it, and motioned them to follow her up the stairs.

'Do you feel that?' Marie whispered in Tim's ear as the two began their ascent hand in hand. 'It's like champagne bubbles bursting all over.'

Tim would have said it was more like insects crawling on his skin, but investment bankers and farmers thought differently, no doubt. 'I thought it might be just the herbs Fiori gave me,' Tim whispered back.

'It is the herbs, among other things,' Sky replied. Tim didn't think he'd spoken loud enough to be heard. Sky continued, 'Marie was given the same. What you're feeling is the thinning of the veil between worlds, a phenomenon that occurs when high magic is done, but one that can be enhanced by certain herbs, even alcohol and drugs carefully used. And certainly by sex. The herbs you've been given will aid you on this first journey through the veil so that you'll be able to relax and concentrate more fully on the experience.'

The stairs felt as though they wound upward for ever,

150

another symptom of the herbs, Tim figured. At last Sky led them into a large round chamber. Inside candles sparkled like fairy lights around the room. Tim blinked and rubbed his eyes as he realised that in reality there was only a single candle at the centre on a hulk of a wooden table. It reflected off a circle of full length, ornately carved mirrors at the perimeter of the room. With a resounding click that made both him and Marie jump, Sky closed the door behind them, and it was as though they had been set adrift on an empty sea, just them in the round room full of mirrors.

'This is our sacred space,' Sky said.

Tim was surprised to find the other three Elementals were already there.

As his eyes grew accustomed to the gloom, he could see that Tara alone stood in the middle of the room. With a smaller candle, she lit what appeared to be a silver bowl filled with dried grasses and herbs, which sparked and glowed red while she gently blew on it. The glow softened to an ember, and a thin swirl of smoke wavered, then rose like a coiling serpent from the dish. The scent of fire gave way to the sweet smells of a Cumbrian meadow in high summer, a scent that seemed to writhe upward and outward and curl its way around Tim until he could almost feel it inside him.

From two earthenware bowls, which looked to be full of salt, Tara and Anderson each took an amulet suspended on a silver chain.

'These are the tools of a rider.' Tara said. As she approached Tim with hers, he could see as it caught the light of the candle that it was a small silver mirror. Anderson settled a similar one around Marie's neck.

'They were made especially for the two of you, and they will align to the energies of your bodies and respond to your desires only.' Tim could barely hear Tara above the thrumming in his ears as she eased it around his neck. It wasn't just in his ears, but he felt it in his body. Marie felt what he felt. He knew it. He sensed it at almost the same second she did.

'The amulet is a bit disorienting at first,' Tara said. 'That'll pass quickly. But the feeling will be stronger for the two of you. Because you've shared love, your bodies know each other, and because you're both riders, it's not just your bodies that have bonded. As the veil between worlds thins, so will the veil of the boundary that separates the two of you. It may be a bit disconcerting at first, but two witches working as one are more than twice as powerful, as you may well have occasion to appreciate.' She eyed them both for a second then shot a glance at Anderson, then Fiori. 'Inadvertently you've both created a double bond, Tim, you with Fiori, and Marie with Anderson. Such bonds within the coven are encouraged. With the situation we now face, any added strength is appreciated.'

She continued, 'As you may have guessed from this room, the mirror is the tool of a rider. Not just your amulet, but any mirror or anything that might capture reflection. Our lives are only reflections experienced through the mirrors of our personalities and our psyches. Our minds give substance to those experiences over and over again. We give them life and breath, even flesh. This is the heart of enfleshment, the secret of the Love Spell.'

As Tara spoke, Anderson moved to flank her and the other two women took up positions at the perimeter of the circle of mirrors. Fiori took Marie by the hand and led her to stand next to a large mirror trimmed in silver. Tara motioned Tim to her, and on legs that were none too steady, he moved to her side.

'Men have no place at the Quarters, Tim Meriwether. If Marie is willing and worthy, she will become the Guardian of the West and of the Element of Water, a position that has long been vacant within this coven. And, as Anderson is the Guardian of all things below and the realm of the hidden, so you will become the Guardian of all things above, and all things to be revealed, if you will.'

He was just about to make some lame-arse comment about club membership dues when she raised a hand to him so swiftly that he thought she would slap him.

'Don't mock the trust placed in you.' She took a step closer and he felt the fine hairs on his body rise, and his skin buzzed with her sudden nearness. 'I'm not Serena Ravenmoor and this is no psychic fair. Don't doubt for one second that Deacon takes you and all of us very seriously, and he's even now planning your death, Tim Meriwether.'

The chill that passed through him made him feel thin on the ground, like water with no container, like death itself had passed through him and left a tiny trace of it upon his flesh. He shuddered, recalling once again the ease with which Deacon had manipulated him and the power Tara had commanded on the fell top when she banished him. And suddenly he was unable to meet her gaze.

'Now then,' she said. 'It's the spell you need. The power to give flesh and to take flesh away is a rider's main tool. And no matter how powerful Deacon is, in the end he has no flesh of his own – no real flesh. And this is his hunger, his desire, and his weakness. That means you both must be skilled at the use of the spell.' She nodded to Marie. 'Since it's apparently hers from birth, then it's you, Tim Meriwether, to whom we must give the spell, and as the high priestess of this coven, the task falls to me.'

It took him a few seconds to realise that while she spoke to him, she had unbuttoned his shirt, and with a flick of her wrists, she pushed it off his shoulders. He tensed, fearing there would be more disrobing, fearing exposure in a neurotic way that made no sense in a place that was all about sex magic.

But it was Tara who shed the thin dress that had clothed her, and he caught his breath at the sight of her, muscle and scars, more scars than any person should have, and womanly curves that made him burn at his centre in a different way than the fire he felt from the ghosts. Instantly, he was hard. Surely she knew, but she paid no attention. 'You have already seen more of my soul than I would have ever had you know, Tim Meriwether. I am exposed to you, vulnerable, and in being so, I offer you the gift of the Love Spell.'

She was nearly as tall as he was, and when she took him in her arms, it was eye-to-eye. Her lips brushed his earlobe, and he strained to hear what she said, but the room seemed to be full of whispering, and there was fidgeting, restless fidgeting. Why was everyone fidgeting?

She rested a hand low on his belly so that her fingertips slid just below the waistband of his jeans, and suddenly it felt as though her fingers had reached inside him, deeper than skin, deeper than blood and bone. His muscles tightened, his cock surged, and she reached still deeper, deeper than he knew himself to be, dizzyingly deep, frighteningly deep. Suddenly it was as though all that made him solid, all that made him substantial vanished and he was left to the mercy of the press and flow of the air around him desperately trying to hold himself together, desperately trying to keep from flying apart into all of the directions the Elementals so carefully guarded. And damn it, the fidgeting grew still more restless and the whispering rose to murmurs. Wasn't there some sort of magical protocol to keep witches quiet when a man was being taken apart one molecule at a time?

The panic was worse for having no substance with which to embody it, and just when the last bits of him threatened to pass through the cracks in the floorboards and dissipate for ever, he felt the ticklish trail of her hand up over his ribcage and his sternum, up over the exposed flesh of his throat. In the time it had to move around his neck to rest at the base of his skull he was overwhelmed by the sudden weight of his own flesh, expanding back into itself like stone.

'Flesh is most precious to those who have none, Tim Meriwether.' There were murmurs of agreement, a shuffling of feet, a rustling of clothing, which Tara seemed to have no trouble ignoring. She continued calmly, 'And flesh is the precious gift you may give. And here is how you will offer that gift.' The murmuring crescendoed, sounding more like a party at the local pub than the working of high magic.

Just when he feared his whole body was turning to stone, just when he was about to clutch at his throat for breath, she took his mouth, and with her kiss oxygen rushed to his brain and his whole being; air that was clean and pure and life giving. It was just a brush with her lips, and only just barely, and yet it filled him, opened him, focused him. And at the second brush of her lips, as her hand at the base of his neck curled lightly in his hair, he heard the whisper in his head, in some language long dead, some language he should not have

154

understood, and yet he did.

As her kiss became more insistent, he saw in his mind's eye what she spoke in his head. And as it took shape, like mist rising off Derwent Water in the early morning, he knew it was the spell. And it was not just with his mind that he knew it, but as he pulled her into his arms and kissed her back, as he felt the press of her breasts against him and the expansion of her ribs with her breath, he knew it in his body, like knowing how to breathe, like knowing how to sleep and wake and eat and drink and love.

'I understand,' he breathed against her lips. 'I see it. I know it.'

There was a murmur of approval, and it was only as she stepped back that he realised the Elementals and Marie had not moved or spoken, but the mirrors, each mirror, was crowded with dim reflections of people he could just barely make out, people who seemed to move and shuffle and press forward from just beyond the reflection.

Tara watched him silently as his gaze fell upon the crowd looking out through the dark glass. Then she took him by the hand and led him close to the mirror opposite the door. His reflection was still visible in the surface, but through it he saw all of the others who looked out at him with anxious eyes.

'Ghosts?' he asked.

She nodded.

Ghosts didn't frighten him any more. Not after having lived with their constant presence for the past three months. He reached out his hand expecting to touch the mirror. There was a shifting and a collective intake of breath, and it was as though the mirror turned to water beneath his fingers.

'The mirrors are only a tool, Tim, choose one person, and use the spell.'

Almost before he fully realised he had set the spell in motion, a cold hand snaked forward and grabbed him by the wrist.

The feel of it was shocking, and he cried out and pulled backward, but Tara steadied him. 'Don't be startled, all ghosts feel cold when they first take flesh. You can already feel warming, pulsing, the flow of blood pinkening the skin.'

Tim felt all those things in an overwhelming avalanche of sensations pressing in from all directions. He swayed, and a sudden wave of nausea threatened to embarrass him in his first real attempt at magic. Anderson moved forward to steady him, and the mirror was once again solid. The shadows within faded away. Tara shoved a piece of shortbread between his lips as Anderson settled him onto the floor, and instead of being repulsed by it, he was suddenly ravenous.

'It's enough,' Tara said. 'And considerably more than I'd hoped for.'

'Hungarian Goulash in the slow cooker,' Fiori said. 'And I think we could all use some sustenance.'

Tim just barely managed to keep his eyes open while he ate, in spite of being ravenous. He remembered being led to a bed in a quiet room with a window full of moonlight, and he remembered pulling an equally exhausted Marie into his arms, but he didn't remember much else.

Somewhere long toward morning, he rose to follow her into the garden. The heat had barely dissipated and the air smelled of roses and night blooming jasmine. The fells loomed like giant temple guardians all around them. He followed her through the wild profusion of green shrubbery deeper into the garden, feeling the odd scratch of bramble and sting of nettle against his naked thighs. He knew the garden was big, but he hadn't imagined it to be this big, nor this untended. Every time he reached for her, she was just beyond his fingertips.

He walked endlessly, the heavy heat of the night dissipating around him to a fetid chill, the brambles drawing blood, the nettles stinging low in his belly. He followed her into a cave, its floor littered with slate leavings, which cut his feet as he slipped and slid over them to get to her. It was dark, so dark he could feel the lack of light like another presence in the cave, brushing against him. Yet even in the close blindness pressing in on him, he could see her, pale like anaemic moonlight through the mist on the fells. The burning in his groin did not dissipate, but grew stronger with each step he took until it felt like fire blooming in his gut. Marie disappeared around a bend into the darkness and he heard her moan. Oh yes, he heard her moan. The need, the hunger in her voice vibrated through him like a heatwave. His heart raced, his cock felt heavy, desperate for her. He hurried to catch up with her ignoring his bleeding feet, stumbling and slipping on the slate.

Then everything inside him froze. There in front of him on a ledge like a stage, there displayed for him to see, was Marie, kneeling, head thrown back, breasts rising rapidly in a desperate pull for oxygen. At her back, looming in a pall of darkness that felt thicker than the deepest part of the cave, yet burning brighter than fire was Deacon. One hand stroking her cheek, the other roaming freely over her body.

And Tim couldn't move. It was as though he had turned to stone like the very slate beneath his feet. Deacon's laugh echoed off the walls of the cave. 'She is mine, Mr Meriwether, and has been since the moment I first touched her. She now lives only to satisfy my will. And we both know what my will is, do we not?'

The scream, the rage, the fear that roiled beneath Tim's breast bone were as trapped as he was. He could neither close his eyes nor look away, as Deacon lovingly, tenderly took Marie's face in his hands, and with one sharp twist snapped her neck. Her eyes fluttered, she uttered a single gasp of surprise, then she slumped.

The cry was feral, erupting from his throat like gravel on bare flesh, as he shoved his way up from the dream world fighting off the duvet, desperately looking around him struggling to remember where he was.

'Tim! Tim it's all right. It's a dream, just a dream.' And Marie was there in his arms alive, warm, breathing, not making him burn low in his belly, but making him ache in ways living flesh ached for other living flesh, in ways the living needed each other. He scooped her in his arms and held her so tight that she squirmed for breath, held her so tight that he was reminded of his own aches and pains.

Then with a visceral need that felt as though it would break him apart, he pushed her down on the bed and she yielded as he opened her legs with his knees and found her warm and slick

157

and ready.

He could offer no more than a few thrusts before he shuddered his release into her in harsh grunts that made his injuries hurt, but those wounds seemed minor as he gathered her to him, finishing her with his fingers while she whispered calming words in his ear, words that barely registered in his fevered brain and mattered most because they were humid with the body heat of the living breathing woman in his arms.

Afterwards she slept. He did not.

Chapter Sixteen

'DO I HAVE TO do this again? You see I can do it. I just don't like it.' Marie chaffed her arms of the goose flesh that engulfed her every time she had to force Anderson out of the flesh. And this time Sky had insisted that she not let him come back into the flesh until she instructed her to do so.

'Do not fret so, my love,' Anderson was saying as he came back into the flesh at Marie's command. 'It is no hardship for me, and I do not suffer from it.'

'Perhaps not.' She shivered. 'But I do.'

'Please feel at ease, my darling. It is to your great credit and for your protection that you do this. That you can keep me out of the flesh at will is unprecedented. And that without the aid of your mirror,' he shivered slightly. 'The experience is extraordinary.'

'I think it's just your manly charm that gets her all goose pimply, Anderson.' Sky laid a hand on his shoulder. 'Perhaps you should let me. I'm not noted for my manly charms.'

Anderson lifted her hand to his lips and kissed it. 'A fact I would not argue, my dear Sky, but in truth, I think you are perhaps a little jealous that Marie is lavishing her exquisite attention on me rather than you.'

Tim could hardly sympathise with Marie's plight when, so far, he'd not even managed to bring a ghost into the flesh, let alone take that flesh away. Several ghosts, apparently volunteers for the training session, milled around the study of Elemental Cottage. Perhaps it was only his imagination, but he was sure some of them were starting to grumble under their breath, or lack of breath, and he was certain he was beginning to get a few barbed looks from some of the more surly ones. If

159

that didn't make things bad enough, he'd been left under the tutelage of Fiori, who was cool and neutral, and very much the professional he'd never known her to be.

Tim found it difficult to concentrate in the touchy-feely presence of the Elementals, and seeing Marie's rapport with them, especially with Anderson, was in no small part, responsible for his sour mood. He liked Anderson. He liked the man a lot. More than he was really comfortable with, actually. But he wasn't nearly as relaxed in the company of the dead as Marie seemed to be. He figured that was his problem. He still felt like an outsider. He couldn't get past his memories of arguing with Fiori one day in the flesh, then seeing her the next and knowing that she was dead. The thought still churned his stomach and made him ache inside.

He and Marie were attended only by the three ghosts at the moment, and the volunteers. He didn't know where Tara was, but there was little she could add to the exercise, since her flesh was as permanent as his and Marie's.

Maybe if Fiori would lighten up a little and be a little more touchy-feely, a little more playful, like he remembered her, he would feel less like an outsider. But she was all business. Oh, she was endlessly patient, providing him with astute advice, which didn't seem to help. But she provided no extras.

No extras was the real problem. She was still Fiori. She was round in all the right places, she had eyes he could drown in and lips that could do things he hadn't even known lips were capable of. And her legs, my God her legs were endless and her hair smelled of geranium. Well it used to anyway. And soft, so soft. He remembered how it cascaded against his groin when she took his cock in her mouth, how it tickled when she bobbed up and down, how it fell over her face when she straddled him and rode him how he curled his fingers in it when he kissed her, when he couldn't hold her tight enough as he was about to come. Christ! Why did he have to think of all those things now? She was dead. That was the problem. She had been destroyed by some bastard of a demon, and he'd not been able to help. Just like in the dream, he'd not been able to help.

A yelp from Marie drew his attention as Sky groped her

breasts just before vanishing into thin air.

Anderson chuckled. 'I must admit, Sky, darling, I lack your finesse.'

Tim tried to ignore Anderson snogging Marie like he would swallow her whole and keep his focus on the slender female ghost in a black cocktail dress reaching out her hand to him. With one hand he grasped the mirrored amulet, with the other, he reached out to her, seeing the spell in his head, feeling the beginnings of it weave together like ribbons around a maypole. He felt the cool of her hand, solid in his, then the gradual warming of the flesh, he heard her sigh, and he was just getting ready to pull her to him when his vision blurred, for an instant his mind flashed on Fiori and Deacon. The ghost cried out in alarm and vanished into thin air. Tim fell backward on his arse, and Fiori's patience snapped.

'Damn it, Tim! Pay attention.'

'I am paying attention,' he growled. 'That's the fucking problem.'

'You need to eat something. You're getting tired,' she said, pushing the hair out of her face.

Eating something was not what he needed, but he didn't argue. He felt like the room was closing in on him and on his cock. He pushed past her and out the back door into the quiet of the secluded garden that looked more like a miniature wilderness. He shuddered as he recalled the dream of the night before and took a deep breath. It was a dream, just a fucking dream!

When he was sure he was alone, he released a shaky sigh and fumbled with his fly, cursing under his breath that he should be reduced to this. No matter how hard he tried, his focus seemed to remain on his cock. Even last night, how could he have taken Marie, and so harshly, after such a hideous nightmare, but his need had been nearly unbearable, as it was now. There was no help for it. He released his penis into his hand and sucked a heavy breath at the feel of his own lust. My God, he'd been horny every second since he'd been here. It didn't matter if it was practising a simple binding spell with Anderson and wanting to rip the man's clothes of and play show and tell, or helping Sky lay the table and wanting to flip up the little skirt she wore and bury his cock in her soft spot. He wanted sex, he craved it. Jesus, how he craved it! Perhaps he was just overly tired, and that messed with his self-control, but still, how could he be as tired as he was and need to fuck so badly?

He shrugged his jeans down far enough to release his balls, and then he found his rhythm, cupping and kneading himself with one hand and dry humping his fist with the other. It wouldn't take him long to come, not as full as he was. Then maybe he could focus enough to actually cast the spell he could so clearly see in his head before he needed to stop for another wank. Or maybe he and Marie could have a nooner. God, was she anywhere nearly as horny as he was? So deep was his concentration that it took him a second to realise Tara was standing next to him.

'You need some help with that?'

'I don't need any help. Go away and let me finish.'

'This is my house, I don't have to go anywhere.' She slapped his hand aside. 'That's your problem, Tim, you never seem to figure out that you don't have to do this alone, you need help. We all need help. And sex magic, especially, is not a one-person job. Get used to it.' Then holding his gaze, she spat in her hand and gave him a long hard stroke.

'Jesus!' he breathed.

'Feels better, doesn't it?'

He thrust and mumbled something incoherent. With his free hand, he reached out and stroked her breasts, and instantly her nipples beaded beneath her blouse. Still holding his gaze, she unbuttoned. There was, blessedly no bra, and his hands were suddenly like homing devices, cupping her, kneading her, feeling the exquisite weight of her. Surprisingly the scars he'd seen last night in the Room of Reflection were not there.

Noticing his gaze, she forced a smile. 'They weren't physical scars you saw last night, Tim. I told you I was exposed.'

With the hand not fisting his cock, she undid her shorts and slipped her fingers down inside. He watched as she shifted and wriggled until the hitch of her breath and the flutter of her eyelids told him she'd found what she wanted.

'Did you fuck Marie last night?' she breathed.

'That's hardly your business is it?' God, he didn't want to argue, at least not until after she'd made him come.

'It is my business,' she grunted, now undulating her hips in circular movements around her fingers. 'You're no good to anyone if your cock hasn't been taken care of.'

'Yes! I fucked her last night? All right? And this morning. Twice. And it seems I'm still no good to anyone. Are you satisfied?'

'Apparently *you're* not.' She offered him a half smile.

'It's just that, bloody hell, it's not enough.'

'It never is, Tim. That's why we have each other.'

Between her tugging at his cock and finger fucking her cunt, her breasts juddered and bounced against his groping hands. Her nipples were gumdrop stiff, a thought that invited taste, and she didn't deny him as he settled in to nurse.

She spat again and the feel of her warm saliva and her tight, powerful grip, the grip that wielded a sword, was too much. Three hard thrusts in her bruising grasp, and he grunted his load in arc after arc out over a pink tea rose, as she shuddered her own release into her hand.

Then she wiped her fingers on her panties and zipped her shorts.

'I'm sorry,' he breathed, as he watched her. 'I could have offered more than a wank session.'

She gave him a pained smile. 'Perhaps you could have, but I couldn't.'

He ran a hand through the cascade of dark hair, something he'd wanted to do ever since he met Tara Stone, and her breath hitched.

'I don't understand.'

He had never seen Tara blush before, and though the emotion that crossed her face was so fast most people would have missed it, he didn't. She stepped away from his touch and avoided his gaze as she buttoned her blouse. 'I don't fuck the living. It's a bond that costs too much.'

Before he could respond, she was suddenly all business as usual. 'In future, if you're too squeamish to take your pleasure with a ghost, find Marie or myself. We'll pleasure you, but don't let it go too long like you did today.'

He nodded toward the house and it was his turn to blush. 'Why can't I do what I'm supposed to?'

'I can't tell you that, Tim. You have to work it out. You know the spell. You can use it. I promise you can. You have to find your way to it. And really, you and Fiori need to get over what happened. We don't need past hard feelings giving Deacon something else to sink his teeth into. Now, go to the house and eat something, then get back to practice. Tomorrow you'll have your first ride, so there's not a lot of time to spare.' She turned on her heels and disappeared into the depth of the garden leaving him to tuck himself back in. He wished he had as much confidence in what was supposed to happen as she did.

'We've had three peaceful days now, three days with no sign of Deacon, and every day that passes, I get a bit more nervous. If circumstances were different, we'd have a lot more time to prepare you two, but we have what we've been given, and I don't think we dare wait any longer.' Tara took a deep breath and paced the carpet in the study. The others all sat around, watching her, waiting.

'Traditionally, as you both know, a ghost rider's magic is for the enfleshment of ghosts, to offer them, for a time, the pleasures of the flesh.' She raised a hand as she saw Tim bristle. 'There was never an exchange of money, nor was the gift ever given with any conditions attached. However, the gift freely given comes with some pretty powerful fringe benefits. Each ride makes the rider age more slowly. Each ride makes the rider stronger, less vulnerable to human disease and more quickly to heal. Each ride strengthens the magic of the rider, and it's the last two fringe benefits we're after right now.'

Tim wondered how the hell he was supposed to reap any of these fringe benefits when he still couldn't do the spell, a fact which everyone in Elemental Cottage had managed to avoid talking about as though no one had noticed.

'There's a mutual sharing that takes place between the rider and the ghost.' Tara's gaze settled on Tim and Marie, but Tim felt like she was staring at him. 'The ghosts desire the pleasures of the flesh, the release they cannot obtain without a body to obtain it in, and riders have unusually high libidos, the need for sex is constant, though often transmuted into other forms of magic. That sexual drive, that desire to fuck, to put it crudely, is what drives all of the magic we do. It's the creative energy at work in us.'

She paced some more, then came to stand in front of the two of them. 'We've given you all the training we can for what must happen next. But the ultimate test of a rider's power can come only through the ride.' She heaved a sigh. 'And that is what you both still lack.'

All eyes were on him, Tim was certain of it. He felt a blush crawl up his throat and over his cheeks. He could feel the heat rising around his neck and ears. 'I can't do it,' he blurted. 'You know I can't do it.'

'Of course you can do it.' Fiori practically shook with her anger. 'If you'd just get over yourself and get on with it. Or is it that you just don't want to fuck ghosts?'

'Fiori, no one has asked for your opinion on the subject,' Tara said with an even voice. 'And if you can't be civil, there's the door.'

Sky took the redhead's hand, settling her on the sofa.

Tim ignored her outburst and turned his attention to Marie. 'Marie, I know you're ready. You were ready from the beginning. But I can't. I really can't.'

Fiori cursed under her breath.

Tara silenced her with a glance, but she said nothing.

Marie took his hand and gave it a reassuring squeeze. 'You just need a little more time, that's all. And you're exhausted. You haven't been sleeping well and –'

He shot her a sharp glance He felt a tight constriction around his throat and the air in the room felt too thin to breath, too close around him. He stumbled to his feet and stepped away trying to keep calm. 'Look I'm grateful for everything you've done for me, Tara, for everything you've all done for me, and I'll gladly do whatever I can, which it seems is damn little. But you saw. You all saw. I just can't do it. I'm sorry.' He found himself backing toward the door, suddenly wanting to run, suddenly needing desperately to be back at Lacewing Farm, to be in his own space. 'I'm going home now. I'll be there if you need me, but not for this. I can't help. I'm sorry.' His gaze came to rest first on Marie, then on Tara, and finally on Fiori. 'I'm sorry, I just can't.'

Both Marie and Anderson started after him, but Tara raised a hand. 'Let him go. We knew this would be hardest for him, and we know why. We can't force him to go there until he's ready.'

Marie noticed that Fiori was crying quietly.

'Marie, are you still all right with this?' Tara asked.

Marie nodded, finding it difficult to speak.

'You do understand what it will entail?'

'I understand, yes.'

'And when you've finished.'

'When I've finished, I'll be a rider, and that's not something to be taken lightly, even for Deacon.'

Chapter Seventeen

AS DUSK SETTLED OVER the fells, Tara and Sky, along with Fiori, took Marie to a secluded field behind Elemental Cottage. Anderson had been left to monitor the ride in the Ether. To one side of the field where the rock flank of the fell rose up there was a cave barely visible amid the tangle of vines and shrubs. A quick tour assured her that the Elementals had equipped it for rider use.

'Our house is off limits unless we invite ghosts. Ghosts follow the same rules that apply to the living in polite society,' Sky said. 'There are several other rendezvous points, but this is our favourite.'

'You're to wait here,' Tara said. 'Sleep if you can so you'll be rested when Michael arrives. Begin casting the spell the moment he reaches out to you, and once it's cast the rest will be easy.' She took Marie into her arms in a tight embrace. 'I know you'll do well, darling.' Neither Sky nor Fiori touched her. She had been told that a touch from another ghost could interfere with the spell.

Marie wore a simple summer dress, no fancy ceremonial robe, no jewellery other than her amulet. She had removed her shoes just inside the cave entrance. Enjoying the fading evening light before she entered the confines of the cave, Marie settled onto the soft moss near the entrance and watched the Elementals walk away. She expected to be frightened, or at least a little bit nervous. But instead, she fell asleep.

She awoke in the rain feeling the familiar flush and tingle of heat deep in her pelvic girdle. 'Wake up, Marie Warren.' A soft male voice spoke close to her. 'You'll catch your death, then you'll be a ghost like me, and that won't do.'

She sat up, shivering. Through the driving rain she could barely make out the shape of the ghost who knelt next to her. As he reached out, she cast the spell with an awareness of what was happening that hadn't been there before her training. As with Anderson, the first touch of his fingertips was icy, but the thaw had already begun as he helped her to her feet, and as he gathered her to him she found herself already clinging to his warmth.

'Shall we get you out of this rain, then?' To her surprise, he lifted her bodily into his arms, her head resting against the rapid beating of his heart through his warm chest.

Inside the cave glowed in the amber light of kerosene lamps. Michael tugged the clingy wet dress up over her head, leaving her standing goose fleshed, nose to nose with him. 'It's you,' she spoke between chattering teeth, 'The ghost from my dream that first night. Well, I thought it was a dream back then.'

'It pleases me beyond measure that you remember me, and that, at last I may touch you, flesh to flesh.' He eased her back onto a pallet of pillows and blankets, opening her legs as he did so with large, warm hands. Then, almost before she knew what was happening she felt him grunt and strain and push inside of her, still fully clothed except for his thrusting cock. The sudden thickness of his penis shoved completely into her so abruptly and without foreplay took her breath away, and she cried out at the shock of it.

'I am sorry. I am so very sorry,' he gasped, 'but I need you so badly. Bear with me but a little, and I will be less savage, I promise you.' The second thrust felt like someone had shoved a policeman's baton into her cunt.

She bit her lip and tried to relax, knowing that tensing would only make matters worse. The man was warm against her, his clothing was dry, as Anderson's had always been, though she could smell the rain on his jacket as he groaned and pushed. The intensity of his need drove him with a force that seemed near agony. And her own discomfort gave way first to compassion, then to empathy. Then, amazingly quickly, the urgency of his need physically became her own. As her pussy became slick and dilated, she matched his rhythm and bore down on his thickness with equal desire.

Even as her arousal grew, she could tell by the tension in his shoulders and the tight thrusting of his hips that he wouldn't last long enough to give her any relief, and somehow that only intensified her own need.

'Please forgive me, but I must take my release now,' he grunted. Then he let out a deep groan as shudder after shudder took him and she felt the flood of him, first in her pussy, then spilling onto her thighs, until at last he collapsed on top of her. As he caught his breath, she lay beneath him, deliciously aware of the growing thrum in her pussy.

At last he spoke, holding her in a pale blue gaze. 'You must think me an animal to take you so rudely. Please forgive me. It is so long since I have been with a woman, and the need, the need is so great.' He dropped a kiss onto her lips. 'And it is your first ride. It was foremost in my mind to be gentle, but I could not.'

As he made an effort to pull out of her, she wrapped her legs around him. 'Gentle isn't necessary. I understand your need.' She tightened the muscles of her cunt around his still erect penis, and he gasped. 'I think with a need such as yours, you best stay where you are because I'm not finished, and I know you're not.' She arched beneath him and cupped her breasts watching his pupils dilate still further as she stroked her nipples between thumb and forefinger. 'You're so thick,' she sighed, as he shifted against her with a little thrust. 'You nearly split me in two till I got used to you, and now that I am used to you, I'm not so anxious for you to leave.'

And that was all it took. He was thrusting again. This time she managed to shift enough to get the right friction against her clit so that when he came, she came too.

The cottage was dark and chilled when Tim got home. It didn't matter. It was home, it was the place where he knew who he was. Well as much as he ever knew who he was. Besides, at the moment, dark and chilled fit his mood, he thought, as he set about building a fire in the fireplace. That always cheered him up, though it occasionally drew one or two nostalgic ghosts. That sent a surge of guilt clenching at his gut. But nothing had really changed, he told himself. He had never fucked ghosts, couldn't have if he'd wanted to, and he still couldn't. It was a lie, though. Everything had changed. Before, he had nothing to offer the ghosts who were drawn to him but his own frustration. Now he could add the guilt at his own failure in knowing that he should be able to help but couldn't. All he really wanted was for them to go away and leave him to get on with his life, to go back to how it was before. How it was before? He could barely remember how it was before.

And now. Now that he'd given in, gone to the Elementals for help and training, he was no better off than he ever was. He could see the spell in his head so clearly. He knew it like he knew his own breath, he felt it in his bones, and yet he couldn't bring it to fruition. Why? Now if the ghosts asked for his help, how would they ever understand his refusal as anything other than mean-spirited?

His stomach growled loudly and he suddenly became aware of how hungry he was. There would have been dinner in the big dining room at Elemental cottage after the ill-fated meeting in the study if he had stayed. Fiori's Lasagne Florentine. Her own recipe. The house had smelled of Mediterranean herbs and rich tomato sauce. His stomach growled again. He doubted there was much to eat in the house. Contemplating ordering a curry, he reached into the refrigerator for a much-needed beer and discovered it was well-stocked, bacon, eggs, cheese, sausage, even veg and fruit in the crisper drawer.

'There's some nice seeded loaf in the pantry, the kind you like for you sandwiches.' He wasn't startled, he didn't turn, but he was amazed to find himself smiling at the chime of Lisette's voice.

When he did turn to face her, she offered a shy grin. 'Fiori did the shopping. I just told her what you liked. Though I think she added a few items she thought you might appreciate, a couple of bottles of some kind of wine she said you liked, and, what was it? Oh yes, blue vinny cheese. I told her you'd prefer cheddar, but she said that you have fond memories of blue vinny.' The little ghost blushed.

He found himself battling emotions, the wine, the cheese, they were things he and Fiori had shared when they were ravenous from love making, when they talked all night about horses and sheep and what it meant to live in Cumbria. He pulled out a chair from the kitchen table and dropped into it remembering. He didn't love her. There hadn't been time. But he might have grown to if things had been different.

'Tim, make yourself a sandwich and go sit by the fire.' Lisette offered him a smile, the one that always flashed before she dazzled him with her wicked sense of humour. He found himself shocked to realise that she *did* have a wicked sense of humour, and he liked it, though he had missed it in his surliness toward her. 'I would make a sandwich for you,' she added, 'but I'm useless in the kitchen.' She hugged herself as though she felt the chill. 'I'm pretty useless in any room actually, but I look nice.'

What he did next happened so fast that he could scarcely believe it himself. He reached out his hand and took hers, weaving the spell as he did so, and finding it effortless, like he had done it all his life, like he could do it in his sleep.

A little moan caught in her throat and ended softly with a sigh and a shudder, and he could already feel her fingers warming beneath his. Suddenly she stood before him as solid as he was, her pale skin glowing alabaster, her body heat deliciously inviting. He brushed her cheek and swallowed back the knot of emotion in his throat. 'Make me a sandwich, Lisette. I don't care what kind. And make yourself one too.' He took one of the bottles of wine Fiori had bought and two glasses. 'I'll be waiting by the fire.'

For a long time he sat gazing into the flames, listening to Lisette rattling about in the kitchen, humming Gershwin, Porgy and Bess. The experience wasn't at all unpleasant. Why had he always pushed her away? And why had he struggled so with something that was as easy as his own heartbeat?

She was breathless when she came into the lounge. Her cheeks were flushed and her china doll eyes were round with excitement. She carried a tray adorned with two enormous ham

171

sandwiches, a bowl of neatly arranged fruit, and a small bud vase containing a single pale rose. She blushed heartily when he looked up at her. 'I hope you don't mind, but I picked the rose from the climber by the door. It smelled so lovely, and it's been so long since I smelled a rose.'

He was sitting on the throw cushions on the floor, his back against the sofa. It was always his favourite place to enjoy the fire. He patted the extra cushion that he'd arranged next to him, and poured them both a glass of wine. 'Sorry. It could have used a little more time to breathe, but I'm being spontaneous.'

'Aren't you just,' she said. 'Besides it won't matter if the wine hasn't breathed enough. I won't know the difference, will I?'

They ate in companionable silence, which surprised him, until he realised she was savouring every bite, every texture, every taste. He felt the tightness return to his throat as he thought about how often he ate his food without tasting it, gulped back his tea without savouring it. 'Do you like it?' he asked, feeling her excitement tingle over him, then down low in his belly.

'I love it, Tim Meriwether. I've never tasted anything so grand.'

He found his own delight in watching her eat and drink, in seeing her excitement at the feel of the cushion, at the warmth and the scent of the fire. She was so alive. Had this been who she was before she died, this beautiful, vivacious, wickedly funny woman who sat next to him savouring her first meal in maybe 80 years.

When they were finished and she started to take away the tray, he took her hand. 'Leave it.'

Her eyes were full of question. 'You don't want coffee or tea. Fiori bought chocolate too.'

'Maybe I'll want all those things later, maybe I'll want to see you enjoying chocolate. But for the moment, I have everything I need right here.' He lifted her fingers to his lips and felt her whole body shudder beneath his touch.

He turned her hand and kissed her palm, then the place where her pulse raced like a wild thing between the slender bones of her wrists. 'I never got a chance to thank you for what you did.'

She tried to pull her hand away. 'I did what any decent person would do, Tim, I didn't do it for –'

He stopped her words with a kiss, just a brush of his lips, but enough to silence her. 'I know that, Lisette, and I know that I've been a fool, and I'm sorry. You're the best of people and you deserve good things, Lisette, you deserve good things.' One kiss dissolved seamlessly into another and another interspersed with the little bird sounds escaping the throat of the woman in his arms. And she was exquisite, tiny compared to the other women he had been with, like a fairy, so delicate he feared he would break her if he held her too tightly.

As he lowered her onto the floor in front of the fire and pushed the top of her dress down to caress small breasts with enormous flower bud nipples, she arched up into his hands and whispered, 'I could die a happy woman now, Tim Meriwether, if I wasn't already dead.' Then she added, 'That tool of yours, the one you're always playing with in front of me, does it work as well on a woman as it does in your hand.'

'Shall we find out?' He shoved up her skirt and slid silk panties down over her hips, feeling her grind her bottom against the floor as he ran his fingers through her tightly trimmed pubic curls and then slid them down into her open pout, which was slick and dewy and grasping at him with little shudders.

'Tim,' she whispered. 'I've had 80 years of foreplay. Please, don't keep me waiting.'

As he reached to undo his fly, she pushed his hands away. 'Let me. It's like unwrapping a present at Christmas.'

He liked that image. He lay back on the cushions, feeling the weight of his own need as the little ghost undid his fly and eased his trousers down over his hips with a moan of appreciation for what she saw.

Then she stood and lifted the flapper dress off over her head. From his angle on the floor the view of her vulva, flared and dark with arousal, was exquisite. Her large clit was marbled hard at the apex of her pussy, and the sheen of her

173

need was slick and heavy between her folds.

His cock jerked and his balls clenched as she straddled him still standing, offering him one last enticing view before she opened her pussy with two fingers and squatted onto him with the grace of a ballerina and the tight fit of a surgical glove.

He gasped in sudden shock at the burn, the burn the presence of ghosts always brought on, but as she began to thrust and undulate, the burn was transmuted to fire like he'd never felt before, fire that threatened to incinerate him to nothing but ashes and he didn't care. He grabbed her hips and thrust up to meet her writhing and grinding, feeling as though molten lead filled his balls, feeling as though his whole world had been reduced to the delicious tight wet grip of Lisette's pussy.

He didn't know when she had actually started orgasming. Her grip, her spasming, her cries of passion were all blended together. He knew that she only stopped shuddering and fell forward onto his chest after he had emptied what had felt like an ocean of semen into her tight hole. As she lay gasping and sweating against his chest, she breathed, 'Don't you dare fall asleep. I'm not nearly done with you yet.'

And she wasn't lying.

The women Serena was staying with were supposed to be witches. There was supposed to be some kind of protective force field cast around their flat. They had given her some kind of herbal concoction that was supposed to take the edge off, but she couldn't lie still, she couldn't concentrate, she couldn't focus, and worst of all she couldn't satisfy herself no matter how hard she tried. She felt like someone had kindled a fire between her legs and every time she tried to quench it, they added more fuel.

The witches, they gave her stuff to help her sleep. She suspected it was strong magic. And she did sleep, but she always dreamed of him and of the relief he would give her when he found her. Sometimes she'd wake terrified from dreaming that he *had* found her. She could no longer quite remember why that was. He was so good to her. Hadn't he only ever wanted to serve her, to please her? These two crazy women pretending to be witches were just jealous, that's all. They were trying to keep him away from her because they wanted him for themselves.

Without the herbs, she couldn't sleep. With the herbs she had bad dreams. And no matter what she tried, she couldn't come, even though she was certain she would die if she didn't get some relief soon.

Stupid women! They said it was just his spell on her. They said she had to be strong, that even now the Elementals were working to help her. The Elementals! Tara Stone hated her, probably was envious of her, probably wanted Deacon for herself.

But Deacon belonged to her, and she needed him, desperately needed him. She checked in the bathroom again. A silver wedge of the waning moon was just now peeking around the edge of the open bathroom window. Her heart raced in her throat. Down the hallway in the lounge, she could hear the telly. They were watching *Casablanca*. That's all they ever watched, old films. She'd had dinner, tried to be sociable, but had finally feigned tiredness so she could prepare. She told them it was the herbs that made her so sleepy. They wouldn't bother her, she was sure.

She shut the light off in the bathroom as the moon moved more into the frame of the window, but it quickly became evident the angle was all wrong. With trembling hands, she started to fill the sink, hoping the moonlight would reflect in the water, but the angle was still wrong. In the end it was the reflection off the old porcelain tub that drew her attention. Practically crying with relief, she filled the tub, hoping they wouldn't hear her, but then again, she'd just tell them she thought a hot bath would help her sleep.

It didn't take much, a couple of inches of water and the moonlight reflected just enough off the surface to allow her to work the magic. She settled next to the tub on her haunches so she could see her own reflection. When she felt like her skin would crawl off at any minute, it took every ounce of concentration she had to remember the spell he'd taught her.

The strain of it drenched her in sweat, and she stared so hard into the water for so long that dark spots swam like fish on the surface interfering with a clear view. But she didn't need a clear view. She just needed him to find her. Dear goddess, she needed him to find her and relieve her suffering.

She didn't know how long she had been in the trance. The moon had moved beyond the frame of the window and the stars were overlaid with thick cloud. It was an icy chill blowing over the water that brought her back to herself, naked and shivering. But beneath the ripples of the water, she was certain she could make out his image.

'Oh my poor darling, such a tremendous need you have for me. I can feel the ache of your womanhood across the miles.' His voice was not just inside her head but inside her whole body. 'I cannot bear your suffering, my love, take your ease.' Her nipples tensed hard, her sex convulsed and soaked itself, and she uttered a muted cry.

'There, there, my darling, hush my little bird. You feel better now, don't you, my love? Go to your bed now and rest. I shall come for you shortly.'

Trembling and sobbing with relief, and with something else she couldn't quite remember, Serena Ravenmoor found her way to her bed, closed her eyes and slept like the dead.

Chapter Eighteen

THE FIRE HAD DIED back to embers, and Tim was struggling to stay awake. His cock was still buried inside Lisette's tight pussy, and she was wrapped around him almost like a second skin, her lovely taut nipples gouging deliciously into his chest.

'You'll sleep soon,' she whispered, brushing a kiss across his lips. 'And you've earned it. I'd love to wake up next to you in the morning and feel that wonderful soreness that one only gets from a night of long, hard lovemaking. But the memory, Tim Meriwether, the memory will keep me going for a long time.'

'There'll be other times, Lisette,' he said cupping the mound of her arse and pulling her still closer.

'I'll look forward to it, but I won't count on it. A full-fledged rider's very busy. I'm not the only ghost on the farm, after all.'

She spoke as though there would be a future, as though at some point life would be normal again. He wasn't sure he believed her, but he took comfort in the thought.

'Have good dreams, Tim.' Her last words drifted off into the soft, even breathing of sleep. He figured even sleep must be numbered among the pleasures of the flesh. He stroked her short, soft hair and ran a hand down her ribcage and along her flank. He *was* now a full-fledged rider, he supposed. There had been none of the tawdriness he had pictured in his mind. It hadn't even been an act of mercy or kindness, really. In the end it had been two people giving each other pleasure because it was what they both wanted. A man could do worse than that, he thought. He stroked the face of the woman lying in his arms one last time. Her cheek twitched softly at his touch and she offered a half smile from the dream world. He could stay awake no longer, and he knew when he awoke, his arms would be empty. He could live with that. He could happily live with what he felt about being a rider right now. As he drifted into unconsciousness, on the distant periphery of his last waking breath, a shadow stirred and paced. He would have been disturbed if he could have stayed awake long enough to witness.

There were bright flashes of dreams weaving their way through Serena Ravenmoor's deep sleep, and they always involved her dark angel, her Deacon. Strange how dreams are. She dreamed of a long taxi ride, and such a deliciously nasty dream it was with her and Deacon making love, endlessly making love in the back seat, the driver oblivious. Or maybe he wasn't. That thought made Serena's orgasms all the more yummy. And Deacon, sweet Deacon, was holding nothing back from her now. It was as though his whole purpose was to satisfy her over and over again. How could she have ever doubted him?

Then there was another long stretch of deep oblivion. No doubt her exhausted body needed it after her scrying efforts. Besides, she hadn't eaten. Why hadn't she eaten?

And then they were at her house in Keswick. Strange how so many dreams are house dreams. And this one was so vivid. She could see her tools shining on her altar. The fresh flowers she had put there before Tara Stone had whisked her away were now wilted and dying. She made a note to cut new ones in the morning. She could see her unmade bed where she and Deacon had had sex so often that she stopped bothering to make it up. She could see one stocking still partially bound to the headboard of the bed. The marks on her wrists had faded. Other bruises had not.

But tonight in the dream his touch was gentle. He undressed her so tenderly and kissed her bruises and abrasions, wounds he said she'd gotten on Raven Crag when she had taken a tumble. But she didn't remember any tumble. And then he watched, stroking his cock, while she dressed in a wisp of a white negligée he'd picked out for her. He said it made her

178

look angelic. Though she reckoned gowns for angels would have been made up of considerably more fabric. The material was soft and sheer and clung to her so deliciously. Then he asked her to take her scrying mirror. He said there was some very important magic he wanted her to do for him. He had held her so close in the dream, and it had been so real. He told her that this was why he had come, that this was why he had been sent to her. He told her that at long last she was ready to fulfil her purpose, what she had lived her whole life for. She had been so excited. Dear goddess, such a dream! The sort of dream one never wants to wake up from.

And then she was driving her car with Deacon sittingnext to her endlessly stroking her. Surely he must have kept her safe because she couldn't possibly concentrate on driving with what he was doing to her. In her little white negligee, she was driving, and he was fondling her while he told her things, stories of his past lives, stories of how he died, of his terrible murder, stories of power that she could barely imagine, power that made her tremble at the very thought, power that he said now dwelt in him. And she wondered how he could contain such a frightening thing without going mad. She would have asked if she had been able to focus on anything other than his hand between her legs.

Then the dream became more chaotic, like the dreams one has in the throes of a fever when one is very ill.

Her feet hurt. They were bleeding, and she was cold. Were they on Raven Crag? And where were her shoes?

He told her yes, they were indeed on Raven Crag because it was there she must perform her great magic. He told her she had such strong magic within her that the pain of the walk and the cold were as nothing to her now. Perhaps that was true, but she wondered why she was crying? She would have thought strong magic could have kept emotions at bay, and yet every once in a while, just for the tiniest of moments, she felt as though she were drowning in a deep well of emotions.

She didn't know how long they walked. Dreams are like that. In the dream, she was in a deep trance, one in which time truly seemed to disappear. Perhaps she really had reached a level of magic that she'd only ever fantasised about until now.

And Deacon kept reassuring her that magic is only ever limited by our doubts and our fears. He promised her that she could heal, that she could commune with spirits, that she could even fly if she believed strongly enough. And Deacon said that Raven Crag was a place to test just how strong her magic was. And when the magic was done and she had fulfilled her destiny, the world would be changed in ways she could scarcely imagine. And Deacon said she would open doors to realms of power she couldn't come close to comprehending. And Deacon said that she had served a power so great that her life and her death would be celebrated.

But her feet hurt; they were bloody. And she was cold.

And Deacon said it didn't matter. Deacon said she had no need of feet when she would soon fly.

He guided her with the gentlest of touches until the very tips of her toes curled over the edge of the precipice and the breeze of coming dawn was so sweet she couldn't get enough of it.

And Deacon said something about fulfilling her duty, about magic greater than she could imagine, about her death opening the doors.

Her feet hurt, and her hand ached. It was then that she noticed her lovely scrying mirror clasped tightly in a white-knuckle grip. She raised it to look into its sacred depths, and swayed slightly forward. It was not her face that she saw, but it was Deacon's face there over her shoulder filling the mirror, looming large and terrible.

When she woke from the dream, the first intimations of dawn stained the fells pink.

As Marie watched Michael walk away and vanish into a nearby copse of hawthorn, the sky was greying with dawn. She stood breathing in the fresh air, wondering how so much time had passed. She smiled to herself. What had she expected, a quick fuck and a hand shake?

Though it hadn't done much to cool things off, the rain of last night had left everything freshly cleansed and jewelled in droplets of water, and the air felt like warm velvet. Almost the

180

moment Michael was gone, Sky materialised and Anderson next to her, both taking her into their arms and kissing her.

'There is no denying, my darling, that last night, you did indeed bring the Cumbrian heatwave into the Ether.' Anderson offered her a wicked smile. 'You alone would have been enough to make it difficult for a man to contain himself, but Tim Meriwether's ride only added to my struggle to keep my mind on the task at hand and keep my hands away from my member.'

'Tim? Had a ride?' Marie's heart raced at the thought.

'Tim Meriwether is notorious for doing things his own way,' Sky said. 'But damned if he didn't enflesh Lisette last night and reward her for putting up with him all this time. Tara suspected, and Tara's seldom wrong.'

Anderson nodded his approval. 'Tim Meriwether's compassion is far greater than he would let on, and what happened to him with Fiori cannot but have left deep scars.' Then he added. 'Tara is with him now, though it is likely he still sleeps, unaware of her presence.'

A sense of relief washed over Marie that nearly took her breath away. 'I was so worried about him.'

'We all were, sweetie,' Sky said.

'News is already filtering through the Ether that there are two new and powerful riders in Cumbria, and they are not to be trifled with,' Anderson said. 'Shall we return to Elemental Cottage, then?' He reached for Marie's hand. 'I believe Fiore is preparing a celebration breakfast.'

'I'm starving,' Marie said. 'Just let me get my shoes from the cave and I'll be ready to go.' She ducked inside.

Tim woke on the floor to find the fire stoked and the smell of bacon wafting through the house. He was just beginning to think perhaps the spell had not dissipated as he slept and that Lisette was still in the flesh. Then Tara stepped through the door from the kitchen carrying a mug of coffee. 'You need to eat, Tim, the magic of a rider is hard work,' She handed him the cup and nodded to his cock, which was already half saluting her.

181

He pulled himself into a sitting position and contemplated covering up with the throw, but he liked Tara seeing him naked.

She offered him a half smile and nodded to the kitchen. 'Even you flashing your fine package at me won't get you breakfast in bed.' She folded her arms across her breasts, barely hidden in a thin vest and no bra. 'However, I won't make you dress for the meal.' She turned on her heals and headed back into the kitchen offering him a very fine view of her lovely arse clad in khaki walking shorts. Even if he hadn't been famished, he would have followed that into the kitchen.

But his exhibitionist streak didn't quite extend to eating breakfast in the buff, so he slipped into a pair of track bottoms, which afforded his burgeoning cock a little more breathing room than his jeans.

In the kitchen, Tara was just placing full plates on the table, and the sight of bacon and eggs made his mouth water, though he wasn't sure how much of his salivation was due to the meal and how much was due to the chef. She took in his less exposed state, offered a knowing smile, and nodded for him to sit.

'Fiori's the cook in the house, for the most part, I can't be arsed, but even I can't mess up bacon and eggs.'

She watched him as he tucked in. 'First peaceful night's sleep you've had in a while.'

He swallowed a mouthful of egg and nearly scalded his mouth on the coffee. 'You been talking to Marie?'

'Didn't need to, Tim. Dream magic is my specialty, and your dreams were enough to have the whole house on edge.'

'I'm sorry,' he said, blushing hard. 'I didn't mean to disturb anyone.'

'Well you should have. You should have disturbed us all loudly. I told you this isn't a journey to take alone. How long have the dreams been going on?'

He avoided her gaze, and chased his eggs around his plate with a fork, suddenly not sure he could get food past the knot in his throat. 'Since he … since Deacon started hurting Fiori. They got worse after he … after her death.'

'Bloody hell, Tim, no wonder you couldn't work the spell. It's a wonder you're still sane.'

He forced a smile, more like a grimace of relief. 'Not sure I am really. Certainly not sure you are.'

She chuckled softly and looked up at him from beneath thick lashes as she buttered her toast. 'Ever been to a three-D film? Notice how things almost make you dizzy until you put the glasses on, then everything's not only clearly focused, but it's three-D.'

He nodded.

'We dreamers have to learn to filter, Tim, or we let in everyone, everything, and some things we don't want in our heads. You're a witch. You have a feel for magic, whether you like it or not, and after last night there'll be all sorts of new tools on the shelf for you to play with. But your gift, your true gift, as is mine, is to traverse the dream world and to understand it.'

He suddenly felt dizzy. 'Dear God, I hope that's not true because –'

'Because you saw Marie die the way you saw Fiori die. I know. It's not prophecy, Tim, and in your case, Deacon has been getting to you in the way you were most open. He invades your dreams and shows you what you most fear. That's why you need to filter, set guardians around the perimeters of your sleeping world, protect yourself. You have a lot to learn, Timmy Boy, and you have to let us in so we can teach you.'

The sigh of relief was so damn near a sob that he would have been embarrassed if circumstances had been different. But Tara had seen him at his most vulnerable, and she was not squeamish at looking into dark corners. His stomach growled, reminding him that he was ravenous.

He was half finished with his eggs before he thought to ask the obvious, and even then he felt silly asking. 'I'm a rider, then?'

'That's right, you are, and it can be a bit disorienting to come down from the first ride. We always make a point of having someone there when the new rider wakes up, or soon after. And since you're a dreamer, I was the best choice.'

He laid down the toast he'd just spread marmalade on and wiped his hands on the serviette. 'Did you know? That I would do what I did, that it would be Lisette?'

'It wasn't planned, if that's what you mean. But I had a hunch that perhaps, if you were in your own space, you would be able to relax a bit more and do what we all knew you could do given the right circumstances.'

'And you provided the right circumstances?'

'I didn't have to, Tim. In fact, I didn't have to do anything. Anderson picked up on the magic while monitoring the Ether for Marie's ride. You followed your instincts, as I suspected you would.' She held his gaze. 'You followed your heart.'

He stuffed half the piece of toast in his mouth and swallowed without chewing. 'It wasn't a sympathy fuck, if that's what you mean.'

'You're hardly the sympathy fucking type, Tim, give me a little credit for being smarter than that.' The mocha maker on the stove began to gurgle, and she stood to pour fresh coffee.

He wondered if Fiori had purchased that for him too. He wondered if he should be offended at the way the Elementals seemed to be barging right into his life. Give them an inch, he thought. And yet Tara dressed so invitingly, so unassumingly, making him breakfast after he had fucked all night didn't seem like too much of a hardship to endure.

When she leaned over to set his cup on the table, he pulled her down onto his lap, and his anxious cock pressed upward against one deliciously round arse cheek. She responded with a lingering kiss that tasted of coffee and marmalade all blended up with her own intriguing taste. He could smell the last residual of her own foray into the dream world on her skin, between her breasts, in the pits of her arms as she encircled his neck in a lazy embrace.

She pulled away with a flick of tongue and repositioned herself so that she straddled him face to face. 'I won't fuck you, Tim, no matter how damn sexy you are.'

He ran a heavy finger down over the crotch of her shorts, easily tracing the swollen splay of her cunt. She uttered a soft grunt and shifted against him. The heat of her radiated over his fingertips. 'You hide it well, I'll give you that, but at the end of the day, you're even more neurotic than I am, Tara Stone.'

She raked her khakied pussy hard against his erection and he gasped at the exquisite agony of it. 'I'm more neurotic than anyone, Tim Meriwether, and it won't be you who psychoanalyses me to the cure.' She nipped his lower lip between her front teeth. 'But that doesn't mean we can't help each other come.' She raked him again then found a rhythm that made it feel as close to fucking as it could get without being the real thing, a rhythm he was happy to match. Shockingly he could even feel the grip and release of her swollen lips through the thin layer of khaki, as it rubbed his cock solicitously. As he ploughed his way, mouth first into her cleavage in a nosedive toward the nearest nipple, he wondered briefly if she was using some kind of magic on him, but he didn't care.

She wrapped her thighs around him and gripped the legs of the ladder back chair with her ankles for more leverage, enough leverage to convince him that with their combined efforts they would grind right through their clothes and end up fucking anyway. But he wasn't going to last anywhere near long enough for that, and she was already spasming. The grip and release and slip and slide of her shuddering slit through scant layers of clothing was enough to send him. He grabbed her arse and held her splayed so that as the front of his track bottoms darkened with each spurt of semen, his wetness rubbed against her until her own crotch seam was dark and soaked. He hoped it was as much from her juices as from his.

He didn't know how long they sat wrapped around each other gasping and groaning for breath. They might have drifted off there, in each other's arms, at the breakfast table, and Tim couldn't think of a better way to end a great breakfast.

It was the beeper for Mountain Rescue that brought him back to reality. And it wasn't a nice one.

'What is it? Tim … What wrong? Your hands are shaking.' Tara's voice dragged him back to the kitchen and he released the breath he didn't know he was holding.

'Some walkers found a body. They think maybe a suicide

off Raven Crag. Tara, where's Serena?'

Tara was instantly on her mobile, which she'd left lying on the credenza. He hurried off to dress. When he returned, her face was pale, her lips set in a tight line. 'Serena's gone, Tim. They thought she was asleep in her room until my call.'

Chapter Nineteen

'SO THIS IS WHAT you've been reduced to, Marie Warren, offering your cunt to rutting ghosts like some whore.'

Marie had just bent to pick up her shoes. There'd barely been time to feel the burn in her belly when she saw Deacon's reflection in the globe of the kerosene lamp still burning low inside the cave. The skin prickled up her neck as she whirled around to find no one there. But she felt the warm breath of laughter against her ear.

'Remember, Marie, I can be wherever I want to be. And I can choose if you feel me or not.' And suddenly the physical press of his body forced her back against the wall of the cave. 'As I recall, you rather enjoyed the feel of me, even though you wouldn't admit it.'

His invisible hand splayed wide against the small of her back, and she could feel his hard cock against her belly as the press of him rucked up the front of her dress. 'Serena Ravenmoor finds that gift of mine intriguing, incidentally. She likes what I can do to her in public places, in plain sight, that no one else can see.' She felt his chuckle against her neck. 'Rather, I should say she did like it. Serena Ravenmoor is dead now. She jumped off Raven Crag.'

'You're lying,' she gasped, struggling in vain to push the weight of him off her. 'Serena is safe away from you.'

She felt the brush of his lips against her nape and a hand moved up over her neck and throat with just enough pressure to feel threatening. 'My dearest Marie, your first mistake is to assume that Serena wanted to be safe away from me. Though she was a bit of a dolt when it came to her craft, even she could manage an elementary scrying spell, enough to call me to her rescue. Oh, don't look so distressed, my dear. Serena Ravenmoor's last hours were the highlight of her life. I kept her happy, made her feel valued, satisfied her voracious appetite, and that was all she really wanted. Even to the very end as she stepped off over the edge of the fell, her heart was full of her Deacon, of her dark angel, as she called me.

'Oh, the coroner will say it was suicide, Marie, and they will find her lovely scrying mirror, the one you threatened to send me back through, shattered into tiny little pieces. In fact it will be Mr Meriwether who finds her. Well, it was actually a couple of unfortunate walkers who found her, but Mountain Rescue is already on its way to retrieve her poor shattered corpse, and Mr Meriwether, being a faithful member of the team, is with them. Such guilt he'll feel. I shall savour the memory of such delicious self-blame for months to come. Ah, but his guilt will be as nothing compared to Tara Stone's. You look pale, my love. Have you not been feeling well?'

He tut-tutted. 'I must have a talk with Fiori. Perhaps she's not feeding you well. Perhaps now that she's dead, she has forgotten the nutritional requirements of the living. But that's not the reason I've come, my dear Marie.' He stepped away and she nearly fell forward at the sudden release. Still he was only visible in the shimmering globe of the lamp. Leaning heavily against the wall of the cave, she kept her eyes on the reflection.

'The reason for my visit is to thank you and Mr Meriwether for finding me such an extensive list of Help Meets.'

'Help Meets? What are you talking about?'

'Not being a product of the technological age, I was completely unaware of just how many, so called, witches there are in Cumbria until you and Mr Meriwether put your heads together for a little online research. Nor did I know how desperately some of them long for someone from the other side to guide them, comfort them, satisfy their carnal lusts, nay even abuse them. Oh how they long to be martyrs for their respective deities.'

Marie found herself suddenly fighting like hell to keep from hyperventilating. Her heart went into overdrive hammering against her throat. 'Why? Serena did nothing to you. None of them have?'

He moved back close to her and slid a curled finger down the curve of her throat and her heart accelerated still further. 'Oh, I have nothing against any of them. But until I get what I want, I will make do with what is available to me. I have my eye on a lovely witch over in Rosthwaite at the moment. Well she considers herself a witch anyway. A good divorce settlement from an over-controlling husband has converted her to Paganism.

'Can you imagine? Back in my day being a witch meant something. And even though Tara Stone and her lackeys have you spreading your legs for rutting ghosts, I cannot deny that it takes a certain skill to manage such. In my day, you certainly didn't brag about being a witch unless you were anxious to meet a fiery death. You kept your skills to yourself. And yet in your modern world, you can purchase a few trinkets from a local curiosity shop and *voila*! You are a witch, and very proud of it, indeed. And you may freely advertise it all over the internet without fear of retribution and without the least bit embarrassment at your complete and utter lack of skill. Ah, such a brave new world, Marie.'

Dark spots swam in front of Marie's eyes and there was not enough oxygen in the cave, as cold sweat broke on her forehead and between her breasts. Damn it! She didn't need this right now! She struggled to listen to what Deacon was saying.

He laid a hand against her clammy face. 'My dear, you really aren't well, are you? If I didn't know better, I would say perhaps you are suffering from a panic attack. Yes, I believe you are prone to such maladies, are you not? You had them often in your silly little world of material wealth and money grubbing where there was nothing at all to fear really, not in the grand scheme of the universe. Such a foolish waste of energy when there are so many truly marvellous reasons for fear and panic.' He brushed her nipple with the tip of his finger and her heart felt as though it would hammer its way out of her chest. 'Now then, my dear Marie, I will make my meaning

189

perfectly clear. I gave Serena Ravenmoor an easy death because in spite of being an imbecile, she served me well. However, our lovely divorcee in Rosthwaite will not be so lucky, I fear. And the one after her. Well I shudder to think.'

'Why are you doing this?' Marie managed between gasps for breath. Her heart jackhammering in her chest had become painful.

'Simple, my darling. If I cannot have what I want, I will take what I can get.' He tut-tutted again. 'I can be such an unpleasant fellow when I don't get what I want.'

'What do you want, damn it!' It took all she had to force the words up through her tightened throat.

'Why, my dear, I would have thought you would be smart enough to figure that out. But then it is terribly hard to think when one is so overwhelmed by fear. Is it not? I want you and Mr Meriwether.' He waved a hand as though he were shooing away an insect. 'Oh, I have no interest in either of you personally, but Tara Stone does, and that, my lovely, is enough to intrigue me terribly.'

He pressed tight against her. 'I will eventually have my way, Marie Warren, and the sooner I get it, the fewer curiosity shop witches I shall have to play with to appease my bad temper.' Suddenly he spoke so close to her ear it felt like he was inside her head. 'Their lives are in your hands, Marie Warren, yours and Mr Meriwether's. Remember that when next he is called to Raven Crag, for I promise the next corpse he finds will not be so easily identifiable when I've had my way. Oh, and Marie, you are exquisite when you're terrified, perhaps even more so than when you're flushed with arousal.'

As quickly as he came, he was gone, and Anderson and Sky found Marie in a foetal position, trembling on the floor of the cave.

Tim's face was pale and drawn when Anderson let him into Elemental Cottage. 'Where's Marie,' he asked. 'Is she all right?'

'I'm here.' She took him in her arms, savouring his warmth and his solidness, but knowing he was as shaken as she was.

She swallowed hard and found her voice. 'It was Serena, then.'

She felt him nod against her shoulder and tighten his embrace. He really didn't need to say. They all knew.

'Marie's had a visit from Deacon, while you were away,' Tara said. 'He was only too happy to crow about Serena.' Whatever Tara added under her breath, Marie figured probably wasn't fit for proper company.

They all adjourned to the study, and when both Tim and Marie finished telling their stories, the room was silent for a long moment, everyone lost in their own thoughts. Tim spoke at last. 'Everything was exactly as Deacon said it would be, except for the scrying mirror. We never found that. Do you suppose he took it?'

'He couldn't have,' Tara said. 'When ghosts leave the flesh, they can only take what they died with.'

'Still,' Tim said, 'I can't help wondering why he felt it was so important to mention the mirror unless it really was possible for Marie to put him back the same way she released him.'

'Come to think of it,' Marie said, 'other than our first encounter on Maiden Moor, Deacon has only ever approached me through mirrors or glass.'

'And you said your compass was misplaced, is that not so?' Anderson asked.

She nodded.

'You usually wear it around your neck, do you not?'

She nodded again. 'I suppose it would be reflective enough but it was overcast.'

'Not at the beginning of the day, it wasn't,' Tara said.

Marie felt the skin crawl up the back of her neck. 'Then you think he was that close to me all the time?'

'Wait a minute,' Tim said. 'He's never used a mirror with me.'

'Of course not. It's easiest, and best for him to approach you through your dreams,' Tara said. 'Like we talked about this morning. He's using both your strengths and your vulnerabilities. He can do this because you're not yet well trained. Until you are, your strengths will also be your weak points. On the other hand, he fancies approaching at that juncture where your strengths lie. It's sort of a power play, if you will, a way of demoralising you, demoralising all of us.

'Marie, I want you to try something for me, if you would please?' Tara said.

Marie nodded, leaning forward in her seat.

'Look into your mirror and think about Serena Ravenmoor. Think about her as you knew her in as much detail as you can.'

Marie pulled the silver chain with the mirror on it from between her breasts, where it had warmed to her body temperature. For a few seconds, she breathed deeply, gazing at her own reflection, as if by doing so she could feel the ebb and flow of her own body. The room around her was silent, but she could hear the breath of every one present, including the ghosts. She could hear heartbeats, shifting of clothing against skin, even blood flowing through veins. And then a current of heat started low in her sacrum, shot upward through her spine and burst in her head in a flash of blue black darkness, leaving only the mirror itself visible to her.

A swell of sickness clenched cold and tight in her belly rushing down past the darkness and dissipating like waves receding on a beach, leaving her breathless and drenching her in cold sweat. Somewhere from a long way off she heard Tara encouraging her to stay with it, to focus on Serena Ravenmoor.

Struggling to keep from disgracing herself further than she already had with the earlier panic attack, Marie did as she was asked, clenching her jaw tight, trying to breathe deeply, focusing on the mirror until her eyes hurt.

'Marie, trust me,' she heard Tara say. 'I know it feels bad at the moment. But please trust me. It'll be all right.'

These days, Marie wasn't so confident that anything would ever be all right again, but she did trust Tara.

There was a roar in her ears like a waterfall, and suddenly the blackness shifted and changed. There were night sounds all around, and she was on Raven Crag, standing on the very edge of the precipice. She was chilled and she hurt. She hurt badly, and yet she had set aside the pain, as though it belonged to someone else. Her fingers cramped from clutching the mirror so tightly. And when she lifted it to her face, it was his face she saw over her shoulder leering at her with eyes like fire.

And she knew him. For the first time since he had come to her, she knew him for what he was. And for a split second she was alone in the universe, in a place where he couldn't touch her. That was all the time she had. He wanted her to jump. She knew he did, and in the end he would drive her to it in terror, though not before he had the chance to fully reveal himself to her. But she already knew who he was, what he was. He wouldn't forgive lightly her stealing his revelation.

But for this split second she could deny him that satisfaction. For this split second she could deny him the pleasure of hurting her further. For this split second her will was her own. Clutching the mirror with his image caught in it, she stepped into emptiness, and as she fell, she had the presence of mind for one last act. She flung everything he had been to her, everything he had done to her, all of it back through the mirror, and in her mind, called out the only name she could trust. Tim Meriwether.

That was all.

Marie came back to herself in Tim's arms, her mirror still clutched in her hand. For a second the faces of the others swam in and out of focus, then everything became clear. 'I saw his face,' she said, amazed at how calm she suddenly felt. I mean his real face, the way Serena Ravenmoor saw him just before she jumped to her death. And I saw all of what he did to her.' In spite of herself she blushed, and in spite of the fact that she couldn't stop shivering, she felt aroused. 'She jumped to get away from him, and she did it with a clear head.'

Fiori brought her a glass of water and she drank it down in thirsty gulps, then Anderson settled the throw from the sofa around her shoulders. In her head, she sorted through everything she had seen in the mirror. It was as though she had actually been Serena Ravenmoor for the few days she had known Deacon. The detail of it all would have been terrifying if she had not also found herself so drawn to him. Every time he made love to Serena it felt as though it had been her he entered. And suddenly it hit her.

'He never came.'

Instantly all eyes were on her. 'What?' Tara said.

'He never came. In all the times he was with Serena Ravenmoor, in all the times they had sex, he never came, not once, and yet he was hard all the time. When he was with me, he was always hard.'

When Fiori realised the attention in the room had turned to her, she shifted uncomfortably in the chair and raised an unconscious hand to her throat. 'We had sex a lot,' she said avoiding everyone's gaze. 'But no. He never came. He said he was holding his energy for when it most mattered.' She forced herself to look up at everyone. 'He said the power of sex could build upon itself indefinitely, and he bragged about how long he'd held himself, how long it had been since he last came.' Fiori shook herself as though she were waking up from a deep sleep. 'I'm sorry, I don't know why I never told anyone. It's just that …' Her voice drifted off and her eyes misted. 'I really don't like to talk about it.'

Tara moved to her side and pushed her hair away from her face. 'But you have to talk about it, Fiori. We all know what we face. The tiniest detail may be important.' She turned her attention to Sky, who shook her head.

'He never came with me either, though I wasn't alive long enough to think that so strange.'

Still shivering a bit from her scrying experience, Marie pulled the throw tighter around her shoulders. 'He came before he died. It's the last thing he did.'

The room was suddenly deathly silent, all attention on Marie, as she continued. 'When he tried to take me at Lacewing cottage the last time, I saw a flashback, almost like what I saw just now through my mirror. There was a woman, a blonde. She had a lead pipe in her hand. He grabbed it from her, almost with his last breath, said something about a sacrifice. Then he shoved it up his arse.' Marie found herself blushing hard. 'And I saw him ejaculate just before his heart stopped, just before his breath left him.'

There was a long silence. Both Tim and Anderson moved closer to Marie, and she found comfort in their nearness.

194

'So he feeds on sexual energy and holds on to it,' Tim said, thinking out loud. 'And he's been holding on to it for all these years. Is that possible?'

'The holding of sexual energy is an ancient practice,' Tara said. 'In some ways that's what celibacy is supposed to be, holding that sexual energy for another kind of creative force. Some eastern religions practice it, and of course, Catholicism. In some places it was traditional for soldiers to abstain before battle, for players of sport not to have sex with their wives or lovers before they played. It's not unusual. But that he's held it for all of these years while at the same time he's drawn to and feeds upon the sexual energy of others is staggering.'

'And may offer a clue to his possible demise,' Anderson said, as though he were reading her mind. 'Clearly he is drawn to the sexual energy with which Marie and Tim Meriwether have infused our little family. They are the only living members upon which he can feed. As far as I have seen, he has no interest in the sexual energies of those of us who no longer live, and of course it is not Tara's sexuality in which he is interested.'

Tara bit her lip and nodded agreement. 'I'm the captive audience for whatever show he intends to put on involving Marie and Tim.'

'We're the entertainment,' Tim said, squeezing Marie's hand.

'If we're the stars in his performance, and at the same time he's drawn to our sexual energy,' Marie said, 'then we can also be the bait to draw him in.'

'Marie,' Tara held her gaze. 'You do understand what that means, what you're up against.' She looked up at Tim. 'What you'll both be up against.'

Suddenly both Tim and Anderson held Marie's hands in a suicide grip, and she gave as good as she got. 'We've known from the beginning what we're here for,' Marie said, 'and I think I can speak for both of us when I say I've had enough. I want it over with. I want Deacon gone.' This time the trembling that shook Marie was not panic but anger. Everyone in the room nodded agreement.

Tara blew out a harsh breath. 'We aren't sending you as sacrificial lambs, Marie. Not this time. You may be the bait, but we know what you're capable of, and what you can do together has yet to be tested. You won't just be the bait. You'll also be the trap.' She looked around at the three ghosts who sat silently. 'And the Elemental Coven, well we're not to be trifled with.'

Marie squared her shoulders. 'Then what do we do?'

Tara studied both Tim and Marie for a long moment while fingering the pentacle at her throat. At last she spoke. 'You'll need to go home to Lacewing Cottage, both of you. And you'll need to take Anderson with you, and the three of you should have no problem drawing Deacon in.'

'The three of us? I don't understand.'

Anderson laid a warm hand on Marie's shoulder. 'It is sex magic, my love.'

Tim shifted nervously next to Marie, but said nothing.

'I need you to be all right with this, Tim,' Tara said.

He spoke between barely parted lips. 'I'll do whatever has to be done. Nobody wants the bastard gone more than I do.' He shot Fiori a quick glance.

'Good. Deacon will be drawn to the hottest part of the flame, and you three, I have no doubt, will generate an inferno. Add to that the fact that Anderson is a master of Ethereal magic, and I think we'll be ready for him.' She sighed. 'As ready as we can be, anyway. The rest of us will cast the spell and make ready to draw him in and bind him.'

Chapter Twenty

FIORI WOULD NOT ALLOW the return to Lacewing Cottage before stuffing everyone with roast chicken and all the trimmings topped off with raspberry and white chocolate pavlova. They would all need their strength, she said, and none of the Elementals ever argued with Fiori where food was concerned. But by the time the last of the pavlova was eaten and the coffee was served up, Marie had the sneaking suspicion something else other than the fabulous meal was going on.

She sat between Tim and Anderson, and even if she hadn't been able to see that they both had fly-bursting hard-ons, the way they both squirmed and shifted and the smell of Tim's heat would have been a dead giveaway. She was sure they both could smell her lust, even above the delicious scent of the meal, and she was more than a little bit worried that the cushion on her chair would be wet before the table was cleared. It was early evening when the three finally left for Lacewing Farm, amid a flurry of embraces and well-wishes from the three remaining witches.

Anderson took Marie by the hand and pulled her into the back seat of Tim's Land Rover. Before Tim had the engine started, the ghost had her blouse open and a heavy-nippled breast excavated and pressed to his lips. Up front Tim adjusted the mirror so that Marie could see his eyes. Then before he started the engine, she heard the zip of his fly, and he wriggled and shifted in the seat. She saw his eyelids flutter, heard the hitch in his breath, then he revved the motor and they were off.

It wasn't a long drive, but Marie was sure the windows would have been steamed had they not been wide open. Anderson had greedily freed both her breasts and suckled them alternately while one hand found its way up under her short denim skirt and into her panties. All the while his erection, straining at his black trousers, rubbed and gouged against her thigh. Though she couldn't see what Tim was doing, he was definitely driving with one hand on the wheel, and the way he was struggling to breathe left little doubt where his other hand was. That only made Anderson's stroking and tweaking feel even hotter.

They barely got out of the Land Rover before Tim, making no effort to zip himself in – though Marie doubted he could if he wanted to – dragged her bodily from Anderson's gropings. Then he took her mouth for himself and yanked aside the crotch of her panties to finger his way in between her creamy folds.

Anderson shoved in next to him, as close as he could get, and went to work kneading her breasts and kissing and nibbling any bare skin he could find. There was getting to be more and more of it by the second, as they all three stumbled and pushed their way toward the door of Tim's cottage.

'They did something to us, didn't they?' Tim gasped when he came up for air. 'Some sort of spell.' Then he went back to eating her mouth as though he hadn't just had Fiori's four course meal.

'Magic was not necessary,' Anderson breathed, nipping at a tender spot on Marie's nape. 'We three are not in need of their assistance where the pleasures of the flesh are concerned.'

They shoved and groped and pushed their way into the lounge. There was a fire built in the fireplace and an open bottle of wine breathing on the coffee table, accompanied by three glasses. Marie figured Tiggs and Finney had taken care of that on Fiori's orders.

As both men tugged her down into the pile of cushions on the stripped wood floor, she took the initiative. She guided Anderson's right hand from her breasts down to rest on Tim's erection, which was shoving at her thigh. And it was as though everything was suddenly freeze framed. The only sound, the only hint of motion was their own desperate breathing and the crackle and dance of the fire.

Tim shoved his way free of the tangle of arms and legs and crab-walked back against the sofa, his chest heaving like it would explode, his eyes locked on Anderson.

Marie held her breath, not knowing whether she should apologise or laugh and blow the whole thing off. She didn't have to do either.

Anderson gave her hand a reassuring squeeze and moved to sit next to Tim. 'Intuition has long been one of my gifts, Tim Meriwether. Am I wrong in believing that you wish more from me than just to watch me share the pleasures of Marie's body with you?'

'No. No, you're not wrong.' Tim ran shaky fingers through his hair. Then he took a deep breath, and glanced from one of them to the other, his gaze coming once again to rest on Anderson. He squared his shoulders and offered a twitch of a smile. 'No. You're not wrong.'

Anderson didn't give him time to contemplate. His large hand slid to the nape of Tim's neck, and he pulled him into a series of kisses, at first gentle and fleeting, little more than brushes of the lips, flicks of the tongue, like dragonflies skimming the surface of a pond. Tim's nervousness was palpable in the charged atmosphere of the room. But so was his arousal.

'I've never been with a man before,' Tim whispered. 'God that sounds so cliché.'

Anderson cupped his stubbled cheek. 'But you have imagined how it would be, have you not? All men have. It is a part of our nature to love our own flesh and the shape of it. Therefore we cannot but love it in others of our sex, though it may not be a love we consciously allow ourselves to feel.' He nodded at Tim's still bare penis. 'If this is the gift you have been regularly offering up to our Marie, then I most certainly understand why sharing your bed pleases her so.' He spoke no more, but took Tim's erection deep into his mouth in long hungry slurps. And Tim's startled gasp was quickly transmuted to little grunts of pleasure. With one hand, Anderson cupped and caressed Tim's full balls, and with the other he stroked his own cock through the fabric of his trousers, Marie was amazed his fly could maintain integrity under such pressure.

Tim curled his fingers in the ghost's dark hair and ground his hips into the cushions as each tight thrust of Anderson's mouth expertly brought him closer and closer to the edge. And when Marie was no longer sure if Tim was even coherent, he surprised all three of them by bringing his hand to rest against Anderson's penis, and the ghost sighed his pleasure at the touch. 'Shall I show you my manhood, Tim Meriwether? Shall I let you touch my flesh?' He didn't wait for an answer but released his erection for Tim's inspection.

Cautiously, A little awkwardly at first, Tim caressed and fondled Anderson's heavy cock. 'Is this for me or for her?' He nodded over his shoulder to Marie, who now watched in voyeuristic bliss.

Anderson gave Tim's penis a solicitous stroke. 'By now, Tim Meriwether, surely you are aware how effortlessly and completely either of you can harden me.' He took Tim's mouth again, this time with no doubt as to where their foreplay was leading.

Marie had fantasised about watching her two beautiful blokes have sex, but she never imagined it would actually happen. With a shudder, she pushed back the sudden thought of why they were actually in this position. Before she could dwell on it, Anderson pulled away from Tim's tongue kiss, still caressing his cock. 'My dear Tim, can you not imagine the affect our lovemaking must be having on our Marie's burgeoning womanhood? I think we can both attest to the deliciousness of her swollen arousal even before we fondled each other's members. Can you not smell her delectable scent like perfume on the air?'

'Mmm, like perfume,' Tim agreed breathlessly.

'Would you not then like to taste the seat of her pleasure while I familiarise myself with your anxious sex?'

Tim scrambled to pull Marie into the rough and tumble, shoving up her skirt and pushing aside the crotch of her panties to bury his face in her pussy. Meanwhile, Anderson tugged at the farmer's jeans until they were down over his hips and Tim practically went through the roof at the first feel of Anderson's tongue against his anus. He murmured something warm and incoherent that vibrated intriguingly against Marie's clit.

'Does it please you, my tongue on your nether hole?' Anderson whispered against Tim's arse.

'God yes!' Both Tim and Marie spoke in unison.

Anderson chuckled. 'My dear Marie, somehow I knew my attention to Tim Meriwether's lovely backside would please you. Only move to one side ever so slightly, Tim and do not be so greedy, for I long to look upon our Marie's dewy, sweet sex.'

Tim shifted slightly to one side, and Anderson sighed his appreciation, then with his eyes locked on Marie's wet pussy, he licked his middle finger and applied it with a single wet thrust to Tim's anus.

'Oh God,' Tim breathed and shuddered so hard, Marie feared he would come.

'Shall I continue,' Anderson said, kneading Tim's arse cheeks.

'Please,' Tim gasped, raising his butt closer to Anderson's efforts.

'Then perhaps you would do us the honour of pushing aside Marie's blouse and fondling her exquisite bosom. The swell of her nipples through fabric teases me so terribly. Good. Very good indeed, and now tell me, Tim Meriwether, is she not very close to her first release?'

'I think you might be right,' Tim grunted.

'And shall you do the honours?'

'It would be my pleasure,' Tim said, giving her breasts a good kneading before he lowered his face once again to her pussy. He slid his tongue up from her perineum the length of her gash as deep as he could reach, then at the apex of her vulva, he pulled her distended clit into his mouth and suckled hard, and she nearly bucked him off with her orgasm.

Anderson chose that moment to drizzle Tim's anus with warm saliva and insert another finger. And Tim froze.

'Shall I stop, Tim Meriwether,' Anderson's voice was tight with his own arousal, 'or do you wish me to continue?'

'Will it hurt?' Tim asked.

'Perhaps a little, but if there is pain, I promise it will be quickly forgotten in the pleasure that follows.'

'You don't mind?'

Anderson smiled down at Tim's backside. 'My dear Tim Meriwether, I have had such delicious fantasies of penetrating your lovely nether hole as you can scarcely imagine.'

Tim laughed nervously. 'Oh, I think I can imagine just fine.'

'Then I shall take that as a yes.' But as Anderson began to move the two fingers inside Tim's anus, Tim cried out and shoved the ghost away, rolling onto his side in a foetal position. 'No,' he gasped. 'Not yet. I don't want to come yet, but I'm too close.' His breath came in great racking gasps. 'Just please, just give me a minute.'

Marie slid down and took Tim's head in her lap, caressing his hair, while he reached upward to cup and fondle her breasts. Anderson moved into a spoon position and laid a careful hand on Tim's flank. His own breath was rapid, and Marie could tell it was difficult for him not to thrust against Tim's bare arse, but he held very still. 'We are at our leisure, Tim Meriwether.' As he spoke, he eased Tim's jeans and underpants the rest of the way off and wriggled out of his own as well. 'It is for this purpose we have come.' He snuggled close again. 'We may share our pleasure as long as you desire it, and as long as our Marie gives us leave.' He looked up at Marie and gave her a hungry smile. 'Perhaps it would please you if I should penetrate her lovely sex until you are ready. That is if she would be so kind as to allow it.'

The words were barely out of Anderson's mouth before Tim was shifting her, positioning her until she was on hands and knees with her legs wide apart, giving Anderson the perfect view of her heavy pussy lips, While Tim continued to caress her breasts. She heard him gasp at the sight of Anderson pushing into her accommodating hole with a satisfied grunt. Then the ghost began to tweak her clit with one hand while the other kneaded the swell of her arse cheeks in turn.

'Is she not the epitome of loveliness, Tim Meriwether?' Anderson breathed. 'And I think she shall relieve her needs once more on my manhood. Ah, such a pleasure it must be for the fairer sex to have the gift of release at their will as often as pleases them. And such an exquisite lust our Marie has. I think that she could endure such pleasure endlessly. Come, Tim Meriwether, come and pleasure her lovely tight nether hole with your mouth, and we shall bring her to release together.'

The addition of Tim's tongue to her arsehole made it impossible for her to hold back, but just as the orgasm burst through her, Anderson pulled out. 'Show our lovely Marie her release.' He nodded to Tim's amulet. Immediately, Tim understood, lowered his face so that he could see her pussy, then angled his mirror so that when she looked down between her legs she could also see the trembling writhing of her engorged splay, dark and slick and convulsing.

But it was Tim who gasped and would have lost his balance if Anderson hadn't steadied him. 'Oh dear God,' he breathed, trembling all over. 'Is that –'

'That is what our dear Marie is feeling, Tim Meriwether, yes indeed. And I feel it too.' Anderson was once again fondling Tim's anus, as they all watched until Marie's cunt had calmed to small tremors. 'Now then, I think that we shall make use of her abundant ambrosia,' Anderson said. And in Tim's mirror, they both watched with tight breath as Anderson fingered in between her pussy lips until the cup of his middle three fingers was drenched with her cream, then, he inserted those same three fingers into Tim's anus.

Tim growled like an animal, pressed back hard onto Anderson fingers and nearly in the same instant shoved forward into Marie's wet cunt.

Anderson chuckled between tight breaths. 'I have such appreciation for a man who knows what to do with his member and when to do it, Tim Meriwether.'

So did Marie.

'Jesus, I haven't had this much sex in ages,' Tim breathed.

'I think you will find the days of your celibacy have come to an end, my dear fellow.'

Tim shot Anderson a look over his shoulder. 'You mean if we all survive.'

'Indeed. If we all survive. If we do not,' Anderson shrugged. 'Being a ghost is not without its merits.'

Then Tim took a deep breath and nodded. 'Do it. I want you to do it now.' He thrust hard into Marie for emphasis, and she wrapped her legs around him.

With one hand on the shaft of his penis and the other on Tim's flank, Anderson positioned himself, then he looked up at Marie. 'You shall not need a mirror to see what I do to Tim Meriwether, my darling, nor to experience our lust. The link between you and me will show you all. The link between you and Tim will let you feel what I do.' Then he turned his attention back to Tim. He spat heavily on his hand and rubbed the saliva liberally over his cock. 'Push out, my dear man,' he instructed. 'As I push in, push out.' Then with a soft grunt, he shoved his cock into Tim's gape.

'All the way,' Tim commanded, holding his breath. 'I want to know what it feels like.'

Anderson obeyed. The force of his body shoved Tim to new depths inside Marie, who gasped at the sensation, the sensation that was dwarfed as the avalanche of what the two men were feeling added to her own lust.

'Oh my God!' Both Tim and Marie cried out. His voice was tense with pain, which, though she felt, was tempered by her own arousal and his thick cock in her pussy.

'You must relax,' Anderson instructed, holding very still. 'If you do not relax you will not feel the pleasure, but only the pain.'

At last Tim caught his breath. 'All right, I'm ready.' He sounded more in control. Slowly, carefully, Anderson began to thrust very gently. For the first few strokes Tim held very still, but as his anus dilated to better accommodate Anderson, he began to move against the ghost, then found the rhythm that allowed him to thrust back against Anderson and let Anderson's momentum drive him forward deep into Marie's gripping cunt. Both men accelerated the rhythmic in and out, faster and faster, and Marie responded by pushing back against both of them with each thrust. 'I can feel you,' she gasped. 'I can feel both of you, everything you feel, I feel.'

204

'Me too,' Tim gasped.

'It is one of the fringe benefits afforded bonded ghost riders, and it is powerful magic that can rock the very foundations of the Ether.' Anderson's voice was stretched tight and the thrusting of both men had become muscle-wrenchingly tense. 'I think that we shan't wait long now for our release.'

The words were barely out of his mouth before Tim convulsed his load into Marie, and she was gripped with her own spasms just as Anderson shuddered over and over, filling Tim's stretched anus with his semen. And Marie felt their combined orgasms like they all belonged to her personally, shaking and trembling as waves of pleasure broke over her again and again.

When at last everyone could breathe, the two men shifted so their combined weight wasn't on Marie and the three of them settled down onto the pile of cushions for a post coital snuggle. In a brief moment of guilt, Marie thought of Deacon. There had been no sign of him, no feel of him, though their lovemaking, combined with the magical bond they shared must have surely shaken the whole universe, let alone the Ether. What was he up to? But the thought did little more than register before she dozed.

Chapter Twenty-one

MARIE WOKE CHILLED, UNCERTAIN of where she was, at first. She rolled on her side to find the fire had gone out, and she was nearly naked on the floor. The memories of the evening's passions rushed back to her, but the warmth at her centre was fleeting. The house was cold and dark, and she was alone. 'Anderson? Tim?' she called. But there was no answer. She fumbled for her clothes and dressed quickly, then walked from room to room, flipping on light switches as she went, feeling a sense of being watched. But there was no one else in the house, and there was no burning between her hip bones to indicate the presence of ghosts.

Cautiously, she opened the kitchen door and stepped out onto the porch. The night was silent and star-dusted, with the crescent moon hanging heavily just above the fells. Tim's Land Rover was parked exactly where he had parked it when they arrived earlier. 'Anderson?' She called out again. There was nothing.

She stood for a second holding her breath, contemplating whether she should hop in the car and go to Elemental Cottage, or stay put. Just as she stepped off the porch toward her house, the mare screamed from the stables and she froze in her tracks.

The paddock was well lit, and there was electricity in the barn. Without giving herself time to think, she slipped into her sandals and made her way as quietly as she could into the paddock, hand clenching at the amulet around her neck. Something definitely wasn't right, and yet, she felt no presence of ghosts. That in itself wasn't right. Tim had told her there were always ghosts around Lacewing Cottage, had been since they found out what he was, and even more so since she had arrived. And yet she felt nothing.

She slowed her pace at the door to the stable, scarcely daring to breathe. She could hear the mare kicking and snorting and whickering in her stall. Carefully she felt for the light, and when she could see, she went straight to the horse who tossed her head, wide-eyed and shifted nervously from foot to foot.

'Easy, easy, girl.' She spoke softly, hoping the horse couldn't smell her own nerves. 'Sh! Shhh. It's all right.' She grabbed the lead rope and threw it over the horse's neck so she would at least have a little control over the animal. She pulled her close until the mare's head was near her chest, then gently she stroked her neck and face, holding her securely and speaking softly until the horse had calmed a bit. 'That's it, girl. It'll be all right,' she whispered, hoping she wasn't lying, but pretty sure she was.

It was then she noticed Tim sprawled in the dark corner of the stable and he wasn't moving. But before she could go to him, fire flashed low in her belly like nothing she had felt before, doubling her over, taking her breath away, causing the hair to rise along the back of her neck. The mare jerked away, reared, and then stood trembling at the back of her stall, nostrils flared, eyes wide. Very slowly Marie straightened and turned. She knew what she would see, what she most didn't want to see.

Deacon loomed larger than life, backlit from the stable yard light and standing in the open door between her and escape. He beckoned her. 'Leave Mr Meriwether, or I shall kill him now before your eyes, and it will be you who is to blame.' His voice vibrated up through her with a heavy cold thrum.

Feeling like her skin would crawl off her, she moved slowly toward him. He chuckled softly and took her into his arms in an embrace that, in spite of herself, she longed to return. 'Come, my darling. We are not strangers. I know your body, do I not? I smell your heat. Do I not know how to ignite it, how to stoke it, how to make you lust?' He stroked her hair, and she wanted him desperately, she felt like her world would end if she couldn't have him. Then she remembered Serena, and grasped her mirror in a white knuckle grip, an act which made him laugh out loud.

'Oh, my dear, how you tremble. Do I frighten you? I do, don't I?' He guided her hand to the bulge in his trousers. 'And your fear is exquisite, Marie, deliciously fine-tuned and elemental. A woman who fears as exquisitely as you do cannot but bring me pleasure untold. Even more so than your lust or your pain.' He yanked her to him with a fist curled in the back of her hair.

His breath was hot, yet sweet against her face, so close to her parted lips that she could almost taste it, and it was the quick, harsh breath of a man aroused. 'No one can help you, Marie. The ghost you've been so happily fucking is now trapped in the Ether he is such a master of. Whether or not he will ever be able to find his way back, I cannot say. The Ether is a very large place. No one at Elemental Cottage knows that anything is wrong. I've made sure of that. They are happily casting their worthless binding spell, thinking that they may trap me as they did before, thinking that they may take away my flesh as easily as they do with simpering perverted ghosts.' He pulled her still closer until his erection raked at her through his trousers, and the heat flared and burned like desire held too long. 'I assure you, they are not concerned with you or your friends. They think you are spreading your legs in orgiastic bliss.'

He took her hand, still gripping the mirror, folded his enormous fist around it and squeezed until bones cracked and glass shattered. The mirror broke with a pop and a scrape, and pain sliced through her palm. She sucked a sharp breath between her teeth and felt her blood, warm and sticky, in her fisted hand. As he relaxed his grip, the broken mirror slid from her fingers and shattered further as it hit the concrete floor of the stable.

The laugh that rose from deep in his chest was anything but humorous. 'Do you really believe that you have any power over me, you foolish little girl.' He tightened the fist in her hair to a painful grip and half dragged, half marched her into the paddock with her clenching her bloodied hand against her chest. There he shoved her onto the ground in front of the water trough and knelt next to her, still holding her by the back of the neck. For a frightening second, she though he was going to force her head under.

'Look! Look,' he roared. 'And I will show you what has come to pass at my hand, Marie Warren.' He forced her head closer to the dark surface. 'Then I shall show you what the future holds, and I shall bask in your fear.'

The surface of the water shimmered, then stilled and darkened. A panicked face rose from beneath the water, as though it were her own reflection, a beautiful face, eyes wide, hair floating wildly through the water, mouth open in a desperate plea that would never be heard.

Marie yelped and tried to pull back, but Deacon held her there, only a breath away from the surface of the water. 'What? Do you not recognize your predecessor, Marie? Rayna, Guardian of the West and of Water.' He chuckled. 'Not a very good guardian, I fear, but you cannot imagine how much pleasure I had with her in her element of water, nor how long it can take one to drown when one is not pressed for time. Perhaps I will show you one day.' He pulled her to his chest and tenderly stroked her hair, then her back. 'But that shall not soon be your fate, my darling. With Serena's unfortunate demise, I am left without a Help Meet, a companion, if you will, and though my lovely witch at Rosthwaite is brighter than my poor little Serena was, she is nowhere near as interesting as you are, with your delicious aroma of fear, and your spirited defiance – when you're not pissing yourself in panic, that is. I find the combination so very intriguing.'

He lifted her chin with a finger, forcing her to meet his gaze. 'Are you skilled with a knife, my darling? No I suppose you wouldn't be, would you? Never mind. You will become so after enough practice.' He pushed her head down toward the surface of the water again. 'And I have devised such a perfect training exercise for you.'

The water rippled, then cleared and she saw Tim tied to a post, his hands above his head, his body exposed to the knife she wielded.

'When I lived and breathed as you do, Marie Warren, I used

to hunt for sport,' Deacon whispered next to her ear. 'I took many trophies in my day, and my skills at skinning an animal, any kind of an animal, were admirable. I am so longing to pass on that skill to a worthy servant.'

Her stomach lurched and she swallowed bile. 'I would never –'

The hand in her hair migrated to an uncomfortably tight caress of her throat. 'Ah, but you will, my darling.' He pressed closer to her, in a tight embrace from behind that forced the breath from her lungs. His voice was a humid whisper against her ear. 'Soon, I will fuck you, Marie, and you will beg me for it, you will want it as you have never in your life wanted anything. And when I have given you ecstasy you cannot yet imagine, you will gladly do my bidding. Oh yes, you will wield the knife gladly, all the while your lust will burn for the reward you know only I can give you.'

The image of Tim on the dark surface of the water writhed in anguish as she watched herself take the knife to the tender skin just below his navel.

'You will know what you are doing, and you will loath the very act, my darling, but you will not stop, you will not stop no matter how Mr Meriwether begs, for he will never be able to reward you as I can.'

'No!' With an effort that wrenched muscles and practically dislocated her shoulder, Marie thrust her bloodied hand into the water and it shimmered and sizzled and the image darkened and disappeared.

Deacon caught a sharp breath, roared like a maddened bull and back-handed her, sending her sprawling on the earth. 'Stupid child! I make the future this night, and neither you nor any of your paltry friends can undo what I foresee, what I …'

His words died in his throat as Tim tackled him from behind and the two rolled and tussled, while Marie struggled not to pass out from the panic.

'He's doing this to you, Marie. Fight it!' Tim gasped from the fray. 'It's just panic. Fight it.' For the briefest of seconds, Tim was mounted astride Deacon punching him in the face, and there was blood, Marie couldn't tell who it belonged to.

Frantically she looked around the paddock for anything she could use as a weapon. She tugged and pulled at the brick that had been set beneath one corner of the water trough to level it, but before it gave into her hand, Deacon rose from the dust, with Tim in front of him, a beefy forearm locked around his neck.

He laughed as though he had just heard the funniest joke ever. 'Impressive, Mr Meriwether. And I do like a good brawl on occasion, a part of my journey among the living that I miss from time to time. You acquitted yourself well, and I am diverted. Perhaps it is you I shall compel to be my servant. Men, after all, do understand each other so much better, do they not?'

'Leave her alone, Deacon.' Tim forced the words up through his constrained throat.

'Of course, Mr Meriwether, I will gladly leave our Marie alone if I can have you.' He ran a hand down Tim's chest to rest against his cock, and Tim shuddered. It was not the shudder of pain.

'Fight him, Tim. You have to fight him.'

'Shut up, little girl!' Deacon's voice was softer now, but it chilled Marie to the bone. 'If you will give me what I want, Mr Meriwether, I will let her go. For now.'

'He's a liar, Tim. Don't listen to him.'

This time, as he back handed her, Tim lunged for her, but Deacon held him tight. 'Of course I am a liar, Mr Meriwether. And no one knows better than you how easily I twist the truth to fit my needs.' He guided Tim's hand to the erection pressed against his trousers. 'What I offer you is time. Perhaps you will be able to fight my influence for a while. Certainly our Fiori did.' He waved a hand as though he swatted away a fly. 'I could kill you both now this very instant, and it would cause a certain amount anguish for my dear Tara Stone.' He stroked Tim's cock again. 'But like any good lover, I want the pleasure to last as long as possible.'

'Then take me and leave her alone,' Tim repeated. 'I'll take my chances that Tara and the Elementals will kick your arse long before I become your boot licker.'

'Are you crazy?' Marie shouted, coming to her feet, this time with the brick in her hand. 'Tim, you don't know what it's like, you don't know what he'll do to you, what he wants. Please.'

But Tim was already pulling down his jeans, his eyes locked on Deacon. As he turned to offer the demon his arse, Deacon shook his head. 'I don't fuck men's arses, Mr Meriwether, and that is why you are so perfect.' He reached out and stroked Tim's penis and it was instantly erect. 'You are a rider. You will have no problem keeping yourself hard enough to pleasure me. And I promise, when you have emptied yourself into my backside, you will know pleasure you have only ever dreamed of. And though you will try heroically to be loyal to your friends,' he took Tim's face in his hands and held his gaze. 'You will be mine with every fibre of your being.' With that, he lowered his trousers and offered Tim his arse.

As Tim positioned himself, suddenly Marie's injured hand throbbed and burned. In truth she had barely been aware of the pain with everything else that was happening. It was slick with blood, and the copper sweet smell of it hit the back of her throat like whiskey, making her eyes water. With her other hand, she held the brick. She wasn't sure why. It wasn't really any threat to Deacon.

The heady scent of her blood made it feel as though her whole body were pulsing, as though it were her Tim were about to push into, and she knew without a doubt he felt what she felt. Her heart raced, and this time not from fear, but from something else. She opened herself mentally, squeezing her hand shut until it throbbed angrily, and Tim was there, and suddenly she understood. As her hand throbbed with the beat of her heart, with the beat of Tim's heart, she understood completely. Their struggle wasn't about getting Deacon out of the flesh. What they had to do now was keep Deacon *in* the flesh. She didn't know how she knew, but she knew it as surely as she knew her own breath. And in her mind's eye, she could see the spell she needed as clear as day. Slowly, carefully, she began to weave it. She would only get one chance.

'Put your cock in me now!' Deacon roared.

Tim spat on his hand and lubricated his cock. His eyes locked on Marie's. Her hand, warm and slick with her life's blood, pulsated with the beat of their two living hearts. They both understood, and Tara was right, two were so much more powerful than one.

Slowly, deliberately, she moved in front of Deacon, unbuttoning her blouse as she did so.

He chuckled. 'Shall I have you both then? It is, after all, what you really want, isn't it, my dear Marie.'

With a slight nod of his head, Tim pushed in hard, Deacon groaned, and as he opened his mouth, Marie pressed the tip of one bloody finger against her chest, against her racing heart, then she slipped it between his parted lips. She felt the sizzle along every nerve ending in her body, she felt it race down Deacon's spine and up through Tim's groin. Tim thrust only once, Deacon roared like thunder and ejaculated in heavy spurts onto the dusty earth.

As understanding dawned in his eyes, Marie squared her shoulders. 'I don't want you out of the flesh, Deacon. In fact I have every intention of keeping you in the flesh. Forever.' She lifted the brick and with the force of all of her rage and Tim's, slammed against his temple. He shuddered and dropped to the ground like a stone.

It was Fiori who appeared first. She was already rucking up her skirt, as she moved toward Tim. 'You need relief,' she said. 'And it's not the kind that would be safe for the living to give you.' She took his hand. 'If you'd be more comfortable, we can go in the barn, but it's best not to wait.'

'Best not,' he said, pulling her into a hungry kiss that seemed somehow tender in spite of his need. Then he leaned back against the fence, lifted her onto him and began to thrust as though he really didn't care who saw.

It didn't take long. Marie knew only too well the intensity of his need, and so did Fiori. Before Tim grunted his release, Anderson was already tending to Marie's hand, reassuring her that he had never been lost in the Ether, that it was only another of Deacon's lies, Sky and Tara arrived immediately in the Land Rover and knelt to inspect Deacon's body.

'Is he dead?' Marie asked.

'He's been dead a long time,' Tara replied.

'What then,' Tim said, tucking in his shirt. 'A coma?'

Tara shook her head. 'You're mountain rescue, Tim. If we had called you for him, you would say he's dead. There are no vitals, and he's cold.' Tara studied the body lying sprawled in the stable yard. 'However this flesh won't decay, nor change, not if we leave it here in your paddock for a thousand years. It's conjured to be the perfect, incorruptible vessel for a demon, and demons, for the most part, aren't at all pressed for time. As Marie intuited, the perfect incorruptible vessel is also the perfect, inescapable prison when just the right blood magic is added to sex magic.'

'Then what do we do with him' Tim asked. 'I don't want him left in my paddock for a thousand years.'

'No, I imagine not.' Tara heaved a sigh and looked around her. 'We'll bury him on the boundary between our two properties to strengthen the binding, cast as many protection spells as we can and hope that his slumber is a very, very long one.' She ran a hand over his face and closed his eyes. 'For now, at least, he won't be bothering anyone.'

Chapter Twenty-two

MARIE AND TIM SLEPT in each other's arms most of the way there. In fact, they didn't even know where there was. They slept in the bed Sky had made out in the back of a little camper van that belonged to the Elementals. Marie remembered very little of what happened after she'd hit Deacon with the brick. She remembered being aroused at the sight of Tim fucking Fiori. She remembered stuffing a sandwich in her mouth like a starving woman. She remembered Anderson and Sky carefully tending her hand, which didn't seem to be nearly as badly cut as she feared it would be. In fact, it seemed to be healing at amazing speed. One of the fringe benefits of being a rider, Sky had reminded her.

She vaguely remembered a hot shower with Anderson carefully scrubbing away the grime, steaming out the aches and very gently bringing her to release, which she needed in spite of, or perhaps because of, all that had happened. Then she and Tim were loaded into the van, stripped naked and tucked into clean sheets with lots of kisses and caresses, which she was sure she would have appreciated a lot more had she not been so exhausted. They were told to rest.

It was late afternoon when Tara woke them both. She was naked. Without offering them clothes, she led them out to the edge of a tarn sparkling like glass against the bronzing sunlight. Insects buzzed in the warm air and the resident blackbird sang from the top of an oak tree. Marie would have asked about Deacon, but Tara stopped her words with a lingering kiss. 'We'll not speak about that now. It's been dealt with, as we said it would be.' She smiled and opened her arms as though to embrace the lovely landscape. 'The heatwave has made it warm enough for us to do our ritual outdoors in comfort, something we seldom get the chance to do in Lakeland. Come.' She led them to the edge of the water. Anderson, Sky and Fiori, all equally naked, were already waist deep in the tarn.

Tara joined them and motioned Tim and Marie to do the same. As they stepped into the water, the Elementals moved to circle them. And Tara spoke. 'The two of you have borne a burden that should not have been yours to bear. You have, in doing so, come in contact with anger, hate, bitterness, and all manner of unwholesomeness. Our hearts rejoice that you've returned to us successful, but most of all we rejoice that you've returned to us safe.

'You've returned to us. You belong with us. You're a part of us. And it's with joy and celebration that we offer ourselves to ease your weariness and cleanse away the efforts of your trials.' With that, she took each of them into her arms and gave them a long, lingering kiss. She laughed softly at Tim's surprised look. 'You're about to learn the cleansing powers of sex, Tim Meriwether.' She shrugged, 'Though the water is a nice touch, I thought, especially in this heat. Welcome to the Elemental Coven.'

The other coven members followed Tara's example and suddenly it was as though the water effervesced with tiny shimmers of gold, tiny droplets of sunlight that caressed and lingered on their skin wherever they touched, and the groping and stroking and fondling by the rest of the coven made certain that the effervescing waters didn't miss any place.

When the waters had done their job, the party migrated, still wet and dripping, to a place in the shade of the large oak where the Elementals had spread blankets and pillows on the moss.

Tim wasn't sure if it was magic or just lust, but the tangle of arms and legs on the makeshift bed seemed to buzz with power he felt not only between his hip bones, but up his spine and into his head. It was better than any alcohol induced buzz he'd ever remembered feeling. Before he could think about it very much, Fiori straddled him and settled herself onto his cock. 'I've wanted to do this for a long time,' she said, as she began to undulate against him. 'And it feels like you might just be all right with it now.'

He reached up and caressed her breasts, loving the way her dark eyelashes fluttered over amber eyes and her already erect nipples pearled still harder against his thumbs. 'I've been all right with it for a while. You've been the prickly one.' Then he rolled with her, pinning her beneath him. She wrapped her legs around him and giggled breathlessly. 'I might just get prickly again, so I would suggest you fuck me hard while I'm not.' Then suddenly her eyes were serious, misting slightly. 'I'm sorry, Tim. I'm sorry it all had to happen this way.'

'Shh.' He dropped a kiss onto her lips. 'I'm sorry too, that I couldn't understand, but it doesn't matter now. Now it feels right, and it hasn't felt that way in a long time.' In his peripheral vision he could see Anderson riding Sky from behind while Marie writhed with Tara's face between her legs.

'Is it always like this?' Tim grunted as Fiori put the squeeze on him.

'No. Sometimes there's a lot more sex.'

He came then, and she with him. He eased his weight off her just enough to maintain the connection. Before they both dozed, he whispered next to her ear, 'I don't want to lose you again, Fiori.'

'You couldn't even if you wanted to now,' she sighed. 'You're stuck with me, stuck with all of us.'

He couldn't really imagine there being more sex. That's all they did, and it was bliss. By the time they broke for the delicious picnic Fiori had packed, he'd romped with everyone, and so had Marie. Bonding, Sky had called it. She said it was very important for healing and for coven morale. She had said that when she came up from sucking his cock while Marie licked her from behind. No one had made any attempt to pack up when the sun set. There had been talk of training, talk of the new dimension the coven now had with two new living members, and it felt as though the pain and the suffering of the last few months and especially the last few days had been washed away, or at least pushed back a bit to where it didn't hurt quite so bad to think about.

Long toward morning, Marie woke feeling as though someone had called her name. She could just make out Tim and Tara in mid grope sitting by the tarn. Any other time, it would have felt rude to approach a couple so intimately involved, but tonight it seemed like the thing to do. In spite of herself, the voyeur in her lingered just a little while to watch. Tim was practically on top of Tara, their mouths were engaged in mutual exploration and he was alternately nudging her legs open and fingering her hole. His cock was like a homing missile right on target, until Tara pushed him away and caught her breath. 'There you are, Marie,' she breathed, 'and just in time. Tim has need of a pussy.'

The look of confusion on his face was followed in rapid succession by irritation, then pain. Tara held his gaze. 'I'm sorry, Tim, really I am. But Deacon's not gone, and until he is, or until so many years pass that I can forget what he's done, then I still won't fuck the living. It's a bond I can't afford.'

Tim kissed her hungrily, then gently, caressing her face as he pulled back. 'You're fooling yourself, Tara. You've already made that bond, and you know it as well as we do.'

'Perhaps, you're right, but it's a deception I can live with for now.'

There was a shuffling on the blankets behind them and Anderson disentangled himself from where he slept between Fiori and Sky and came to Tara's side. She gave Tim one more kiss with lots of extra tongue and pulled Anderson down next to her. 'Besides, I don't think either of us will suffer overly much from lack of … comfort.'

Anderson was already worshiping her nipples with little darts of his tongue, cupping and releasing, cupping and releasing each breast in turn, while the other hand slipped down between her folds. 'Perhaps I may be of service by offering you comfort now, my dear Tara.'

Marie's already wet pussy got wetter, as it always did, at Anderson's delicious poet-speak. Watching the ghost lift Tara into his lap, holding her open with one hand and guiding his cock with the other only added to Marie's own growing need

218

for said comfort. She reached for Tim, and whispered in his ear, 'I like it both ways.'

'The paragon of versatility, you are, Marie Warren,' he said, biting her earlobe. As Tim pulled her down kissing whatever part of her body happened to be in the path of his lips, for the briefest moment, she thought about Tara's reasons for refusing Tim's cock, and though she felt safe and secure, she knew Tara was right to be wary. But then Tim pushed inside her, filling the space that had been empty for so long, the space that wasn't just her womanhood, as Anderson would call it, the space that was her heart. And it wasn't just Tim who had found a space there. It was the whole Elemental Coven. That she loved and lusted for them all didn't seem the least bit strange, knowing what she knew. As she wrapped her legs around Tim and lost herself in the feel of his body, she reckoned that was enough for now. More than enough. And at the moment, now was exactly where she wanted to be. She knew, as Tara did, that it would be all too brief.

A free chapter from K D Grace's next book!

LAKELAND HEATWAVE SERIES

RIDING THE ETHER

K D Grace

LAKELAND HEATWAVE: BOOK TWO
RIDING THE ETHER

Chapter 1

'There will come a time, my dear Tara, when you must let him use his gift.' Anderson nodded to Tim Meriwether, who sat naked meditating on the edge of the dream bed in the cave. 'You have said it yourself that he is ready. He has progressed even more quickly than we had hoped, once he made peace with the difficult circumstances in which he finds himself. In which we all find ourselves.' He lifted the high priestess's chin, forcing her to meet his gaze. 'And it is possible that I may not always be here.'

She pulled away and continued to loosen the plait of her hair. 'What, are you planning a holiday away from all this fun?' As was common when he broached the subject of permitting Tim Meriwether to perform the task that fell to their masculine sex, in the coven's dream magic, she made no pretence of hiding her irritation. In truth he knew her irritation was focused inward. Irritation was the most effective disguise Tara Stone could manage for her fear of becoming too attached to the living. In fairness, Tara had done all in her power to see to the proper training of Tim Meriwether and Marie Warren, since they had been added to the coven. And they were quickly becoming formidable witches because of the training.

But on this one subject, she would not be moved. Tara Stone would not have intercourse with the living. She allowed herself sexual congress only with ghosts. And though Anderson, being himself a ghost, benefited greatly from what Tim Meriwether referred to as Tara's sexual neurosis, he worried about her still, worried about her as he had the entire 130 years they had been together. The burden she bore would have broken anyone else long ago, and yet she shouldered it. His heart ached for her at the thought. He brushed a dark lock of her lush hair away from her cheek.

'I have heard that Tahiti is lovely this time of year, and I think I should quite enjoy a bit of warmth after the long Cumbrian winter.'

She gave him a look that told him she neither believed him nor was she impressed. 'You're a ghost.'

'A ghost who is at this moment fully in the flesh, and I assure you, my darling, my flesh does not appreciate the cold any more than yours.'

She forced a smile. 'And yet your flesh is doing a lot more complaining about it than mine is.'

'My dear Tara, you have once again successfully directed our conversation away from the topic I endeavoured to broach.'

She shook her head slightly, and the last of the plait collapsed into a soft torrent of deep auburn which reminded him of the peaty waters in the fast-moving streams on the fells. 'Clearly not as successfully as I'd hoped,' she said, 'or you wouldn't be bringing it up again.' She took him by the hand and led him toward the dream bed. 'Now, do you think we could focus on the magic we're here for instead of my choice of sex partners?'

He thought it wise not to remind her that the magic had been precisely the topic of their conversation, aware as he was that in her heart she knew that fact, even if she could not bear to admit it. And in truth, his timing had been poor. But Tim Meriwether was truly gifted in dream magic, while Anderson had come to practice it only by default being, before Tim's arrival, the only member of the coven equipped with a penis. Anderson was more at home in the Ether. He was trained in ethereal magic and, in truth, it had been 130 years since he'd had need of what was now referred to as REM sleep, that sleep in which dreams occurred, that sleep which kept the living sane and healthy. Not for the first time he wondered if it would not be more expedient simply to allow him to journey into the Ether and seek out with more direct methods the information they desired. But Tara had forbidden it as too dangerous at the moment. And in spite of the unease he felt, he would do his high priestess's bidding.

He brought his attention back to the circle that had been cast earlier and let the full weight of the magic rest against the flesh he wore as comfortably as the living wore theirs. He immediately felt his penis stiffen and tense with the growing urgency of the rising magic. He became aware that Marie and Tim Meriwether were now entwined around each other, naked and sheened in perspiration in spite of the winter outside the cave. Through their act of pleasure, their task was to prepare the way for the magic that was to be worked. Sitting next to them with their arms around each other in a caress of their own were Sky and Fiori, theirs the responsibility of witnessing all that was to happen.

Anderson watched as Tim Meriwether positioned himself between Marie's pale thighs. She moaned softly and lifted her legs to his hips. Tim's buttocks clenched with his first thrust, obscuring, for a brief moment, the lovely back hole with which Anderson had grown quite familiar in the passing of the six months since they had fought the demon together.

Could it have been such a short time since Deacon had been bound in the flesh, in the strange lifeless limbo in which Marie and Tim Meriwether had trapped him? Anderson's stomach clenched as he thought of how very close he had come to losing the two he had so grown to love.

He knew them both intimately, and memories of making love with them served only to tighten the growing weight of desire in his own loins, as he knew it did with Tara and Sky and Fiori, as it was intended to do. It was the foundation set in motion, the drive to rut, the ancient need that brought humanity to the very edge of ecstasy while at the same time driving it to the brink of its own destruction. And in between ecstasy and destruction, the next generation was birthed into existence. And there, on that knife edge in between, the magic happened as it could happen nowhere else. Again and again Anderson had experienced it, always new, always wild, always almost beyond his control.

With the weight of the magic pressing in on him along with the desperate need it created, he shrugged off his robe and eased aside Tara's, then drew her down onto the bed of cushions, kissing each of her heavy nipples before beginning his descent to the Gateway. He nibbled at the base of her sternum where her ribs yielded to the rise and fall of her belly, which tightened with the touch of his lips and teeth. The caress of his tongue forged the path to her navel, sinking in, darting, probing in sympathy with what his penis would soon do. He traced the soft goose-fleshed skin down to the pillowed curls of her pubis, down to the very bud of her pleasure. In his mind's eye he could see clearly the Gateway as he reverenced it with a kiss to the keystone. He worshiped at its entrance with long lavings of his tongue, preparing the way.

Tara curled her fingers in his hair and spoke words, ancient words, words that could be understood in no other context than this; words that would never be uttered in any other space but the space they now created in their intimate act.

And when he was certain the Gateway was fully open, fully inviting, he rose on his knees and positioned himself, one hand on his member, the athame in flesh, the other bracing himself. Then he entered the Gateway with a shifting of his hips and a sigh of pleasure laced with fear of the unknown, fear of the Dream World, which was always unpredictable, never completely safe in its revelations.

From a long distance, he heard Tara moan, heard the rush of her breath, felt her legs tighten around his hips, but he was already through the Gateway, speeding forward with each thrust deeper and deeper into the dream. It was familiar territory, a journey he had made with Tara many times before. He found himself poised there on the threshold of the unconscious waiting to be drawn under, waiting to uncover secrets. He felt a slight tightening in his chest, an acceleration of his heart, and the scraping of flesh against stone, solid and bruising. His pulse accelerated further. The hair on the back of his neck rose. Someone called his name from a long way off, but it was not Tara. His last thought before he was catapulted from the flesh with a force violent enough to take his breath away, if there had been breath left, was that he was no longer in the Dream World.

He was unsure if he had lost consciousness, but Anderson knew immediately, when he had gathered himself enough for the knowing, that he was in the Ether, though how he got there he could not tell. Immediately he cast the counting spell his mother had taught him when she finally agreed that, even though he was no daughter, he had wit enough and was gifted enough in the Old Ways to walk safely in the Void. He had already crafted his own counting spell, for, until she had relented, he had visited the Ether in secret without her permission. More efficient than his, her spell allowed him to set a small clock in the back of his mind, a clock that kept track of time in the World of Flesh, the only way to mark the passing of time in the Ether. If the counting spell were not cast, one could very easily die. While starvation set in and the comatose body withered away in the World of Flesh, no time passed at all in the Ether. Time was simply not a concept in the Void.

And though he did not remember casting the special enfleshment spell, the one he always cast for himself in the Ether, he was fully in the flesh, completely naked, and fully, nay, outrageously, aroused. The pressure in his groin was both agonizing and exquisite. He reached for his manhood, knowing full well he was in need of wit that he did not possess when his lust was so great. But before he could stroke himself to release, a voice spoke out from the Void. 'That belongs to me.'

He was not startled that the woman appeared out of nowhere. After all this was the Ether, but he was very startled, if most pleasantly so, that she was as naked as he, and it was no hardship for him to look upon her. Before he could utter even a cry of surprise, she knelt next to him, slapped his hand away and took his member into her mouth.

'My dear woman,' he gasped as her tongue snaked up the underside of his manhood. 'I do not believe we know each other.'

She stopped pleasuring only long enough to reply. 'We will very soon.' Then she returned her efforts to his great need.

'I fear this shall end quickly if you do not stop what you are doing.' He tried, though only half-heartedly, to push her away.

After all what manner of man saw to his own release before the pleasure of his lover?

'I know you.' As she spoke, she continued to stimulate him with her hand. 'It may be over quickly this time, but then,' she lifted her head enough to brush a quick kiss against his lips, enough for him to catch the tiniest glimpse of dark molasses eyes, 'when it's over we'll begin again, and then,' she gave him a squeeze. 'Then I'm sure I'll be well compensated.' She spoke no more, but took the length of him deep into her throat and tightened her grip until there was nothing for it. He shuddered the weightiness of his release into her throat, and she drank it back like fine brandy. And when she had drained him as surely as if he had been the glass containing her drink of choice, she slipped up next to him, her tight roseate nipples brushing against his ribs. And when she kissed him, he tasted himself on her lovely tongue. This time she kissed him with all of her mouth, nay, with all of her body if that were possible, and he felt lust already returning to his loins.

When she pulled away, he spoke in one breathless sentence, fearful that if he did not find his voice immediately, the lady's own greed for the pleasures of the flesh might make him forget that he even possessed the power of speech, might make him forget why his voice would even be of importance. 'My dear woman, might I at least enquire who it is that pleasures me so well and in such unusual circumstances?'

Once again she held him with the deepest, darkest eyes he had ever seen on a woman so pale of complexion. 'I'm Cassandra, Cassandra Larken, and I've been waiting for you.'

'Then it is clear you have most definitely found me, Cassandra Larken.'

Though it was usually fear and uncertainty that drove those who rode the Ether to complete the task for which they had come, and return to the World of Flesh as quickly as possible, those who were more adept at journeying in the Ether knew that passions and desires were always more difficult to control in that vast space. Therefore it came as no surprise that his desire should return so quickly.

Though in truth, he had never taken his pleasure in the Ether before, and he was certain other practitioners of ethereal magic would not approve. But at that particular moment on his internal spell-induced clock, he could think of nothing in the Ether he would rather be doing than sharing pleasure with Cassandra Larken. Though he was much more in control of his manhood after she had so deliciously emptied him, he would most definitely be the first to agree with modern theories on human sexuality, stating that the brain is the seat of desire. And this slender woman, pale of flesh and hair, dark of eyes, was truly intoxicating. He wondered if her appearance in the Ether was as her appearance in the World of Flesh. Some, he knew, chose to appear differently when riding the Ether.

He felt her hips shifting and rocking with her unsatisfied need, and as he lifted himself onto one elbow rising above her, for the first time he became aware of the bed on which they lay. It was devoid of colour, like the emptiness in which they found themselves, but it was a bed nonetheless. Anderson could not but admire the woman's attention to function, much more important in ethereal magic than form. And at this moment, hers was the only form in which he was interested, though he wondered why that should be when there was important coven magic in which he ought to be participating.

She guided his hand to the soft warmth between her legs, and he eased a middle finger into the slippery wetness of her ardour. His thumb caressed the heavy node of her pleasure and she trembled like a leaf on water, honeyed eyelashes fluttered over dark eyes. She opened herself to him, shifting her buttocks until he could see the heavy folds and hillocks of her womanhood pouting open before him, until he could smell the heat of her rising up from below her belly at the seat of her desire.

She lifted her arms around his neck. 'Anderson,' she pressed his name up through her chest and past her lips with laboured breath. 'Anderson, it's all right for me to have you here in this place, and I need you. Please. I need you.'

His own need grew with the feel of her beneath him, and he did not deny her the release she so needed. He cupped her buttocks, felt them tighten in his grip, felt the strain of her anticipation as he positioned himself, the head of his member pressed tight against her womanhood. 'Please,' she whispered again.

He pushed into her until the sigh of her breath was a sob, then she wrapped herself around him and pulled up to meet him, pressing her mouth to his, whispering against his lips. 'Ride it with me, Anderson. I need you to ride it with me.'

The power of first contact drove fire up his spine and up into his head until the very fabric of the ether sparked with it. Then, as he thrust, it was as though she had inhaled all of him into herself, right up through the very core of her womanhood all the way to the beating of her heart. And then she gave it all back to him again, each time driving the fire up into him hotter and brighter than the time before. His bliss was such that he wondered if it was her intention to burn him until he was but ash to be blown away into the nothingness of the Ether. But he was too far gone for his possible destruction by fire to matter, and when she began to shudder and tremble with her release, driving her heels into his kidneys, digging her nails into his back, he allowed himself to tumble into the abyss with her. The bed she had created quite literally vanished and they were falling, endlessly falling into the heat of their release.

For a time, they floated in nothingness, wrapped around each other. The clock in his head warned him he had been gone too long, that there were important responsibilities he must return to, but still he clung to her.

'Are you all right?' she whispered against his ear.

He chuckled softly at such a question. 'As ecstatic as the experience of sharing pleasure with you is, my dear Cassandra, it was only le petite morte and surely you are aware that I am already dead, and therefore undamaged by your ardour.'

To his surprise, she wept, only a little, but he appreciated the ways of women. Their ease with their own emotions was a thing much to be envied. And she did indeed weep, and hold him even closer to her, if that were possible. 'Only le petite morte,' she sighed. 'Of course.' She moved a hand down to rest against his heart. 'I have to go now, Anderson, and so do you.' She kissed him, and in that startling moment colours flashed before his eyes, steamy sunsets, nights dense with stars, an older woman with a cascade of white hair falling over a black robe, ghosts, memories, dark places, the sharp crack of a whip and fire. And once again he slipped out of his body.

When the darkness broke over him, he awoke on the dream bed looking up into the concerned faces of the rest of the coven.

THE LAKELAND HEATWAVE SERIES

9781908086877

9781908262789

9781908262202

THE INITIATION OF MS HOLLY

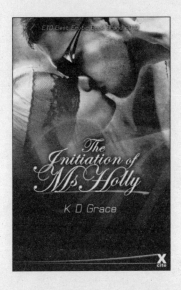

"The Initiation of Ms. Holly is so hot I am still tingling a day after I finished reading this novel. Ms. Grace gives us a tale that is so passionately raw that you will feel as if you have been stripped to the bone" *Coffee Time Romance*

Sex with a mysterious stranger aboard a train leads Rita Holly to an initiation into the exclusive and secretive Mount club. Sophisticated and deviant rituals await Rita, as do the endless intrigues and power struggles deep within the heart of the organization. Rita learns that membership of the Mount Club is not for the sexually repressed. During her initiation, sex with her new lover from the train, Edward, is forbidden but Alex the dance instructor is happy to take his place and Leo the zoo keeper is happy to encourage Rita's animal instincts. With more and more titillating punishments in store and the club's sexy head Vivienne intent on her failing, will Holly succeed in her lengthy and lurid initiation?

THE PET SHOP

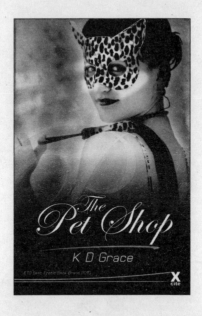

A satisfying mix of romance, kink, and inventive S&M, The Pet Shop reels the reader in, neatly side-stepping clichés, and forcing you to read just one more chapter before you put it down. Oysters and Chocolate

In appreciation for a job well done, STELLA JAMES's boss sends her a pet, a human pet. The mischievous TINO comes straight from THE PET SHOP complete with a collar, a leash, and an erection. Stella soon discovers the pleasure of keeping Pets, especially this one, is extremely addicting. Obsessed with Tino and with the reclusive philanthropist, VINCENT EVANSTON, who looks like Tino, but couldn't be more different, Stella is drawn into the secret world of The Pet Shop. As her animal lust awakens, Stella must walk the thin line that separates the business of pleasure from the more dangerous business of the heart or suffer the consequences.

Join us on Facebook
www.facebook.com/xcite.erotica
www.facebook.com/XciteGay
www.facebook.com/XciteBDSM

Follow us on Twitter
@XciteBooks
@XciteGay
@XciteSpanking

www.xcitebooks.com

Scan the QR code to join our mailing list